The Q Fragments

A Novel

Michael Douglas Scott

Copyright January 2013

To Joel,
My partner in
adversity!
Michael

1

For Barbara

About thirty years after the death of Christ, the Essenes, a small Jewish brotherhood, hid hundreds of scrolls in caves near their settlement of Khirbet Qumran close by the Dead Sea. The first scrolls were discovered by a local Bedouin goatherd in 1947 CE. Over the next ten years, the Bedouins and archaeologists raced each other to find more scrolls, the Bedouins to sell to the highest bidder, the archaeologists to study the ancient writings.

Today, all of the recovered scrolls have been translated. Although expectations were high, they contain no mention of Jesus, early Christians, or anyone from the New Testament writings. However, most authorities agree on one thing: it is not certain that all of the scrolls have been found.

Cover photograph by author - Cave 4, Khirbet Qumran

Part One

Israel, 1951 CE

Khirbet Qumran

Chapter 1

The three Bedouins had been searching since morning, scrambling over rocks and sand on the escarpment that runs north and south from the ruins of Khirbet Qumran. They explored the canyons and defiles, always looking for dark openings and fissures. Although they found a few, none contained much of value. Bones they found occasionally, and a few ancient potsherds, but nothing else, no ancient scrolls. The sun burned the ravines and defiles into a white heavy vessel, baking all within, sucking the moisture from living things as it did the water from the nearby Dead Sea.

"Aiee, it grows hot," said Shareem, a youth of twelve.

"Let us have water," said his uncle Abrihim. "Amal! Bring the water bottles."

The third Bedouin, Amal, older brother to Shareem, slid down a steep dirt hill, scattering rocks and dust beneath his canvas and rubber shoes, darting quickly into the shade where the others waited. He took a glass soda bottle half full of water from an old army pack. They passed it around gratefully.

"This is a good place. We are still close to the old ruins," Abrihim said.

"What if they have all been found, the ancient writings?" Shareem asked.

"Although that is possible, I think not. I believe there are more to be found. Many people lived here long ago," Abrihim said pointing back to the north where the remains of Khirbet Qumran lay partially exposed to the sun. "Surely, those who hid the scrolls must have known of many other caves. They have not all been found."

They finished the bottle and Amal slipped it back into the pack along with the remaining full ones, then they continued their search until the sun swung below the rock cliffs.

"We will stop for today," Abrihim said. "Where is Amal?"

The boy was nowhere in sight.

"Amal!" Shareem called out. "We must go now! Come quickly!"

Faintly they heard Amal's high pitched, excited voice. "Here! Over here! I have found one!"

They quickly moved around a jutting rock wall and into a shallow defile. High on the slope above them was Amal. He was grinning, his hands covered in the brownish dirt of the ravine. "Look!" he said pointing to a small, dark fissure next to where he stood. "I have found one."

They quickly scrambled up to Amal. He had scraped away a little of the thin layer of soft dirt covering the fissure. Working together they made the hole larger. Cool air flowed into their faces. The sun was sliding from view. It was a cave.

"We cannot go farther now. It will be dark soon," Abrihim said.

"What if someone comes before we can return," Shareem said. "With the digging we have done, the cave will surely be obvious."

"We are not leaving," Abrihim said. "We will stay the night and get into the cave at first light."

The next morning they opened the entrance and went inside. They found many clay jars containing scrolls written on leather and papyrus. Some were merely wrapped in leather, lying on the sandy floor of the cave. In the trio's hurry to remove their treasure, they took only the biggest and best scrolls, leaving others behind, some trampled into pieces and ground into the sand by their feet. They knew others would soon come, scavenging what remained.

They loaded them on their donkeys and left the rest for whomever would come after. They would be the first to sell to Olikara, the infidel dealer in Bethlehem, and these new scrolls would command a good price.

Colorado, USA

Present Day

Chapter 2

Walker Burnett sat on a rock beside the Frying Pan River in Colorado, drinking coffee and watching the water for signs of rising trout. His cell phone rang. He took it from his shirt pocket and pressed the green button.

"Go ahead," he said.

"Walker, it's Edith," a voice said.

He recognized her voice. "Good morning. Long time."

"Are you particularly busy these days?"

"Not at the moment. You know, my superior sleuthing skills tell me this isn't a social call."

"No, and it is important. I need to talk with you as soon as possible," her voice said clear and pointed.

Walker looked at the river. Yes, there was a trout working the eddy. A brown, from what he could tell, and a decent size too.

"I got a trout rising. Still kind of cold, but there it is," he said.

"Good for you. When can you come?"

Walker sighed, and stood. "Well, I can get a flight out of Denver this afternoon, or if you're in a rush I could probably get something out of Aspen."

"I've already booked a charter out of Aspen. It will leave when you get there," she said.

"All right. I'm on my way."

"It will be good to see you."

"You too," he said and pocketed his phone, took a last look at the river and the trout and went to his cabin to pack. He filled a small bag with one clothing change and a few personal articles. He selected a compact Ruger 9mm semi-automatic pistol, two loaded magazines and a box of hollow point ammunition from his gun safe. The box of cartridges and one magazine went into the bag. He loaded the Ruger and fitted it into a black holster on his right hip and put one spare magazine on the other side. Locking the safe, he slipped on a thigh-length black leather coat, picked up the bag, lowered the thermostat, armed the security system and locked the door.

Walker stood six feet four inches, weighed two thirty and change, and was possessed of a calmness that belied his size. He kept his brown hair short and was habitually clean shaven. He wore no rings, bracelets, watches, tattoos or earrings. His was not a handsome face but rather ordinary if you didn't notice the scarring over his right brow or his slightly misshapen nose.

Edith was waiting in the sun room of her home to greet him. The windows were streaked with rain but the lights of San Francisco were visible across the bay.

"Walker, it is good to see you," she said taking his hand and smiling up at him.

"What? No California hug?"

"You are not the hugging type. Come. Sit. Would you like something to eat? Drink? Are you still partial to Sierra Nevada?" she asked.

"Love one, thanks."

Edith Donaldson was tall and slim, carrying her seventy-odd years like a much younger woman. Vanity had small claim on her though. Although far more wealthy than even her friends knew, she dressed to please herself and had little patience with trends in style, clothing, jewelry or the latest exercise and fitness fads. She loved to walk and occasionally ride horseback, which she did outdoors in all weathers. She kept her hair short, casual and uncolored since it had long ago faded to gray, sparsely sprinkled with a few fine, dark streaks. "Compliments the wrinkles," she liked to say. It did compliment her blue eyes and open smile.

She brought the drinks back to a large driftwood coffee table. She sat on a sofa, poured his ale into a cold glass and handed it to him and leaned back with her glass of zinfandel, stretching her Levi clad legs out on the table, crossing her ankles, her beat up pair of running shoes dangling over the edge.

"Private jet. A car meets me at the airport. What's so urgent?" he said taking a long swallow of the ale.

"It is a matter of timing, obviously. I need to get some information quickly without anyone else knowing that I am interested."

"I thought you had resources for this kind of thing."

"Yes, but the information I need isn't available here. You'll have to go to Israel," she said looking at him, amusement wrinkling her eyes.

"Sure. I suppose that would be right away, seeing as how you are so much in a hurry. Why couldn't you tell me this on the phone, instead of this James Bond routine?"

"I don't think you will have to shoot anyone, unlike that unfortunate person in Los Angeles, so that isn't really a good analogy."

"Dizzy Bones was about to shoot me at the time. Better him than me and besides, I was working for you, remember?" he said. "What analogy would you suggest?"

"None. I have encountered nothing quite like this. Let me get to the point. A young associate of mine, a scholar I am sponsoring in Israel, called me yesterday. He is working with the Rockefeller Museum in Jerusalem translating old documents. You've heard of the Dead Sea Scrolls?"

"Sure. Very old scrolls found somewhere in Israel, in the desert, I think."

"Close enough. They were discovered in 1947 by a Bedouin boy out looking for his goats, or that's the story. Anyway, after a few years of searching, most of the scrolls were recovered. They are really beyond price, quite valuable in an historical sense. Until now, it was thought they had all been found."

"But, someone found more."

"My associate, Nathaniel Benjamin, came across new fragments, pieces of a scroll. More importantly, it may be that these fragments are special, very special and very valuable."

"If they are real."

"Yes, that's our first consideration. Fake relics surface regularly, especially in that part of the world. Nathaniel thinks these are authentic, but they have not yet been tested. It is not their age but what is written on them that is important. If they are authentic, they could be the most valuable of all the scrolls."

"What do they say?"

"There are are references to important figures and places in the earliest days of Christianity."

"Don't the Dead Sea Scrolls do that?"

"No, there is nothing at all in the scrolls about Jesus or the early Christians."

"Until now," he said. "Maybe."

"Yes, until now. Maybe."

Edith went to a desk and took a file folder from a drawer, walked back to the sofa, sat and began reading from a single page printout.

"This is what Nathaniel has translated so far, '... Legions......Vespasian invested Jerusalem after .... Doomed......the Temple burning everything not ..... fleeing.... many are [passing? Moving?] Qumran on ... [south?] ..... refuge at Masada.... [scrolls?] from the Temple ... hiding for those who cannot .... South ... [if any] of the Brothers survive this terrible time and return here and recover our sacred writings I wish it to be known .... of immense value hidden ... to the north .... message of God .... of Nazareth in G[alilee?] .... friends and followers and enemies ... Jerusalem .... Romans .... executed ....'"

"Seems pretty inconclusive to me. Of course, I'm no historian but if your man thinks this is important…" Walker said.

"These fragments are part of a more complete set. If they are authentic, and there are more references to the early Christians, even to Jesus himself, their value would be beyond price."

"I understand that, but why do you need me? You know the kind of work I do. Sometimes it's not pretty. You're rich, why can't you just buy them and let your man translate them?"

"The fragments were not brought to the Museum by a kindly benefactor. They were in the possession of an antiquities dealer, a man with a history of shady deals and criminal associations. He has the remainder of the fragments and, of course, he wants to sell them, but I don't trust him. Nathaniel is an academic. I don't want him hurt or taken advantage of. And I want those fragments," Edith said. "Also, the fragments we already have mention something else hidden near Qumran. Something of "immense value"."

"Qumran?" he said.

"That's where the original scrolls were found, near the ruins of Khirbet Qumran, an ancient community of the Essenes, a Jewish sect," she said.

"Something of immense value. Maybe treasure, or more scrolls?"

"No idea," she said. "That's why we need the other fragments. Combined, they may tell us, or perhaps describe a location. This is where you come in. I need you to help Nathaniel buy the remaining fragments and get them to a safe place where they can be analyzed and translated without anyone else interfering. If they are authentic, and if they do reveal information about Jesus and the early Christians, they will be the most significant find of the century."

"What about this treasure that is hidden in the desert? Any ideas on that?"

"No, but perhaps when we put all of the scroll fragments together, they will tell us something."

"I can tell you something now," Walker said draining the last of the ale and setting his glass on the low table.

Edith arched one eyebrow and said, "And that would be?"

"Trouble," Walker said. "You mix mystery, religion and hidden treasure and you've got trouble written all over it."

Edith smiled. "And, that's your business, yes?"

"OK, let's say we manage to buy these missing fragments, then what?" he said.

"Nathaniel will translate them and we will know what we are dealing with. Further plans can wait until then."

"If we don't find them, or they are fakes, or never existed in the first place?"

"Then you come back and we'll have a nice dinner in the City, overlooking the Bay. I've booked your flight on El Al. It leaves tomorrow morning."

"One thing we haven't talked about."

"What's that?" she said.

"Why are you so interested in this?"

Edith took a sip of her wine and looked out the window. The rain had stopped and the lights of the city were bright and crisp, outlining the streets winding over the hills toward the riot of lights that marked downtown.

"I'm dying," she said turning to look directly at him. "I have maybe another year, possibly two. If something else doesn't get me first. All of my life I've been a Christian. When I was diagnosed two years ago I began to seriously think about what happens after death and, frankly, the same, sad stories I've heard every Sunday don't seem to matter any longer. Besides, no one agrees on much of anything. Protestant, Catholic, Jewish, Lutherans, Mormons, Jehovah's Witnesses..."

Her voice trailed off. She took another swallow of wine and turned her gaze across the Bay.

"Perhaps there are answers in the fragments. I don't know, but I want to find out," Edith said.

"I am sorry, Edith."

"Yes."

Walker lifted his glass and clinked it against hers. "Here's to the scrolls. Now all we need is a plan."

Chapter 3

Walker enjoyed the flight to Tel Aviv about as much as anyone enjoys spending fifteen hours in an airplane. As he walked through the lobby in the Ben Gurion airport he saw Nathaniel in the waiting area. Walker recognized him from the photograph Edith had given him. Medium height, wavy dark hair, wire rimmed glasses, clothes a little disheveled.

"Nathaniel?" Walker said.

"Ah... yes. And you are Mr. Burnett?"

"Just Walker will do."

"Oh, right. Call me Nat. Everyone does."

They shook hands. Nat looked around and said, "You have more bags?"

"No, this is it," Walker said his travel bag over his shoulder.

"OK, lets get going. You'd be surprised, but there is actually a rush hour and I'd like to get out of Tel Aviv before it starts."

The road climbed steadily to Jerusalem through scrub oak and cypress wooded hills, and smaller towns that melded into the greater Jerusalem metropolitan area. They drove past fine homes, modern apartment buildings, stores, neighborhoods, people walking, some riding bicycles. They passed a gaggle of school children out on a field trip, laughing and playing, bright backpacks and kids clothes just like in the United States, except for the armed teachers at the head and tail of their laughing column, men with automatic rifles slung over their casual clothes.

"Not in Kansas anymore," Walker muttered. Nat didn't seem to notice.

"Mrs. Donaldson booked a room for you at the Knight's Palace Hotel in Jerusalem's Old City," Nat said. He continued past the Jaffa gate and parked near the city walls.

"This is pretty close. If you don't mind a little walk. Parking here is much easier to find than inside the walls. Terrible traffic," he said.

"Fine. It will feel good to get a little exercise," Walker said.

Nat locked the car and they walked across Aqabat Al-Manzil Street into the old city of Jerusalem. The streets were narrow, paved with flat, irregularly shaped stones worn smooth by centuries of use. Motor scooters roared by, weaving among the pedestrians. Three-wheeled carts powered by scooter front ends piled with goods, slowly maneuvering through the crowds. Young people with ear bud wires dangling from their ears, talking and laughing with one another nonetheless. Old men in shiny suits with white shirts, open collars and sandals. Orthodox bearded Jewish men dressed all in black except for white shirts and the fringes of the tzitzit dangling over their waistbands. Jeans, T-shirts, Nikes and cowboy boots were popular with the younger folks. Old Jerusalem, noisy, colorful, the air heavy with the smells of food, tobacco, incense and the fumes of too many combustion engines.

The Knight's Palace Hotel was an old stone building tucked in a corner near the New Gate. The hotel was not pretentious, but it was clean and comfortable. Its high vaulted ceilings and long lobby graced with statues and paintings hanging above comfortable chairs and couches gave it a timeless class.

"This place was a seminary in the nineteenth century, although some parts of the building date back to the eleventh or twelfth centuries," Nat said.

"Never stayed in a seminary before, even a former one," Walker said.

Walker signed in, left his bag with the desk man, and took a city map from the counter.

"How about you show me around?"

"Don't you want to talk?"

"Yes, but not here," he said stepping out into the street. He paused to look at the map then turned right on St. Peter Street.

"This way will take us to the Jaffa Gate," Nat said.

"Crowded is it?"

"Yes. It's one of the main gates into the old city."

"Sounds like the ticket," Walker said.

A constant stream of cars and vans flowed in and out of the Gate. People were moving everywhere. Merchants enticing the tourists and pilgrims into their shops. Crowded sidewalk cafes. Businessmen hurrying with their briefcases. Armed Israeli Defense Force soldiers, male and female, weapons slung over their shoulders, moving slowly through the crowd, eyes alert.

Walker looked at the map and turned down a narrow street packed with merchant shops and stalls. He and Nat followed the flow of people past endless rows of booths and stores, their shutters open, goods stacked, hung and packed into racks for display. Dresses, pants, scarves, shawls, racks of T-shirts with every imaginable logo, chess sets, tea sets, hookahs, incense, candy, jewelry, baked goods. They walked and looked, moving with the crowd through the narrow street. Walker sometimes turned suddenly, retracing his steps for a short distance to check an item in a shop, or to look at goods behind display windows. After many minutes of this, Walker went into The Weeping Camel, a narrow coffee shop empty except for a few customers. They took a solitary table against the far wall. Walker sat facing the doorway.

"OK," Walker said, "let's talk."

They ordered coffee and toasted sesame pastries. Nat took a pack of Camels from his pocket and lit up.

"You don't mind, I hope," Nat said.

"Your lungs. Just don't blow it my way," Walker said.

"I'm trying to quit. Was doing good until these fragments showed up."

"I don't think tobacco is good for stress."

"You're pretty calm," Nat said. "I didn't expect to go on a shopping tour."

"Not shopping. Checking for a tail."

"You think we are being followed?" Nat said turning around to look out the doorway.

"Don't do that," Walker said, "it draws attention. I can see the door fine from here. And, no, I didn't think we were being followed."

"Anyway, I'm glad you're here. I hope you can help."

"I understand there are other fragments on offer?"

"So he says. I think he wants to drive up the price. I don't actually know if there are other fragments or not."

"Easy way to find out."

"How?"

"Let's ask him," Walker said.

"I don't have a phone number or anything. He's in Bethlehem."

"How far is that?"

"Next door, almost," Nat said, "but it's on the other side of the wall. You have to go through a checkpoint."

"That going to be a problem?"

"Not really. An inconvenience more than anything else. It's part of the security fence between here and the West Bank. The Palestinians call it the Apartheid Wall."

"So, if these fragments are as valuable as you think, how much would, ah, what's his name?"

"Chandi."

"How much would Chandi expect?"

"God, if they are what I think, they are worth a fortune."

"We don't want to give Chandi reason to think that. What if the fragments he still has are part of the scrolls you already have? How much would they be worth?"

"Well, I think we could pay, maybe five thousand."

"Five thousand for each set, or for both together?"

"Each. That would be about right."

"OK, when we meet with him, we want him to believe that the fragments are important, but nothing special. When he's comfortable, we're going to offer him more than he expects," Walker said.

"Why do we want to do that?"

"Because we want him to believe you are selling the museum out. That you have a private collector who is willing to pay more than the museum. And we want to give him a reason to keep quiet. If he thinks we are dealing under the table and his end might be at risk if he talks, so much the better. Gives us more time," Walker said.

"I see. OK. I think I can do that. Who is going to be our private collector?"

"That would be me. Now, I think it's time to give Chandi a call and set up a meet."

"Like I said, I don't have his number or anything, and we don't want to ask my boss, Dr. Menahem for it."

"This Chandi have more than one name?"

"Sure, it's Olikara. Chandi Olikara."

"Let's try a phone book."

Chapter 4

The next morning Walker and Nat drove through Checkpoint 300 between Jerusalem and Bethlehem. People on foot were queued up on either side of the Checkpoint, moving slowly through the fenced gates and turnstiles, their papers checked by Israeli security police. Nat inched his car forward between a taxi and a large tourist bus packed with a church group heading for the Christian sites in Bethlehem. The security fence was a twenty-six foot high concrete wall, cast from long rectangular slabs, topped by strands of razor wire and guarded by armed IDF soldiers.

On the other side, in Bethlehem, the buildings were drab and run down. Some areas were pocked with piles of rubble, the demolished remains of buildings left to scavengers and street urchins. Trash was scattered here and there, weeds grew among the rocks, plaster and broken glass. A few people looked at them curiously, one or two with outright hostility, but mostly they were ignored.

Nat parked on the street next to an ancient wagon someone had made into a flower garden. Littered among the flowers were empty beer bottles, cigarette butts and soda cans.

"Chandi's shop is just down the street, not far from here," Nat said locking the car.

As they walked along the sidewalk, Walker turned into a tourist gift shop and bought a wooden crucifix and a large picture book of Bethlehem's churches. The clerk put them in a large green plastic bag. As they pushed through the door onto the street, Nat said, "What was that all about?"

"Security," Walker said.

Nat started to speak but Walker interrupted. "Let's get this over with."

They walked another block in silence to Olikara's Bethlehem Emporium and stepped through the doorway.

"Welcome, welcome," a thin man dressed in a light blue shirt, dark blue tie and pressed black slacks said as they entered. He was tall and wiry, his black hair well groomed. He wore a thin mustache and an enormous gold ring on his right hand.

"Mr. Benjamin, it is good to see you again," the man said.

Turning to Walker he continued, "I am Chandi, and you must be Mr. Burnett."

Walker took Chandi's hand in a strong grip, holding it for a heartbeat too long.

"Yes," Walker said releasing his hand. "Nice shop."

Items of all kinds were crammed into every conceivable shelf, corner and wall, some hanging from the ceiling.

"Yes, it is quite a burden dealing with all of this," Chandi said sweeping his arm to encompass the mess.

"You have what we have come to see?" Walker asked.

"Good, good. Right to the point, eh? Right to the point. Indeed I do. I shall be just a moment," he said and walked quickly to the street door, closed and locked it, and went into a tiny office in the back.

He returned with a small, brown briefcase and set it on the counter by the register. He opened the clasps and removed a manilla envelope containing five scroll fragments encased in plastic document covers and placed them on the counter. Nat carefully lifted a sheet and tilted it toward the light, studying it intently. Walker leaned on the counter and smiled at Chandi.

"Nice, are they not?" Chandi asked.

No one answered. Nat continued to study the fragments, running his finger along the words, occasionally holding sheets against the light to better reveal faded letters. After many minutes, Nat set them carefully on the counter.

"Yes, this looks good. Very good," Nat said.

"Are we interested?" Walker asked him.

"I won't know for certain until I can examine them more closely, but I'd say they are part of the other fragments," Nat said.

"Ah, the IAA is interested in purchasing these also, I see. They are companions to the others I have brought you, yes?" Chandi said.

"I believe so," Nat said. "They will need to be tested, of course, but my confidence is high that they are."

"Do you have an estimate of their worth?" Chandi asked.

"Well, if they are genuine, I would say,... five thousand US dollars," Nat said.

"That does not seem like so much, considering their antiquity and the likelihood that they are part of the Dead Sea Scrolls," Chandi said.

"The tests may prove that to be the case, and if so, we might be able to pay more," Nat said.

"I don't think we need to worry about the tests," Walker said.

"No?" Chandi said. "Why would that be, may I ask?"

"I represent a client who is able to have the tests done independently, and who relies on my judgement in these matters. He is very wealthy and a connoisseur of antiquities, especially those originating in early Jewish history. I am certain that he would place a much higher value on these items than the IAA would be able to meet," Walker said.

"Ah, a private investor in history," Chandi said. "Would this gentleman be American, perhaps?"

"Doesn't matter," Walker said. "He is willing to invest significantly when rare and unusual opportunities present themselves."

"You believe this would be one of those opportunities?" Chandi said. His eyes flashed to the fragments.

"I rely completely on Mr. Benjamin's assessment," Walker said looking at Nat.

"I've examined the other fragments and these appear to be written on the same material, in the same hand. I am almost certain they are from the same scroll," Nat said.

Chandi looked from Nat to Walker. "If I were to consider selling to your... who did you say you represent?"

Walker smiled but said nothing.

"Your client, then, what about the fragments I have already supplied to the IAA. How will your client find full value without those?"

"At this point, as far as anyone else is concerned, those are merely fragments from an old scroll. There is nothing to establish their value," Nat said.

"Besides," Walker said, "what happens to the other fragments isn't your worry, is it? You've done your duty, turned them over to the IAA. Our arrangement now is private and secure, and I am certain we can make it worth your trouble."

"Trouble," Chandi said, "trouble can be very costly. These are uncertain times."

"True enough," Walker said. "What would one require in order to deal with such times?"

Chandi considered. Walker could almost see the wheels turning.

"Twenty-thousand American," he said. "Each."

Nat started to speak, but Walker said, "How about sixty? Forty for both sets of fragments, and twenty for your continuing discretion. Let's call it an insurance policy."

Chandi smiled broadly. "Done! I like the way you do business Mr. Burnett. I am always discreet in my business affairs, not to worry."

"I'm not worried. I trust that a man who buys insurance does so knowing what can happen if his policy gets canceled," Walker said looking directly at Chandi.

"Indeed," Chandi said but his eyes could not hold Walker's.

"Now, it's payday. Nat, put the fragments inside this," Walker removed the large picture book from the green plastic bag. Nat returned them to the manilla envelope and laid the envelope inside the open book. Walker slipped the book back into the bag. He removed a fat envelope from his jacket pocket and handed it to Chandi.

"Consider this a good faith payment against the total," he said.

Chandi opened the flap. His pupils dilated and he looked quickly at Walker.

"Ten thousand American," Walker said, "the rest payable today. In Jerusalem."

"Jerusalem?"

"You did not expect that I would be coming here with that much cash?" Walker said. "The rest is in a bank in Jerusalem. Let's go."

"Now? With you?"

"You want to lock that away somewhere?" Walker said nodding toward the money.

"Ah, yes... in my office. I have a good safe in my office."

"Good, lock it up and let's get moving. I don't want to be late for dinner."

"Tell me where, and I can meet you there within an hour."

"It's best that we all cross through the checkpoint together. You can watch us, we can watch you, hell, we'll all watch each other. No mistakes that way. No unexpected circumstances, if you follow what I'm saying," Walker said.

Chandi stood thinking for a moment, the wheels turning again.

"Of course, if you have changed your mind," Walker said reaching for the envelope.

"No. All is well. Give me a moment to put this away," Chandi said taking the money and moving toward his office. Walker followed and leaned on the door frame as Chandi opened the safe and stowed the money away. As he did so, Walker removed the manilla envelope containing the fragments from the book and slipped it into his jacket pocket. Chandi locked the safe and turned to leave, stopping short when he saw Walker.

"Sorry," he said, "I didn't see you standing there."

"Just making sure everything is all right," Walker said. "Now, you ready to go?"

Chapter 5

Nat parked again near the Jaffa gate and they walked into the old city. Walker led them to The Weeping Camel. They took a table near the back.

"Here is the way it works," Walker said handing the shopping bag to Nat. "Keep the fragments with you. I'm going for the money."

"Will you be long?" Chandi said his eyes flicked to the bag.

"You have someplace else to be?" Walker said.

"Not at all, certainly not," Chandi stammered.

"You seem nervous," Walker said. "Something bothering you?"

"No, I am fine. I fear it is the heat and the crowds. I seldom come to Jerusalem because of the crowds. So many people."

"See the man in the white shirt, near the door?" Walker said.

Nat and Chandi turned to see a big man sitting alone at a small table next to the entrance, his large hands raising a tiny coffee cup to his lips. He sat the cup down gently on its saucer, nodded at Walker, then went back to his newspaper.

"Who is that?" Nat asked.

"Let's say he's a friend having a coffee in a cafe. Maybe taking a break and keeping an eye on things for me while I'm gone," Walker said.

Both Nat and Chandi were looking at Walker now.

"Do we understand one another?" Walker said to Chandi.

"Clearly and most definitely," Chandi said.

Walker disappeared into the street, stopping briefly to buy a black, rectangular athletic bag from one of the stalls, then walked quickly to the Barclay's Bank. He presented his key and was escorted to a safe deposit box. He removed six banded stacks of $100 bills and placed five stacks in the bag and one stack in his inside jacket pocket. He put the envelope containing the fragments in the box. Leaving Barclays, he walked quickly back to the Weeping Camel stopping at an outside table at a nearby bakery. He ordered coffee and a roll. As he sipped his coffee, he closely examined the area and the customers in The Weeping Camel. There was no one loitering about or reading a paper outside. Customers came and went. Inside, two men sat near Nat and Chandi, drinking from white cups and talking. The big man near the door was still reading his paper.

Walker waited until the two men left. He followed them far enough to see that they did not double back. Satisfied, he returned to the Weeping Camel and took his seat. The big man folded his paper and left.

"Wow, that took a while," Nat said.

Walker ignored him, placing the bag on the floor between himself and Chandi. He partially unzipped it and turned back the cover. Chandi's eyes flicked down to the bag and roved over the stacks of bills.

"Are we good with this? Want to count it?" Walker asked.

Chandi, reached down fanned through two of the stacks. He closed the cover and said, "I trust you are a man of your word."

"Indeed, and I trust that your insurance policy will remain in force for a long time."

Walker stood and said to Nat, "Let's go."

"Goodbye," Nat blurted out before dashing after him. Outside, Walker paused to let him catch up, then continued walking quickly through the crowded streets.

"Chandi, did he stay with you in the cafe? Did he leave for a moment, step outside, go to the restroom?"

"What? Oh, yes he did."

"Did what?"

"He excused himself right after you left. Went to the restroom."

"Too bad. Nothing's ever simple."

"What's wrong?" Nat asked, eyes wide.

"Keep walking. I'll tell you later," Walker said weaving through the crowds, heading east, away from his hotel. Turning west at a narrow intersection, he pulled Nat quickly into a store, stepping out of sight behind rolled carpets and rugs stacked in the windows, blocking the view from the street. The two men who had been in the cafe earlier walked rapidly into the intersection, stopped and looked down each street.

"We're being followed. Friends of Chandi. He probably called them on a cell from the restroom," Walker said softly.

"Why would he want to follow us? He knows where I work."

"These guys don't care where you work, they're after the fragments."

"I don't understand."

"Chandi has another buyer on the line. He now knows two things. The fragments are worth big money and we aren't representing the Museum. If he can get them back, he keeps our money and resells them for maybe more than we paid."

"What are we going to do? We can't let them take the fragments," Nat said clutching the bag tighter.

"They aren't in the bag. They are in my safe deposit box."

"How...? When...?" Nat blurted out.

"And even better for us, they don't know that," Walker said nodding toward the two men in the street.

The two men conferred, then split up. The taller one, wearing rubber soled leather sandals, turned down the street where Nat and Walker were hiding. Walker pulled back out of sight. After the man passed, he told Nat what they were going to do.

They stepped out of the shop and followed Rubber Sandals, walking quickly, talking, seemingly unaware of their surroundings, merely two men in a hurry. They moved past Rubber Sandals without looking at him. He fell in behind them and opened his cell phone.

They turned off the main thoroughfare into a narrow side street with few pedestrians. After a short way, Walker led them into another twisting street, the narrow cobblestones winding among stone walls cut by doors almost flush with the street. Rubber Sandals continued to follow, keeping his phone to his ear. As they turned another corner, Walker, seeing that the area was deserted, whispered, "Keep walking. Don't look back. Meet me at the hotel."

Nat moved fast, rounded a corner and disappeared. Walker followed a few steps, then slipped into a dark doorway and waited. Rubber Sandals, muttering into his phone, turned the corner. As he passed the doorway Walker hit him hard below his left ear where the skull meets the neck, dropping him dazed to the cobblestones. Walker stooped and slipped a black pistol from the man's waistband and slapped him softly across the temple with it, knocking him unconscious. At that moment the second man appeared, phone to his ear. He saw Walker standing, facing him and stopped, his eyes going to his partner sprawled on the ground. Walker racked the slide on the black pistol, chambering a round, the sound ringing harsh and deadly in the deserted street.

"Another Glock," Walker said pointing the chunky pistol at the center of the man's chest. "You guys get a discount on Glocks? Everybody's got one, even the police."

The man was shorter than his partner but easily twice as broad. Brown eyes stared at Walker from a face lined and scarred by the hard side of life.

"Don't you think it's kind of ironic, Israelis carrying German guns?" Walker asked.

The man began to slowly lower the cell phone.

"Your problem is, what to do with your phone. Not a good idea to carry it in your shooting hand."

The hand with the phone continued to slowly descend, the man watching Walker closely.

"Drop that phone and I shoot you dead with your partner's gun. Then I wait for the police. Two armed men trying to rob an innocent tourist. One of the robbers getting killed in the attempt. I can live with that."

The man still gripped the phone but didn't speak.

"Too bad," Walker said and raised the Glock, sighting down the slide at the man's head.

"Wait!"

Walker did not move or speak.

"I have a family," the man said "a daughter and a young son. Please…"

"Your weapon, take it out slowly with your left hand and put it on the street. Don't drop it," Walker said holding the Glock steady.

The big man lifted his shirt exposing the butt of his pistol. He grasped the gun with his thumb and forefinger, drew it out and slowly squatting, laid it gently on the cobbles.

"Who sent you?" Walker asked.

"Chandi," the big man said.

"You should take up another profession. This one doesn't seem to be working out well for you. Besides, you've got a family to take care of. Go home."

Walker lowered the Glock. The man took a last look at Walker, turned and walked around the corner and disappeared.

"Amateurs," Walker said.

Chapter 6

When he returned to his hotel, he found Nat pacing back and forth in the lobby.

"What happened?" Nat asked. "Did you lose them?"

"Yeah. They're not a problem. Don't worry about it."

"But what about the..." Nat began.

"Not here," Walker said. "Let's go upstairs."

Walker had Nat stay at the end of the hallway while he entered the room alone. He looked out a few seconds later and motioned Nat inside.

"You're beginning to freak me out," Nat said once inside the room. "You think Chandi knows where you are staying?"

"Probably not, but no sense in being careless. Here, I got these from the bank," Walker said handing the fragments to Nat.

"Well, that's a relief," Nat said. "Now, let's see what we have."

He took a small, folding magnifying glass from his pocket along with a small black notebook, secured by an elastic strap. Turning on the desk lamp he sat, opened the notebook and focused the glass on the fragments.

Walker slipped out of the room quietly, locking the door behind him and went downstairs to the bar.

"Mr. Walker, good afternoon," the bartender said.

"It's just 'Walker'"

"Yes, it is difficult to break old habits, Walker," the bartender said smiling. "What can I get you?"

"Two bottles of a good IPA and a couple of glasses, please."

When the bartender brought the ales and cold glasses, Walker paid in Israeli shekels, then peeled off two five hundred shekel notes and put them on the bar. "This is for your cousin. Tell him thanks. He was very helpful."

"My cousin sends his thanks and asks why it is worth so much to sit, drink coffee and read the paper," the bartender said.

"We Americans have strange ways."

"So I have noticed."

Nat looked up as Walker came in the door, smiled at the bottles and went back to the fragments. Walker set a glass and a bottle on the desk. Nat was writing in his notebook. He ignored the ale. Walker moved to a chair by the window that overlooked a long rectangular plaza, enclosing the playground of a school. Recess was in full swing, the kids doing what kids do everywhere, running, skipping, swinging, playing with balls, talking excitedly in little fluid groups, making lots of noise. Walker sat, watching, his boots crossed on the window sill, sipping his ale and thinking long thoughts about playgrounds far away and long ago.

"This is unbelievable. Unbelievable. If we didn't have these actual fragments, I would seriously doubt this," Nat said looking at Walker.

"You translated it? All of it?"

"All I can make out. I might be able to add more later, but this is enough to, to... I don't know. This is bigger than I thought."

"Read it."

"OK. There are gaps, missing pieces, but this is what I have so far. '... altered beyond all that ... by his followers... brother James who ... Cephas and the Pharisee... God that the Law not...' followed by a long gap, and it continues, 'among the Brothers. The Teacher refused. I secretly led them to a high cave far to the north ... wadi... few venture... south wall ... it is concealed... waterfall step...Qumran settled again... Brothers it would be fitting... us who still remain in this holy ground... Mordecai Teacher of ...'"

"That's it," Nat said. "Freakin' awesome..."

"OK, I got some of it. James..."

"Brother James," Nat said, "the difference is crucial."

"Brother James, something about a Pharisee, I remember that from Sunday School I think. Ah, Brothers, probably not meaning James, and some directions to a wadi and a waterfall and what is probably a cemetery."

"Not bad," Nat said, "but there's a great deal of history involved that puts this in context. Let me try. We know the fragments were written during the First Revolt, when the Romans took Jerusalem and destroyed the Temple. People were fleeing, many running south, where Qumran is located. Some took documents with them, precious to them, and the Essenes hid many of those along with their own scrolls in the caves around Qumran. That's where the Dead Sea Scrolls were found. The first fragments Chandi had mentioned events and people that may be associated with the earliest Christians. A man called Joseph. The village of

Nazareth. Jerusalem and someone who might have been executed by the Romans."

"But, no one named, right? Could have been anyone, far as we know."

"Yes, no one specifically named, but here," Nat said pointing to the fragments on the desk, "the evidence is much stronger. It says, 'brother James who', and 'Cephas'. Do you know who Cephas was?" Nat asked, and not waiting for an answer rushed on, "He was Peter. You know, Simon Peter from the Gospels. The disciple who denied Christ three times?"

"So, why doesn't it just say, 'Peter'?"

"Because 'Cephas' was his nickname. Means, 'rock'. Probably because he was so hardheaded."

"This is important because Peter is mentioned in the fragments?"

"No. It's important because Cephas was the name given to Peter by Jesus."

Walker looked out the window. The children were lining up to go back to class. "Now, that puts a whole new light on things," he said.

"Not only that, but put 'Cephas' alongside 'brother James' and, well, I think this combination provides a really high level of confidence that these fragments relate to Jesus of Nazareth. One of Jesus' brothers was named James. Later called James the Just."

"You're the scholar. Let's say you are right. Why was the scroll written in the first place? What do you think it means, the part about being refused, about something hidden in a cave?"

"I think the author wanted to keep something hidden from the Romans, but it was also something the Essenes didn't want to have around. Look at the part that says, 'the Teacher refused'. He would have been the Essene leader, the Teacher of Righteousness. It goes on to say that the author led someone to this secret cave far to the north. It has to be something valuable, too valuable to be hidden near Qumran."

"All right. I think we need to get these fragments in the lock box and call in the cavalry," Walker said. "The other fragments are at your place?"

"Yes, they are locked in my desk."

"Got a spare bedroom?

"Why?"

"After our little episode with Chandi and his people, I think it would be a good idea if I stayed close."

"You think we are in danger?"

"Maybe. Chandi obviously has ties to the underground antiquities market, and when money is involved, it is always a good idea to be alert and be prepared. I don't mean to alarm you, but I'd feel better if I were closer to you. And your wife."

"Is that what you meant by 'calling the cavalry'?

"Not exactly. I need to call Edith, Mrs. Donaldson, and work out what we do next. She can arrange for whatever help we will need."

"Edith? Edith Donaldson. I never knew her first name was Edith."

"I wouldn't call her Edith, not unless she asks you to. She gets kind of touchy about that," Walker said.

"You call her Edith?"

"Yeah, but we have a history."

"Like what?"

"You don't want to know."

Chapter 7

Walker checked out of the Knight's Palace that afternoon, took the fragments to Barclay's and left them in the safe deposit box. He rode with Nat to his home in Ein Karem, a short distance southwest of Jerusalem. Ein Karem was very old, perhaps as old as Jerusalem itself. It was nestled on a low wooded hill, surrounded by higher hills covered in trees, gardens and houses. After the Arabs were forced out during the 1948 war, it was one of the few former Arab villages with the buildings left intact. Over the intervening years, artists, artisans, musicians and young people turned Ein Karem into a peaceful village town of music, cafes, art galleries, restored homes and accommodations for the three million tourists who visited the Christian churches and holy places there each year.

Nat parked in a neighborhood lot, for which he paid a monthly fee, and they walked past tour busses jammed into a small, circular traffic park. People were trudging back and forth to Mary's Well or strolling along the sunny streets, among the sidewalk cafe tables filled with laughter, talk and quiet music. Nat and Walker walked up a low hill to the house and went through the garden to the door.

"I've brought Walker. Come say hello," Nat said opening the door and stepping inside.

Carol entered the living room wearing a peach colored Gap T-shirt, jeans and sandals. She smiled at Walker and extended her hand.

"Make yourself at home. Nat, why don't you get drinks while I finish in the kitchen."

While Nat got the drinks, Walker inspected the compact house. It had two doors, both with good locks. The windows were street level and protected by decorative but strong wrought iron fashioned in the same pattern as the iron gate. Finished, he plopped onto a leather reading chair. Nat appeared with two glasses of beer.

"Thanks," Walker said drinking off half the glass. "Hot day. Nice place you have."

"We got lucky. Could have ended up in a Jerusalem apartment building," Nat said.

"You planning to stay here long?"

"Not really. We were about ready to return to the States when the fragments turned up. We want to start a family and America would be a better place for us. Besides, both of our families are there."

"Probably a good idea," Walker said. "Be hard to bring up kids here. It's a volatile place."

"It has been peaceful so far," Carol said walking in from the kitchen with a glass of white wine and sitting next to Nat on the sofa. "But, with children, I just wouldn't feel safe. The kids who go on field trips always have armed guards along. The security fence has helped. There are no terrorists attacks now, but you never know when they're going to happen again."

"I suspect that when these fragments become public, you both are going to have much less privacy. That might be a good time to head back home," Walker said.

"You have them, the other fragments?" Carol asked.

"We have them," Nat said. "Oh, not here. They're in a safe place but I did a first translation run thorough. You won't believe it."

Nat read the translation from his notebook while Carol listened intently. Walker sipped his beer.

"Oh, Nat," Carol said giving him a big hug. "You're going to be famous."

"Not just yet," Walker said, "there are a few things to get ironed out first."

"What do you mean?" Carol asked.

"The first set of fragments were given to the Museum. People know that, even though they don't know yet what's written on them. The second set, the Museum doesn't know whether they exist or not."

"But you have them now," Carol said.

"Yes, we bought them. Rather, Walker did," Nat said.

"You bought them for the Museum, didn't you?" Carol said.

"Not exactly," Walker said.

"You bought them for yourself? Or for Mrs. Donaldson? Are you treasure hunters?" she said.

"In a manner of speaking, I guess we are, but we didn't get involved in this to steal Israeli treasures. I am here because Mrs. Donaldson doesn't want a valuable artifact to fall into the hands of private collectors, or to be locked away in a laboratory while the politicians grind away at it," Walker said.

"What does she want?" Nat asked.

"I think we should ask her," Walker said taking his cell phone from a pocket and hitting the speed dial. "I'll give her the run down on what happened, you tell her what you translated and we'll see where it goes."

"Hello. Walker?" Edith Donaldson said.

"Yes. I've also got Nat and Carol here on speaker," Walker said putting the phone on the table.

"Hello," Nat and Carol said almost together.

"Good to hear your voices. I hope all is going well."

"So far," Walker said, "but we need to figure out the next steps."

Walker related their visit with Chandi and what happened afterwards.

"You think Chandi will be more trouble?" Edith said.

"Maybe. I think he has another buyer lined up," Walker said, "so he might make another run."

"I am most interested in the reference to the cave. What do you make of that?" Edith asked.

"I don't know. More scrolls?" Nat said.

Everyone was silent for a moment, then Walker said, "There is one way to find out."

"That would be impossible," Nat said. "You can't just wander around Israel looking for artifacts. There are laws against that sort of thing. Besides, we don't know where to look."

"Not impossible. The fragment says the cave is in a wadi to the north of Qumran, on a south facing wall, near a waterfall step. That ought to narrow down the possibilities quite a bit," Walker said.

"Maybe," Nat said looking doubtful.

"No, he's right. How many combinations of those features can there be north of Qumran?" Carol said.

"Two thousand years. Someone would have found it by now," Nat said.

"Nobody found the Dead Sea scrolls for over two thousand years," Walker said.

"Still, you can't just put together an expedition and go poking around in the desert. Israelis are sensitive about such things. Too many treasure hunters and grave robbers as it is. It won't work," Nat said.

"Then, we will have to become an official expedition. An archaeological survey party, responsible to the Museum I think," Edith cut in. "I will talk to some people and get back to you."

Walker broke the connection and pocketed his phone.

"Do you think she can do it?" Nat said. "Get permission for us to search?"

"Edith Donaldson can be very persuasive when she sets her mind to something," Walker said. "Look at us. We're all here because of her. I doubt that the Museum or the Israeli Antiquities Authority is going to be too much of a challenge for her."

Chapter 8

Jerusalem's Rockefeller Museum and the IAA were happy to accept Edith Donaldson's grant for antiquities research, the first action being the creation of a new archeological survey. While the survey team was being assembled, Walker, Nat and Carol spent hours going over topographical maps of the Dead Sea area north of Qumran. Sometimes they used Google Earth or satellite images to make better sense of the terrain. Obviously, many features of the wadis and stream channels had changed over the intervening two thousand years, but they were hopeful that the major terrain features might still remain. Orem Tamir, their liaison with the Museum and the IAA, was helpful. He was familiar with previous surveys in the area, having worked with a number of them, and his field time with the IDF, the Israeli Defense Force, gave him a personal feel for the area.

They mapped a number of possibilities, good places to begin a general foot survey, but decided that most of them did not closely enough match the description in the fragments.

The last survey team members to arrive were Dr. Maria Chavez, Professor of Anthropology, specializing in southwestern archaeology from the University of New Mexico, her assistant Jimmy Butler, and Andrew Kruzmann, Professor of Religious Studies at Fordham University. Walker had them all camped eight kilometers north of Qumran by Sunday night. Each team member had their own tent. Larger tents were set up for a general work space and a mess tent. Their liaison, Orem, had hired two of his nephews, Taz and Josh, both former IDF soldiers, plus a cook and two men to set up camp, tend to the basic needs of the team and to ferry food, water and any other necessary supplies from nearby Jericho or Jerusalem.

Monday morning they gathered in the mess tent for breakfast and got down to work. On two easels Walker had pinned topographical maps covered with thick, clear plastic sheets. Using grease pencils he went over possibilities for the search areas.

"We're starting out closer to Qumran than perhaps we should. The information we have indicates the cave is located, and I quote, 'far to the north' of Qumran. Since nobody knows exactly what 'far to the north' means, we will begin here," he pointed to a wadi that came down from the escarpment and emptied east into the Dead Sea. "If we find nothing, we move north to here," pointing on the map to another, larger wadi.

"We know that a survey for caves and artifacts was done north and south, to a distance of eight kilometers from Qumran. If there was anything of interest there, it has probably been found. If not by archaeologists, then by the Bedouins," he continued.

"Yeah, and if the Bedouins found it, it is long gone on the black market by now," Jimmy said.

"Sad, but true," Walker said. "We figure our cave is farther north than they went. So, the idea is to split up into three teams of two each. Carol, if you want to go, you can go with Nat. Everybody be sure to take cameras, your radios and plenty of water. If you run dry, come back. We can always go out again. Don't take chances."

"Will these radios work up in the wadis?" Maria asked.

"Hard to say," Walker said. "You might have to walk out a ways, or climb to get reception. I want everyone to check in with base here at noon, and again at, what? Four? That o.k.?"

Silence.

"Don't everyone talk at once," Walker said.

"Yeah." "Sure." "Fine," came back.

"Good. We don't hear from you at noon, we get concerned. No contact by four and we come looking," Walker said. "Questions?"

There were none.

"All right, pick your teams and let's head out."

Maria and Jimmy paired up. So did Nat and Orem. Carol decided to remain in camp and monitor the radio.

"Looks like you and me," Andrew said to Walker.

"Fine. You ready?"

"I'll just get my pack from the tent, be right back," Andrew said striding off toward the sleeping tents.

"Carol, you good with the radio?"

"Dad was a ham operator. I used to operate my own base station in high school," she said.

Walker smiled, "You're the radio boss then. Ask Andrew to wait here. I won't be long."

Walker went over to the big shade awning the men had put up.

"Heading out?" Taz said.

"Yep," Walker said. "You guys gather around, I need to ask you something."

"Problems?" Josh said.

"Maybe. Not sure. A few weeks ago I had some trouble in Jerusalem over the fragments. Could be the guy responsible doesn't give up easily. Have you noticed anything out of the ordinary? Odd people hanging around? Anything like that?"

"There are always Bedouins around the north end of the Dead Sea. Usually nothing to worry about," Taz said.

"Now that you mention it, I did see three guys who didn't fit in. I mean, they weren't Bedouins and they looked more like military than tourists," Josh said.

"What made you think that?" Walker asked.

"You were setting up camp and I was driving in from Jericho with supplies. I saw this Land Rover pulled over a couple of miles up the road. As I got close the men climbed back inside, but before they did I thought I saw one of them looking toward camp with a pair of big binoculars," Josh said.

"Could be nothing," Walker said.

"You don't really think that," Taz said.

"No," Walker said.

"I don't believe in coincidences either," Taz said.

"You want us to go out with the teams?" Josh asked.

"That would be a good idea," Walker said. "Thanks for asking."

"How about you?"

Walker opened his light utility vest revealing the black pistol clipped to his belt.

"What is that?" Josh asked.

"Ruger. Nine millimeter."

"They're o.k. I guess. I like a Glock myself," Josh said.

"Why is it everyone over here carries a Glock?" Walker said.

"What?"

"Never mind," Walker said. "Private joke."

"You be careful," Taz said. "Josh and I will go out with the other teams. We'll stay in contact by radio."

"Appreciate it," Walker said and went back to get Andrew.

"What do you think?" Josh said.

"Seems to know what he's doing," Taz said.

"About the gun?"

"We both have guns. Be fools not to around here."

Chapter 9

The team moved three times, making the last camp near the mouth of Wadi Og, a wide, dry water channel that cut through the desert escarpment for miles, terminating near the northern end of the Dead Sea. Everyone was working well together now. They had found two minor surface sites which they logged for later excavation by the Museum. They also found five caves. All were empty and only one had been inhabited, but the occupants had abandoned it long before the first century.

At noon Walker made his call to Carol and reported their position and progress, which was none. Each team had previously found rock steps that would be waterfalls when the rains came, but there were no caves high on a south facing wall. Walker and Andrew were near another of the steps, higher than the others, also with no signs of a cave nearby. They sat in the shade eating their lunch.

"What do you think," Andrew said, "Should we climb the step or take that branch off to the north?"

"Maybe the northern branch. It's easier than climbing and if we don't find anything we'll have to return here anyway. We can take a look above the step later if there is time," Walker said.

"Sounds like a good…"

"Did you see that?" Walker said.

"What?"

"That bird, the big one, there, flying down the wadi."

"What about it?"

"Looked like it flew out of that rock wall over there."

They got up and walked toward the south wall of the wadi, inspecting it closely. Another black bird emerged from the rock and flew off in the same direction as the first.

"I saw it," Andrew said.

"Yeah. Birds don't just appear out of solid rock," Walker said.

As they got closer, a narrow, dark defile, a huge looming crack, appeared in the south wall, rearing up behind a shoulder of the wadi that had hidden it from view.

"I'll be damned," Walker said. "Never would have seen this except for the birds."

"Look, it's wide at the bottom," Andrew said.

They walked around the rock shoulder into a large crack that opened into a wide bell shaped entrance. This was formed by a boulder the size of a large house, wedged between the shoulder and the wadi wall. Walking through, they came to a small, narrow canyon. On the the canyon's east wall a layer of cream colored rock slanted upward, forming a ramp that ended on a plateau in a compact amphitheater of rock, littered with boulders fallen from the escarpment above.

"What do you think?" Walker said.

"I don't know. I'm getting a creepy feeling about this place," Andrew said.

"Want to go up or go back for the others?"

"Let's go. But be careful."

Walker led the way. In places the ramp was scattered with rocks and they had to negotiate narrow sections where the rock wall intruded onto the ramp. It was slow going as they climbed to the plateau.

"Got to be fifty or sixty feet high up here," Andrew said.

Walker took his notebook from his shirt pocket and flipped to the section where he had copied the text from the fragments. "Let's see… it says 'south wall' and 'concealed'. This place is certainly concealed."

They both inspected the south wall above the plateau. It was composed of a harder rock than the wadi below, covered in a dark brown patina, mostly featureless. They saw no sign of a cave or opening.

"Nothing," Andrew said and sat on a boulder, pulling the water bottle from his pack. "I like the looks of this place. Too bad. No cave. Again." He took a long drink and replaced the bottle. "Want to go down?"

"Not yet," Walker said. "Let's look around first. Lot of rock here. I'd like to see what's at the back of this place."

They carefully climbed, slid and squeezed through and around the tumbled boulders, working their way to the back wall of the plateau.

"Feel that?" Walker said.

"Cool air," Andrew said. "That means…"

"It does," Walker said and stepped around another large boulder lying only feet from the back wall.

"What is it?" Andrew asked.

"You need to see this."

Andrew came up beside him, and there it was. Cooler air drifted from the dark opening before them, wide enough for two people to easily walk through without bending down. Cautiously, they stepped into a high and spacious room with a flat, sandy floor. On the walls they saw faded drawings of stick people and animals with blocky bodies and curving horns. On a low rock bench, sloping above the floor lay a long bundle, covered in dust and what once had been thick cloth wrappings. At the head of this bundle sat a short clay pot sealed with a lid.

Both men stood silent, listening to their own breathing.

"I don't think I believe this," Andrew said.

"What is it?"

"I'm not certain..." Andrew said.

He took a flashlight and moved the light over the bundle. He looked closer, then turned to Walker.

"I think it's a body."

Chapter 10

Andrew dropped his pack on the sandy floor and knelt to get a closer look.

"Well, is it?" Walker asked.

"A body? Yeah, I think so. Look at this," Andrew said moving his light over the still form. "It's shaped like a body, underneath all of this wrapping. See, this is the head, then it gets wider and tapers down to what have to be feet."

Walker inspected the rest of the cave. The room they were in was spacious, but not deep. There were no other entrances and nothing else to be seen.

"Walker," Andrew said.

"Yeah," Walker said still inspecting the cave walls.

"Walker…I found something else." His voice was hoarse and Walker detected a slight tremble.

"What is it?" he said moving quickly to Andrew who focused his light on a flat piece of wood.

"I found this under the body. It was just sticking out, like someone had shoved it underneath," he said.

He held a short wooden plank, leached gray by time, pierced with a small rectangular hole and spattered with rusty brown stains. Letters were carved into the wood.

"That's writing," Walker said. "Can you make it out?"

Andrew looked up at him. He was grinning and his eyes were wide. "Someone carved these letters. They are initials, like an acronym. 'INRI'. In Latin, it means "king of the jews.""

Images of paintings and crucifixes ran through Walker's mind. He could see the little sign, nailed to the cross above Jesus' bleeding head. INRI.

"You're saying this is the body of Jesus Christ. The Jesus Christ of the Bible?" Walker said.

"I know this is crazy, but yeah, I think so," Andrew said.

"I need to get back in the sun. Let's get out of here and talk," Walker said and stepped out through the cave entrance. As he did, he saw movement on the top of the escarpment but before he could focus, it was gone.

Walker took his radio from the pack. Nothing but static.

"We need to call in. Orem and Maria need to get here this afternoon so they can document the area and do what needs to be done to secure it," Walker said.

"I think we have time to get back to camp before it gets dark. We can get everyone together and come back in the morning."

"We could, but if we did, there would be nothing here."

"What do you mean?"

"Treasure hunters," Walker said. "I didn't want to worry everyone. Someone has been shadowing us since our first camp near Qumran."

"Shadowed? You mean, like followed? By who?"

"Don't know, but I do know we've got ourselves a problem."

"Who would want to follow us out here?"

"Fellow by the name of Chandi I expect."

Andrew looked around nervously. "What are we going to do?"

"Way I see it, we've got two choices. We can spend the night here and wait for the others to come looking, or I can make radio contact and get help sooner."

"But the radio doesn't work here," Andrew said.

"True, but if I get down to the wadi floor, it will. Remember, we checked in at noon from there."

"One of us must stay here. This is far too important. We can't leave this unprotected," Andrew said.

"True enough. You stay here and I'll go."

"What if someone comes while you are gone? The robbers I mean."

Walker drew the pistol from its holster. "Ruger. Nine millimeter, semiautomatic. Ever used one like this before?"

"God no," Andrew said. "I don't like guns."

"Well, that could be a problem, but I think I can help you with that."

"Why don't you stay, and I'll go down?"

"Somehow I don't like the idea of you and our only radio down there alone with the bad guys lurking around. Got any hand-to-hand skills?" Walker asked.

"I'm not a violent person."

"I can see that. Most people aren't, which from civilization's point of view, is a good thing."

"Look, it's no use leaving the gun with me. I don't know how to use it anyway. It would be better if you keep it."

"Men like these are dangerous and unpredictable. They might just take what they want, knock you around some and leave. On the other hand, they might kill you first."

"You really think so?"

"Dead men tell no tales," Walker said.

"That's not funny."

"No, it's not. Listen, if nothing else, you should be ready to defend yourself. Here, take this," Walker said handing Andrew a smaller gun.

"You carry two guns?"

"Sometimes. This one isn't so big, but it makes a loud noise and can do some damage. All you have to do is hold it with both hands, point it like you'd point your finger and pull the trigger. It's loaded with seven rounds. Just keep pulling the trigger and it will fire until you run out of bullets."

Andrew smiled nervously and reached for the pistol.

"One more thing," Walker said. "Keep your finger off the trigger until you are ready to shoot."

Andrew gingerly took the pistol and placed it on his pack.

"I'm going down now," Walker said moving toward the ramp. "You might hear some noise but don't worry. It will be o.k."

"Be careful," Andrew said.

"I'm always careful. And besides, I'm a pro," Walker said.

He knew the only feasible way up to the cave was to climb the ramp. There was no way to rappel down from above. He figured there would be at least two men, maybe three. He made enough noise climbing down the ramp to draw attention. He stepped outside the defile near the wadi floor and made contact with Carol.

"We found the cave. And we need backup. There are two, maybe three treasure hunters following us. They've also spotted the cave," Walker said. He gave her a quick description of the defile and the ramp and the plateau above and said to hurry. Turning off the radio, he slipped quietly into the shadows at the bottom of the defile and hid there beside the ramp.

It took longer than he expected. The men were being careful and it took them some time to work their way down to the wadi floor. Walker smelled the stale tobacco on their clothes before he heard them. There were three of them, whispering in a language he did not know.

Walker remained motionless, breathing slowly, relaxed, as the men stepped around the rock shoulder, following his tracks. They passed his hiding place and stopped about twenty feet away, pausing while their vision adjusted to the shadows, inspecting the way up the ramp.

One of the men was large and muscular, his blond hair cut short in a military buzz. The others were smaller, but lean and fit. They wore desert fatigues and carried camouflage packs. Two had Glocks in tactical holsters and small assault rifles slung over their shoulders. The big man, obviously the leader, was armed only with a large Glock strapped to his right thigh and a combat knife duct-taped upside down to a pack strap. Walker figured the guy had watched too many action movies.

The blond man started up the ramp. Walker waited until he had climbed a short distance, then took a solid two-hand stance with the Ruger and said, "What brings you fellows out here?"

The two men below spun around, bringing their rifles up. Walker quickly shot both of them, two rounds apiece. One man went down immediately but the other staggered, lurched sideways, and fired a short burst from his rifle in Walker's direction, the bullets kicking sand and pocking the rocks with dull hammer blows. Walker shot him twice more and he went down for good.

The blonde man on the ramp spun around at the sound of the shots, grabbing for his pistol but his feet slipped on loose rocks. He fell backwards, arms windmilling for balance as he landed on his back and tumbled to the ground below. Dazed, he could only watch as Walker ripped the pistol from its holster, unloaded it and tossed it into the rocks. The knife followed the pistol.

Walker found a bundle of parachute cord in one of the packs and tied the man securely. He unloaded their weapons, carried them into the wadi and threw them on the sand. He turned on the radio and thumbed the transmit button.

"Carol, Walker," he said into the radio.

"Walker, are you OK?" Carol's voice came back.

"I'm fine. Listen, I got one of the treasure hunters tied up at the bottom of the defile. There are two others nearby. They're dead. Tell Orem to call the police. I'll meet you at the bottom. I'm going back up now," he said and turned off the radio.

Walker climbed the ramp quietly and stopped just outside the cave's entrance.

"Andrew. It's Walker."

"Walker? Thank god. I'm glad you are back. What happened? Were those gunshots?"

"Yes," Walker said, "But it's over."

"Was anyone hurt? What happened?"

"We can talk about that later. I'm coming in now," he said stepping into the cave. "The police are on the way. They'll take care of everything. Don't worry about it."

Andrew was sitting cross legged on the sandy floor. His flashlight was on. The pistol still lay on the pack. The pottery jar was no longer next to the body, but was sitting open beside him. A scroll lay partially unrolled on his lap.

"What are you doing?" Walker said.

"I can't get this scroll open any further or I'll break it," he said. "I know, I should have left things as they were until the others get here, but…"

"It's not me you have to talk to about that, I just work here. What is it?"

"I'm not sure yet," Andrew said. "The scroll is written in Latin. How about that? I knew something was strange when I saw this." He held up the scroll's leather covering and pointed to letters cut into one side. "These are Latin. The letters LQ."

"What's special about it?"

"Because it is written in Latin," Andrew said, "and that makes it absolutely special. Not impossible, of course. The Romans were all over this country, but it is very unusual to encounter Latin scrolls in this area. You know what's funny? I read Latin. I also read Greek and German. But not Aramaic or Hebrew. You'd expect to find something written in one of those languages, not Latin."

"What's it about, this scroll?"

"I don't know, I can only read the first part. I need to get it to a place where I can safely open it. Then I can read the entire thing," Andrew said. He looked at the body resting on the shelf. "I have to ask you something."

"Go ahead."

"It's about this scroll. I need your help."

Chapter 11

Carol contacted the police then called the other teams back to base camp. Leaving one of the cooks to man the radio, Carol left with Nat and Orem. It took them almost two hours to reach the foot of the defile where they found Walker waiting for them.

The blond man was tied securely, sitting in the shade of the entrance.

Orem looked at him, then said to Walker, "Where are the others?"

"Follow me," Walker said. "It's not pretty. Carol, you might want to wait here."

"I'm all right. I'll go with Nat," she said.

The two dead men were sprawled where they had fallen. The sand had absorbed most of the blood. Bright shell casings were scattered near one of the bodies. Carol drew close to Nat. Orem walked carefully around the bodies, closely inspecting their wounds and the empty cartridge casings. Squatting, he traced the confused tracks in the sand. He stood, brushing the sand from his hands and walked back to Walker.

"What happened?" he asked.

Walker handed Orem his pistol, butt first, slide locked back and open.

"I figure you'll be wanting this," Walker said as Orem took the gun from him.

Orem looked at the pistol. "This all you used?"

"Didn't need anything else. They were careless."

"They had automatic weapons. These two were shot in the front, one of them about three times I think."

"Four."

"You'll be making a case for self defense I suppose," Orem said looking at the fresh bullet marks on the rocks.

"I won't be making a case for anything until I've talked with my attorney."

"Three men, dressed in combat fatigues, carrying automatic weapons, followed you around, then shot at you. You have a good story," Orem said. "Where's Andrew?"

"In the cave. Come on, I'll show you the way," Walker said then led them up the ramp to the cave entrance. They stepped inside one by one. Andrew was sitting on the sand, closely inspecting the body wrappings.

"Oh. Hello..." he said. "How about this? Can you believe it?"

"This is a body," Carol said walking over to inspect it closely. "That's what they hid in the cave, a body."

"Find anything else?" Orem asked.

"And this," Andrew said holding up the sign.

Orem put his light on the sign. "Is this a joke?"

"Joke?" Andrew said, "No, of course not."

"Why would you call it a joke?" Nat said.

"It doesn't seem possible, what is written on it, and its being here," Orem said pointing to the body.

"It means 'king of the jews'" Andrew said.

No one spoke.

"I had the same reaction," Walker said. "I was here when Andrew found it. I'm no expert, but it looks real enough to me."

"Find anything else?" Orem asked.

Andrew played his flashlight over the walls and floor. "No, just the body and the sign."

"Ok. Now we wait for Maria. She needs to document everything in place. What about the sign?" Orem said.

"I can't very well put it back now," Andrew said.

"We'll ask Maria what she thinks. Both of you saw it in place, correct?" Orem said.

"Yes, it was under the body," Andrew said. "Looked like someone had shoved it underneath. One end was sticking out. That's why I saw it."

"OK, no one else touch anything until Maria and Jimmy get here," Orem said.

Maria was not at all happy that five people had been tramping around in the cave. Walker thought her command of Spanish curse words was extraordinary for an academic. She shooed everyone out while she and Jimmy measured, noted and photographed everything. Walker went down to the wadi floor to wait for the police. He contacted base camp, and arranged for food, water and sleeping bags to be brought up, then sat in the shade thinking about what he had seen and what Andrew had said to him. He might be wrong, but he thought Andrew had a point. He took out his cell phone and called Edith.

"We found it. You sitting down?" he said.

He related the day's events to her, leaving nothing out.

"You shot those men? They are dead?" she said.

"Two are. The other one is alive. I didn't have to shoot him."

She was silent for a few moments. Walker heard a soft sigh then she said, "Listen, there is something I need you to do now."

Walker listened.

"All right," he said. "I'll take care of it."

Chapter 12

After Maria and Jimmy had finished, Orem left with them for base camp. Four Israeli police officers arrived in two Land Rovers and took the blonde man into custody. They inspected the scene in the defile, took many photos and a brief statement from Walker. Before they left, another Rover arrived carrying four IDF soldiers, four sleeping bags, boxes of food and twenty liters of water in plastic jugs. Two of the soldiers stationed themselves at the defile entrance and one climbed to the top of the plateau to stand guard through the night. The fourth soldier drove the blonde man and the bodies away.

Nat found a clear area for their overnight camp. The men ferried the wooden boxes of supplies to the plateau and set them by the rocks. It was still light when they finished their simple meal of bread, hummus, olives and bits of roast lamb. Someone had thoughtfully included two bottles of red wine, cups and a corkscrew.

They settled back on their sleeping bags, propped against the rocks as the sun sank over the escarpment and the shadows worked up the walls above them. Walker made a fire using the boards from one of the packing boxes.

"It's a little spooky here, with that body in the cave," Carol said.

"We will get it out tomorrow. The Museum is sending a recovery team to transport it to Jerusalem," Nat said.

"I agree with Carol," Andrew said. "I don't believe in ghosts or spirits, but this particular body, well… it is what you might call spooky."

"Why do you think that? This is not much different than finding a mummy," Nat said.

"No, this is different. I think I know who the body is," Andrew said.

"You don't know that. That sign doesn't mean anything by itself. Anyone could have put it here. It could have been made by anyone," Nat said.

"Possibly, but look at what we know. What led us here? The fragments, right? And what do they mention? The earliest Christians, like Peter and James. Also, Roman execution. Nazareth. And we know the fragments were written shortly after the time of Jesus' crucifixion. Why else would they describe the hiding place of a body if it wasn't so important?"

"But that doesn't mean it was Jesus' body. Could have been someone else," Carol said.

"Another little problem," Walker said, "wasn't Jesus supposed to have risen from the dead? If that's true, his body wouldn't be here, right?"

"That's just a story. Never happened," Andrew said.

"But, it's in the Bible, in all the Gospels," Carol said.

"Actually, that story is only in one gospel. The other writers took that story and wrote it into their own versions. And, the resurrection account wasn't even in the first gospel until someone added it years later," Andrew said.

"You're talking about the Gospel of Mark," Nat said.

"Right," Andrew said.

"He's right, honey," Nat said. "Scholars discovered over a hundred years ago that the ending of Mark was tacked on by a copyist. In the original version, when the women came to the tomb and found Jesus' body gone, they ran away in fear and told no one. Only later did someone add the part about Jesus appearing to the disciples. Mark was the first of the canonical gospels written. The others borrowed heavily from Mark."

"Why would someone do that?" Carol said.

"No one knows for sure," Andrew said, "but they did. Probably they wanted to convince their followers that Jesus didn't really die. All the Gospels are different, some in significant ways, and many of those differences can't be reconciled. They were all written years after the fact and none of the original authors knew Jesus or even anyone who knew him when he was alive. Except Paul, and he didn't know Jesus. They were writing for different audiences in different parts of the world. For certain, they were not writing for Jews, Jesus' people. What they wrote was intended for early Christians."

"Many of whom were Jews, though," Nat said. "There were many groups of early Christians who believed different things about Jesus, who he was, what he taught, what happened after he died. Most of those were primarily Jews, like the ones following Peter and Jesus' brother, James."

"The people who knew Jesus, didn't write anything about him or what he did. Probably all of Jesus' followers were illiterate. But, if someone who knew Jesus did write about him, no one has ever found it," Andrew said. "Besides, those other Christians, like the Gnostics, everything they believed and all they wrote was condemned as heresy by the group that eventually created the Church."

"It is too bad that we don't have any old accounts, like something written by someone who was actually there at the time," Nat said.

Andrew looked at Walker who was leaning back, his legs stretched out, crossed at the ankles. Walker returned his gaze and took a sip of wine.

"I guess I better tell you about the scroll," Andrew said.

"What scroll is that?" Nat asked.

Walker opened his pack, removed the pottery jar and set it on the sand.

"This one," he said and pulled off the top and gently lifted the scroll from inside.

Nat and Carol looked at it in the fading light then at Andrew.

"You found this? In the cave?" Carol said.

"I did," Andrew said.

"Why wasn't it... why didn't you tell us?" Nat said.

"Or you?" Carol said to Walker.

"Because I asked him not to," Andrew said.

"There better be a good explanation for this," Nat said.

"I don't know how good it is, but I think it is important, extremely important that the existence of this scroll remains secret for a while," Andrew said.

"You can't do that. It's like, stealing. When Maria finds out, you could be arrested. Sued, even. I could lose my job, my grant. I'd never be able to work anywhere," Nat said.

"I'm not talking about stealing anything. Look, I have already translated part of the scroll, the part I can see without damaging it. I need to finish the translation, then we'll turn it in," Andrew said.

"You translated it? You know Aramaic? Hebrew? Is it Greek?" Nat said.

"No. Latin," Andrew said.

Nat looked at him and blinked. "That's not possible," he said. "Latin? Here, in the desert, in Judea?" he said. "How would a Latin scroll be here, with the body and the sign? Doesn't make sense. It must have been put here as a hoax. Someone else found the cave."

"Yes, I think someone else did. But that happened very soon after the body was put here," Andrew said.

"Andrew," Carol said, "that's beside the point. We've got to turn it in. You could be fired. You could be blacklisted by every university in the world. It's not worth it."

Walker put the scroll back into the jar.

"Look, Carol, when you and Nat first entered the cave, did you see this jar?" Walker said.

"No. Only the body," Carol said.

"Who else was there with you?" Walker said.

"Orem," Nat said.

"Right. So, as far as you two know, and Orem knows, there was no jar in the cave," Walker said.

"Yes, but we know now," Carol said.

"No, I don't think you do," Walker said.

"What do you mean? Of course we do," Carol said.

"Hold on," Nat said. "Wait a minute. Walker, if I read you right, you're suggesting that unless we say something, as far as anyone else knows, only you and Andrew know about the scroll. We never saw it, and we were with Orem. He didn't see it either, right?"

"Right. No one else needs to know," Walker said.

"I don't...," Carol said.

"Look, right now, the only things found in the cave are the sign and the body. Unless you tell someone otherwise, you two can't be involved. Walker and I are the only ones responsible," Andrew said.

"What are you going to do?" Carol said.

"We are going to take the scroll to the Museum lab where I can unroll it safely and translate all of it," Andrew said.

"Why not just turn it over to the Museum and follow their process?" Nat said.

"Because this may be too important. Do you remember what happened to the Dead Sea Scrolls? They were kept under lock and key for years. Other scholars throughout the world were not even allowed to see them, or see even photographs of them. Some people considered the scrolls too potentially dangerous to share with the world," Andrew said.

"You think this scroll is dangerous?" Carol said.

"I'm not certain. I've been able to read only a small piece, but what I have seen makes me uneasy. I'm afraid that if other people get involved right away, powerful and politically motivated people, we may never find out what is written on the scroll."

"He could be right, honey," Nat said. "That has happened before."

"How about this? I get the scroll to the museum and open it. I'll translate it and you two can be the first to read it. Then we all decide what to do. I will take full responsibility. If we decide to turn it in, I'll do it. As far as anyone will know, I acted on my own, completely," Andrew said.

"With a little help," Walker said.

"You don't have to be involved," Andrew said.

"I am involved. I said I'd help you and I will. Besides, what are they going to do, fire me? I don't work for them," Walker said.

Carol took Nat's hand and said, "What do you think?"

"I'd really like to know what's on that scroll," Nat said.

Walker pulled the cork from the last bottle of wine. "Let's celebrate," he said. "I think we have a deal."

Chapter 13

The recovery team quietly moved the body and the INRI sign to the Museum's laboratories. Maria and Levi Hartmann, a forensic anthropologist from Tel Aviv University, began carefully exposing the body, slowly removing the wrappings.

"Look at this," Maria said lifting the last piece of cloth from the face. "You can almost make out the features. The hair is still intact."

"This is very strange," Levi said peering closely at the body. "If I didn't know better, I'd say this looks like an Egyptian corpse preparation."

"Doesn't look like an Egyptian, or anyone from Africa," Maria said.

"No, it doesn't, but still…"

"I know. Let's continue and see what we find," Maria said turning back to the body.

As they worked, a technician opened the cloth covering the INRI sign. He took a quick photograph, stepped back and said, "Hey, Maria, we got a problem here."

"Better not be. If that sign is damaged there will be…" Maria said stopping short, staring at the uncovered wooden plank. The wood was new and both ends were broken off. On the piece that remained was stenciled, "…ations. Open caref…"

Maria glared at the technician. "Is this supposed to be funny?"

"Hell no. I just now unwrapped it. Here," he said handing the camera to Maria, "look at the photos for yourself."

Maria took the camera and scrolled back through the photos. Each was time and date stamped. The photo of the unwrapped plank had been taken only a minute before the last one showing the new, splintered plank before them.

"This is bad, this is really bad. Levi, don't touch anything. Come on," Maria said pulling the tech out of the lab room and locking the door behind them.

"You stay right here. No one goes in. This has to be an inside job. Someone is working with the treasure hunters. I'm getting Menahem."

Dr. Menahem quickly doubled the security and called the police. With the lab under guard and attention focused on the missing sign and the body, no one bothered Nat and Andrew while they processed the scroll in the museum's document lab. It took two days to completely open the scroll and make high resolution photographs of the entire document. The following day, behind Nat's locked office door, with the scroll itself stored in Walker's safe deposit box, Andrew began the translation. Shortly before midnight, he called Nat at home.

"It's Andrew," Carol said handing the phone to Nat. He took it, said hello and listened. His eyes flicked to Carol and Walker. They could hear Andrew's muffled excitement.

"OK. Are you coming alone? Should we come in and pick you up?" Nat said. Andrew spoke and broke the connection.

"He's coming here," Nat said.

"And?" Carol said.

"This is crazier than we thought. We're going to have to figure out what to do now," Nat said.

"Time to call Edith," Walker said taking out his cell phone. "She will want to be in on this too."

"Do you think we should wait?" Carol said. "How long will it take her to get here?"

"About fifteen minutes, I'd guess," Walker said. "She's been here since Monday. She's at the King David hotel, keeping a low profile while Andrew finished the translation."

Edith arrived before Andrew. No one talked much until Andrew came through the door. They sat together while Nat read the translation aloud. They were still discussing options when the sun rose on a new day. The house phone rang and Carol answered, then hung up and turned on the television. The early news show was headlining a story by anonymous sources within the Rockefeller Museum about a two thousand year old body found in a cave near the Dead Sea site of Qumran that might be that of Jesus of Nazareth.

"Show time," Walker said. "We better come up with a plan. Today."

Chapter 14

The Museum scheduled a news conference for the next day. Dr. Mayefsky the IAA Director and Dr. Menahem would speak first, then Maria would describe the site, the recovery and what had been so far learned about the body. New concern had developed that a New York Times reporter was working on another story about a missing artifact that had also been found with the body.

The Museum's largest conference room was choked with cameras, wires, microphones and people representing the world's news organizations. Guards were turning people away. Television monitors had been set up around the walls and a large screen had been placed outside to accommodate the crowds that had been gathering since early morning.

Inside, reporters and cameras were still jostling for position when the side door opened and Dr. Mayefsky led a group into the room and onto the raised dais. They took places behind him as he stepped up to a podium, top heavy with microphones. Nat put an old leather briefcase down at his feet. Edith stood between Carol and Andrew.

"Thank you all for coming today. I am Dr. Zev Mayefsky, Director of the Israeli Antiquities Authority. Before we begin, I must ask that you hold all questions until the team has made its presentations. There will be a question and answer period immediately afterwards.

"As you know, a survey team was assembled under the direction of Dr. Evron Menahem, our Deputy Director, and sponsored by an old friend and associate of the museum, Mrs. Edith Donaldson of the United States. The team's mission was to search for potentially valuable artifacts that we had reason to believe were located in the desert area north of Khirbet Qumran, the site where the Dead Sea Scrolls were found. The team, most of whom are assembled here," he turned, sweeping his arm toward the group behind him, "will also be available for your questions."

"Last week we were successful in finding a cave located in Wadi Og in the northern Dead Sea area. Inside the cave was a body, amazingly well preserved. We assembled an extraction team and brought the body here for exposure and analysis. Although that process is still incomplete, we do have some initial information we can announce. For that, I present Dr. Menahem, Deputy Director of Archaeology."

The noise level rose as reporters shuffled for better positions, took notes and talked among themselves while Menahem took the podium.

"Good morning. I will be brief. As of today I can report the following concerning the body recovered from the cave. Although we do not have definitive data as yet, we are highly confident that this individual lived during the first Temple period, the years between the beginning of the First Century CE, and the first Jerusalem revolt, which occurred in 67 CE. The individual was male, somewhat above average height for that period, around 170 to 175 centimeters. Age is estimated between thirty and forty years. From the samples recovered with the body, he was bearded and had black hair. There were, ah... signs of trauma on the body."

"What were they? Was he crucified?" someone yelled out from the crowd.

"As Dr. Mayefsky said, please hold your questions until later..." Menahem began.

"Tell us now! What happened?" another person shouted. "Shut up! Let the man talk," someone else yelled.

"Please!" Menahem raised his voice. "If we cannot have order, I will terminate this press conference now."

Security personnel took the reporter into custody and were escorting him toward the doors.

"Wait," Menahem said. "Hold up." The security team stopped. "We want everyone to hear this. Sir, if you can restrain yourself, you may remain." The reporter nodded and the security team released him.

"Now, to continue," Menahem said. "As to the trauma," he looked down at his notes, "they consist of puncture wounds in both heels, and a fractured radial bone in the left arm. There may be other, less obvious injuries but we won't know until the final analysis is complete. There is some indication that the body may have come from northern Egypt. The methods and materials used in the body's preservation were common to that region and seldom, if ever, found in association with remains from ancient Judea or Sumaria. There will be detailed handouts available as you leave.

"Now, before we get to questions, Mrs. Edith Donaldson, the sponsor of the survey, would like to say a few words, followed by Dr. Maria Chavez who was responsible for the recovery. Mrs. Donaldson," he said stepping back from the podium.

Edith and Nat, carrying his briefcase, stepped forward.

"I am Edith Donaldson, and this is my colleague, Nathaniel Benjamin who uncovered the initial information that led to this discovery. Nat, would you please," she said.

Nat opened the briefcase and removed the scroll, holding it high for the cameras.

"This is another artifact found in the cave with the body. As the sponsor of the survey, I directed the team to withhold this scroll from the Museum until it could be thoroughly examined and translated," she said. The room broke into loud conversation. People crowded closer for a better look.

"What is she doing?" Menahem said to Mayefsky.

"I don't know, but this must stop," Mayefsky hissed and started to move forward but Walker grabbed him just above his elbow and squeezed hard on the nerve sending a jolt of searing pain up his arm and into his shoulder.

"Stay where you are, Doc. You too," he said softly to Menahem. "She'll be done in a minute."

"We believe that the contents of this scroll together with the remains, demonstrate that this is, indeed, the body of Jesus of Nazareth, also called Jesus Christ," she said.

The crowd erupted, everyone talking and shouting questions at once. Edith stood calmly, waiting for the noise to subside. Walker kept his grip on Mayefsky. The crowd began to quiet. Then Edith spoke again.

"The scroll will be available, here, today, and later at the Museum, for all scholars to examine. I am convinced of its authenticity and am certain that those more qualified than I, given the opportunity to examine it, will also agree. I also call upon the Museum to provide their results to the world, and provide access to qualified scholars and scientists to examine the body and scroll for themselves.

"As to the scroll's content, which is the most significant of these amazing discoveries, it is being made available, as

I speak, to everyone. The complete translation is being published right now on the internet, along with high resolution photographs of the scroll itself."

"Questions?" she asked.

A young woman from the London Times beat everyone to the punch.

"The scroll, what does it say?" she shouted.

"The scroll was written by a Roman, Lucius Quintus in the year 53 CE. He lived in what is now Israel and personally knew Jesus of Nazareth. The scroll is the story of what happened, written in his own hand."

Part Two

Rome

30 CE

The House of Quintus

"Lucius Antonius Quintus, you must arise now. Your father is asking for you."

It was Kasha's voice. Lucius could tell with his eyes closed, which they were, and he intended to keep them that way.

"Go away," Lucius groaned. "Too early. Head hurts."

"I am not surprised at this. Why should you be so? Last night you drank enough for both of us," Kasha said.

"You don't drink," Lucius said his voice seeming to come from outside his head.

"You continue to provide me with sufficient reason not to begin," Kasha said. "Now, arise young Lucius, and attend your father."

The bed covers were abruptly yanked away and one of the house slaves drew back the window curtains admitting a painful spill of light. Lucius cracked one eye open and there was Kasha towering above him, his ebony skin bright in the light, smiling broadly at his discomfort. Kasha held a large bronze pitcher over the bed.

"What's in that pitcher?" Lucius asked.

"It is not more wine," Kasha said. "It is cold mountain water to assist with your rising."

"You wouldn't," Lucius said.

Kasha's grin grew wider.

"You would. I am getting up. Egyptians..." Lucius said.

"I am not Egyptian, as well you know," Kasha replied. He stood taller than anyone Lucius had ever seen, his body roped with long muscle, the ritual identifying scars of his warrior family furrowing in three serpentine lines on each cheek. His thick hair was pulled back and secured behind his neck with a gold band. The bright contrast of his white tunic and ebony skin was painful to Lucius' sight.

Lucius rolled upright, the inside of his head seeming to follow a heartbeat later. Kasha motioned to a house slave who took the pitcher from him and poured a large cup full. Kasha handed the cup to Lucius.

"Make haste, young Lucius, your father awaits," Kasha said.

Lucius grumbled but dressed hurriedly. He was not yet thirty years of age, tall, not nearly as tall as Kasha, and, like all Romans who lived and fought with the Legions, he was fit and strong. His brown hair was cut short in the Roman style, his eyes were green and, this morning, bloodshot. Although his nose was rather long and thin, like his father's, he was considered handsome and a good catch for an unmarried woman of equal rank. So far, he had eluded their efforts to capture him.

Lucius' father, Marcellus Rufus Quintus, appeared young for his years. He was tall, strong and always calm, deliberate and always himself. Lucius had never seen him lose his temper, curse the gods or mistreat his slaves, as many others were quick to do. His hair, once red, was now faded and graying after many years in the service of Rome.

"Good day, my son," he said as Lucius entered the sunlit courtyard where Rufus sat with Kasha, Larissa and Helvia taking breakfast.

"And, to you, father," Lucius said kissing him on top of his graying head. "And to you, my sisters."

"Ave, brother!" the girls said loudly in unison. Lucius winced. Rufus laughed at his discomfort and the girls struggled to suppress their laughter. They were pretty and soon to be beautiful young women. Larissa was dark and tall, like her father Kasha. Helvia appeared almost white sitting next to Larissa. She was average in height with the blue eyes of her mother and the red hair of her father.

"You two connived in this. No, do not deny it. I know both of you," Lucius said slumping on a couch next to them.

"Brother, you do look a fright," giggled Larissa.

"One day when you have had too much of Father's wine, I may return the compliment," Lucius said.

"I am teaching her the ways of the proper Roman matron, brother, so you should not depend on getting your revenge," Helvia laughed.

"Regard your sister's instructions well, Larissa. Moderation is the Roman way, moderation in all things," Lucius said.

"Yet, do not become discouraged when you stray from the path, daughter. We are human with merely a spark of the divine within us. We are not gods," Kasha said.

"Even the gods can stray," said Rufus.

"And, when they do, it is we, here, who must pay the price for their transgressions," Kasha said.

"This is certainly uplifting talk for early in the morning," Lucius said motioning to an attending slave for food and drink, "Meno, bring me a cup of the hot tea drink. The dark leaves."

When Kasha and his daughter Larissa had come with Lucius to Rome, they brought intricate wooden boxes packed tightly with dried leaves. When a few of the leaves are placed in boiling water for a brief time and then removed, the remaining drink was both flavorful and either rouses or calms the senses, depending on the leaf.

"Children," said Rufus to the girls, "you may leave us. We must talk."

"Yes, Father," the girls said together, rising to leave. Then to Lucius and Kasha, "We are glad you are home."

They both kissed Rufus, then Kasha, then Lucius. Larissa lingered for a quiet word with Kasha then departed with her sister.

"Larissa has grown these past two years," Rufus said to Kasha. "Do you see much difference in her now?"

"Yes. She is happy and her spirit is growing free. Alexandria was hard for her. Perhaps she is putting that behind her now."

"Such things are never forgotten, but I believe she is learning to live with those memories. Time will continue to heal her and she brings much joy to our family," Rufus said. He rose and motioned for his toga. "Lucius, get your drink, then let us walk. We have much to discuss."

Lucius and Kasha followed Rufus into the busy morning streets of Rome. They made their way through the crowds and the markets, past the slave sellers and taverns to the temple of Saturn at the foot of the Capitoline Hill. They ascended the portico and stopped between two of the massive pillars.

Rufus turned so that his back was to the street. With Kasha on one side and Lucius on the other it would be impossible for them to be overheard. Also, they could observe anyone who might approach too closely.

"Now, let us talk," Rufus said.

"Why the secrecy? Are you in danger? Has this to do with the Emperor?" Lucius asked.

"Yes, but more so with Sejanus. Things are changing in Rome. Tiberius is awakening to danger at last."

"What danger?"

"Sejanus is seeking to replace Tiberius as Princeps. Sejanus has grown powerful. He has the Praetorian Guard and now he courts the Julii. I believe he is maneuvering to become an adopted member of that family, which would give him powerful support and wealth, enough wealth to perhaps to influence certain Senators…"

"To replace Tiberius," Lucius finished for him.

"Exactly."

"How did he manage this without the Emperor's knowledge?" asked Kasha. "Tiberius is no fool."

"Sejanus has taken into his control all communication between Rome and Tiberius, who remains in Capri. Or so Sejanus believes. Tiberius trusted him. His work partner, Tiberius called him, and depended upon him for the functioning of the empire. Until recently, no one dared tell Tiberius the truth of the matter. Now he knows," Rufus said.

"What man braved Sejanus' wrath to bring Tiberius such news?" Kasha asked.

"No man, but a woman who is in a position to know. She is someone Tiberius would not doubt," Rufus said.

"Father, how is it that you know this?"

"I too have my sources, who shall remain unknown. Dangerous times," he said. "Besides, Tiberius told me."

"Tiberius himself?" Lucius asked.

"Not directly, of course, but we maintain secure contact."

"You are certain your communication is secure?"

Kasha smiled. "If it were not, Sejanus would have killed us all by now."

"I see that Kasha remains both your guardian and teacher," Rufus said.

"Yes, he is my most stubborn, wise and outspoken friend. I still thank the gods for the day we met," Lucius said.

"As do I," Kasha said.

"Even so, these are treacherous days. We must trust in our friends. As does Tiberius. He has sent for us," Rufus said.

"Us?"

"You particularly, and Kasha too, of course. I will accompany you."

"He is still in Capri?"

"He is. We sail tonight."

"What could the Emperor want with me?" Lucius said.

"We will discover that from Tiberius himself. Something secret, I suppose," Rufus said.

"And, dangerous," Kasha said smiling.

Old Friends

Tiberius, master of Rome's vast empire, sat alone in a large hall open on three sides to the air and the sea below. He had retreated to the island of Capri four years previously, keeping himself distant from the Senate and Rome's powerful families, leaving the task of ruling to Sejanus. He was long divorced from his first wife, Vipsania Agrippina, whom he loved, forced to marry Augustus' daughter, Julia the Elder. Tiberius was now in his middle years, graying and quiet. His face mirrored sadness. When Rufus, Lucius and Kasha entered he appeared to be asleep, but as they approached he rose and placed a scroll among the others on a table by his chair.

"Ave, Caesar," Rufus said.

"Greetings and well met, old friend," Tiberius said gripping Rufus's arm in friendship.

"Ave, Caesar," Kasha and Lucius said in unison.

Tiberius smiled, "Ah, so you two are together in all things. Rufus told me of your friendship. It does you both honor."

"Yes," said Rufus, "they are both the better for it."

"Good, good," Tiberius said. "We shall eat and drink while you tell me how this friendship came to be."

He motioned to someone standing in the shadows. The man turned and quickly departed and soon servants appeared with couches and tables laden with food and wine. As everyone took their places Tiberius lifted his cup and said, "Well, young Lucius and friend Kasha, tell me how this remarkable friendship began."

"Very well, Caesar. Being the elder, and the better master of memory, I shall begin," Kasha said.

"My daughter Larissa and I were living in Alexandria. My wife, Larissa' blessed mother, had recently died of the pestilence and we were still in mourning. One evening I returned home to find five Roman soldiers in my house. They had followed Larissa home and when I came into the house one had her on the floor. I immediately killed two of them but one of the others had a blade to Larissa's throat, so I permitted myself to be restrained."

"Wait," Tiberius said looking hard at Kasha. "You killed two armed Legionnaires then permitted yourself to be restrained?"

"Yes, Caesar. The first two were not difficult. I have skill with these arts," Kasha said. "The others would have been more difficult had it not been for Lucius. He also possesses certain skills although he does not yet properly value the worth of training."

Tiberius looked at Lucius.

"It was Neuna, one of Parcae, the Fates, that led me there. I had mistakenly turned into the street where Kasha and Larissa lived. As I neared the house one of the Legionnaires fell bleeding into the street. I entered and one of them attacked me. I killed him," Lucius said.

"The others?" Tiberius asked.

"By the time I finished with mine, Kasha had killed the rest," Lucius said.

Tiberius looked more closely at Kasha. "You killed four armed soldiers of Rome?"

"Yes, Caesar," Kasha said.

"Exactly how did you accomplish this?"

Kasha remained silent, looking calmly at Tiberius.

"Your pardon, Caesar," Lucius said, "Kasha is sworn to not reveal those arts to anyone who is not his pupil."

Before the silence grew uncomfortable, Tiberius spoke.

"Rightly so. If I were younger, Master Kasha, I also might seek your wisdom. Now, let us dine. After, we shall talk, neh?"

The food was plentiful and good but plain, with nothing strange or exotic as some were prone to offer their guests. Once they were finished, Tiberius began.

"It is Sejanus," he said. "He is changed. Perhaps I have been too long away from Rome. I have relied on my friendship with him and the good sense of the Senate. Not a wise decision, as it has turned out. I do not know why Sejanus has betrayed me, nor is it now important. I am at last privy to the truth. Sejanus seeks to replace me as Princeps."

"He is grown too bold," Rufus said.

"Yes, his boldness and lust for power reveals his true character. I should have seen this," Tiberius said. "As you have reminded me, old friend, trust can blind one to many things."

"Now the game is in the open."

"Almost, but not quite yet. It is now my move," Tiberius said turning to Lucius and Kasha, "You both will be my personal emissaries to Judea. Lucius, Rufus tells me that from your service in Syria you are familiar with that part of my empire."

"Yes, Caesar. It is my honor to serve you and your house, as always," Lucius said.

"I too am honored, Caesar," Kasha said.

"I have sent word to the Judean Prefect, Pontius Pilate and to the Lucius Vitellius, my Syrian Legate that you will be coming to Judea and that you are my personal representative. Pilate will treat you accordingly. I have told him you are to bring me news of the country and the temper of Herod's people. I indicated to him that my trust in Herod has run thin, and you may be able to discover more of his true purposes with your ease in their language," Tiberius said.

"However, your real task is to keep that fool Pilate in check. He created quite enough difficulties with the Jews soon after his arrival. I want no further problems in Judea, especially now. I plan to move against Sejanus soon, and there will be trouble. I want my provinces to remain undisturbed and the grain to continue to flow, especially that from Egypt. Judea is key to the land and sea routes. Do you understand?" Tiberius said.

"Yes, clearly, Caesar. I speak but little Hebrew, but in the common language of the people there, I am well versed," Lucius said.

"Pilate is no fool. He will know the reason I have sent you, and he will also know that you see and speak for Caesar. He is not so foolish that he will obstruct you or let you come to harm."

"Yes, he will be cautious and careful, but still, he will bear watching," Kasha said.

"Indeed," Tiberius said. "He is crafty, and can be merciless when it suits his needs."

"As can we," Kasha said.

"Well, Rufus," Tiberius said, "It appears we have chosen well. Lucius, you and Master Kasha will leave tomorrow. Time is short, and I will act soon. May you fare well and journey safely."

Tiberius stood and retrieved two scrolls from the table. Handing them to Lucius he said, "This one is for you. It is my authority for your commission. This other you will give to Pilate so he will clearly understand your purpose and his charge to provide whatever you require. Send word to me when you arrive."

"Yes, Caesar. Is there any message you wish me to deliver to Pilate?"

"A personal word, eh? You may tell him that Caesar trusts he will uphold the honor of Rome, as always. Now, off with you both."

As they took their leave, Tiberius said, "Rufus, a word…"

Rufus and Tiberius walked out to the low wall overlooking the drop to the sea below, talking quietly. Kasha and Lucius left them to prepare for their journey.

Welcome

Caesarea Maritima was the major Judean port and the administrative center of Roman control. The Roman governors lived in Caesarea, conducting business from Herod's palace by the shore, enjoying the luxurious baths and entertaining guests. Caesarea was a fine city, the most modern in Judea. Being a hub of commerce and government and a portal to the Middle Sea, all the eastern Mediterranean cultures were present there in some degree. Greek, Hebrew, Latin, Aramaic, Copt and Persian were spoken, often mixed together within the marketplace in a single conversation. The Romans had built a magnificent hippodrome for their chariot races, the largest on the eastern sea, and the theatre held performances almost nightly.

Inland, a few day's journey to the east lay the real center of Judea, the soul of the nation, Jerusalem. The contrast between the two cities was striking. Far from the coastal breezes, sprawled across steep rocky hills, bereft of races or theaters, it drew the faithful and the pious, the pilgrims and the curious. The Second Temple complex, begun by Herod the Great, now nearing completion, dominated the city. The vast enclosure and buildings within it were claimed by many to be one of the world's wonders. Herod had turned the summit of Mt. Moria into a vast platform to support the Temple complex, using Roman, Greek and Egyptian architects to plan and supervise the enormous project. Huge stones were quarried and dragged to the site, then positioned in long trenches dug for the foundations. The labor was immense, and the result was a temple complex to rival anything in Greece or Rome. There, within the inner room of the Temple building itself, dwelt the Jewish god, when he cared to come, marking this place as the soul of his people.

The Centurion Marcus Claudius Strabo strode purposefully through the halls of Herod's Palace by the sea in Caesarea Maritima. Those in his path were careful to give him plenty of room. Marcus' temper was known and feared by all. Powerfully built, tall and blonde, his hair almost white, Marcus was a master with the Roman gladius and pilum, the short sword and javelin, and few dared to challenge him. Rumor was that once, in Rome, he had entered the arena, disguised as a gladiator, and killed all those who opposed him, winning a wreath from the Emperor.

This was, indeed, rumor. Marcus had never been to Rome. Until he had joined the Legion in Gaul, he had not ventured more than a few leagues beyond his village. Now, thirty years later, he had seen half the world and he liked most of it better than he liked Judea.

"The Prefect?" Marcus snapped at a minor official hurrying by with an armload of scrolls. "Where is he?"

"Sorry, your honor, he is, I think... yes, he is in the baths," the man stammered, gesturing with his chin over the pile of scrolls toward the sea.

"The baths," Marcus grumbled as he stalked off, "Hell's own dark gate, the baths. Always the baths. You'd think he'd be clean enough by now." He quickened his pace, scattering servants before him.

The Roman Governor of Judea, Prefectus Pontius Pilate, lay reclined on a delicate cedar wood divan, talking with a small group of similarly reclining men. They were laughing at some joke and eating olives, fish, bread and cheese, washed down with wine in large silver cups.

"Ah! Marcus," Pilate exclaimed, "join us. Pico here has a delicious tale of his evening with Herod's people."

"I swear by the gods, if Herod was dispossessed of that dense beard and those ringlets about his ears, anyone would take him for a Roman patrician's wayward son," said one of the men with Pilate.

Had Pilate grown his hair and beard, he might have been mistaken for a Jew. He kept his hair cropped short which did not conceal the gray beginning to show amidst the black. He was of medium height, but powerfully built, his tanned face broken by wrinkles and a long scar running down from the corner of his left eye, separating the end of that eyebrow into a small, black island, continuing deeper and down across the cheekbone, trailing off before cutting through his upper lip. A handsome face, even with the scar. Handsome, edged with hardness and a hint of cruelty.

"Prefect, I bring news," Marcus said looking pointedly at the reclining guests. Pilate stood.

"Please continue. I must deal with the Empire's business," he said to the others.

He and Marcus walked to the western end of the baths and decorative pools Herod had built on a low promontory by the shore of the Middle Sea. The distance from the others and the roll of the waves breaking on the rocks below gave them privacy of speech.

"They are here," Marcus said.

"Hmm...... Tiberius' spy and his black shadow, at last. No matter. We are prepared are we not? Everyone knows their duty."

"We are ready, Prefect," Marcus said.

"We must be cautious with the Jews. They are a stiff necked lot, and, my bones tell me, are bound to cause trouble before our visitors depart."

"Many Jews have found it in their best interests to obey your counsel."

"True, but that business of the shields in Jerusalem still rankles and Tiberius has not forgotten. Nor, apparently, forgiven."

"The Jews were quick enough to take our gold then. They will again, should it come to it."

"We will deal with them," Pilate said, "but now, tell me your news."

"Two fast triremes are coming into the harbor. They tie up within the hour. They fly the Senate's flag, so it is him, Lucius Quintus. How shall we receive him?"

"As we would Tiberius himself," Pilate said then laughed, "Well, not as the old man himself, more as a demi-Tiberius I should think."

"A reception party of virgins and young boys then?" Marcus chuckled.

Pilate did not smile. "You do not know the old man," he said. "Tiberius cares not for the debauch and wine. Would that he did for his mind would not have rested here, on Judea, on us. He eats simply and drinks sparingly. His tastes run to philosophy and the ways of the Greeks, not the sybarites. Unfortunate for us…"

Both men stood silent for a while, watching the perfect sweep of the ships' three tiers of oars as they appeared beyond the point and made their turn into the harbor.

"Come, let us prepare to greet Tiberius' watch dogs," Pilate said.

As the lead trireme swept into the harbor, white water breaking under her bows, Lucius and Kasha stepped onto the deck for their first view of the port and the city of Caesarea.

"Caesar's messenger was swift," Kasha said pointing to the pier where a cohort of Roman soldiers was drawn up, waiting at attention. Their commander stood relaxed and curious before them as the trireme neared, and the crew made ready to tie the long ship against the pier.

"That one is a fighter," Kasha observed of the Centurion.

"You know this how?" Lucius said.

"I do know it. So should you. Observe, young Lucius. He is relaxed, yet ready. He sees everything without appearing to do so. His gear is used but well cared for. His gladius is plain but exceedingly well made. The grips are wrapped in rough leather, not engraved or inlaid with gold. A sword for fighting, not for show."

Kasha was correct, as usual. Kasha also carried a Roman short sword like that of the Centurion's, but Kasha's was longer and much older. It had belonged to Kasha's master. Lucius had never seen him without it.

"Ave! Lucius Antonius Quintus of Rome," the Centurion saluted as the trireme bumped against the pier and the handlers' ropes made it fast. "I am Decimus Marius Lucullus, Centurion of the Prefect's cohort, your guide, and by the Prefect's order, your guard."

"Ave, Centurion," Lucius said. "This is my friend and companion, Kasha of the house of Quintus. You will treat him as you would me."

Decimus looked Kasha over, head to feet. "Appears to me that your companion will not require much in the way of protection," he said.

"There are times when one cannot prevail against many, and the help of friends is sorely needed," Kasha said.

"May they always prove both brave and true," replied Decimus, giving his salute to Kasha and swinging his open hand toward the palace. "If it please you, I will escort you to the Prefect. He awaits your coming."

"Let us not keep him waiting too long," Lucius said.

The escort troop formed up and marched down the pier. Decimus said softly, seemingly to himself, though he threw a glance towards Lucius as he spoke, "Waiting is not one of Pilate's strong points."

Prefectus

"Ah, Lucius Antonius Quintus and Master Kasha, friend and companion, welcome!" Pilate said striding across the spacious entrance hall to greet them. "We give thanks to Poseidon and his minions for your safe passage to us."

"Greetings, Prefect," Lucius said clasping Pilate's outstretched arm, which was browned by the Judean sun and hard with muscle. A sword fighter's arm. "The Emperor sends his greetings and commands me to give you this," Lucius said handing over the scroll Tiberius had given him to convey.

Pilate took the scroll without looking at it and held it up as a scribe stepped forward and took it from him.

"Tiberius is kind and thoughtful as always. We are honored that his thoughts pause to rest upon us here, so far from Rome. Tell me, how does the Emperor? Is he well?"

"He is," Lucius said. "He appears much as he did when a younger man, even though the cares of the empire weigh always upon him. He bears them well and with much fortitude."

"My manners...Come, forgive me," Pilate said. "Let us rest while we talk and take refreshment. Marcus, join us."

Marcus moved out of the shadows and followed as Pilate led them into a wide garden murmuring with fountains and lush with blooming flowers and fruit trees. Tables and couches were set under a wide blue and white awning. They reclined in the shade while servants rushed about putting platters of food on the tables and pouring wine into golden goblets.

"I present Marcus Claudius Strabo, Centurion of Cohort Prima Augusta here in Caesarea," Pilate said motioning toward Marcus, who was reclining beside him. "I have charged him with keeping order among our stiff-necked Jews. He also keeps me informed about our local troublemakers."

"If you know those who are trouble do you not deal with them so they are no longer troublesome?" Kasha said.

"Some Marcus kills. A few are given to the Jewish authorities to deal with and the remainder… they are convinced it is in their best interests to cooperate with us," Pilate said helping himself to a plate of olives, bread and cheese.

"Most efficient," Lucius said.

"Please, Lucius Quintus, call me Pontius. Prefect is much too formal among friends, neh?"

"You will be Pontius. I will be Lucius," Lucius said.

"And Kasha will always be simply Kasha?" Pilate said.

"You will find there is little simple about Kasha," Lucius said.

Kasha was reclined at ease, eating and drinking his water as if he were the only one in the room.

"Doesn't say much," Marcus said.

"Only as much as needs to be said although he is always free with his counsel to me. I am not yet, as he often reminds me, fully formed," Lucius said.

"Impertinent," Marcus said looking closely at Kasha who merely reached out for a date, his eyes half closed.

"Perhaps. Forgive me," Lucius said arising from his couch, "but the journey was long and now that the deck beneath my feet is no longer pitching and rolling I greatly desire to rest."

"Then I must ask for your pardons," Pilate said and gave orders for them to be shown their quarters.

The following morning, Lucius and Kasha found Pilate and Marcus attending to business.

"You will pardon me, I trust, if I do not accompany you about the city today. There is much to see, but other matters call me. There has been more violence in Galilee. Hard people, the northern Jews. A few of them enjoy killing Romans. At times they also kill their own whom they term collaborators. We find them, eventually, of course, but they must breed regularly for there seems no end to them," Pilate said.

"This is a matter of concern?" Lucius said.

"An irritant, nothing more," Pilate said wiping the subject away with a wave of his hand. "Things have always been thus, at least as long as we have been here, and, I suspect, the Jews will continue to kill one another were we to leave."

"Perhaps this is in their nature," Kasha said.

"That is so," Pilate said, "and their nature is stubborn. We find them and kill them, yet they continue to resist."

A palace servant quietly appeared and whispered in Marcus' ear, then moved aside.

"Ah... yes," Marcus said. "Prefect, the council members you summoned are here."

"Good. Good. We will see them presently."

"They are the Sanhedrin? The Jewish council here in Caesarea?" Lucius said.

"Indeed. There are also a few here from the Jerusalem council," Pilate said. "I often apply a certain persuasion to them in the expectation they will do likewise to their people."

Pilate paused and regarded Lucius with interest. "You are familiar with the Sanhedrin?"

"I know of them. A few of them from Jerusalem once came as a delegation to Quirinius in Antioch while I was there," Lucius said. "They are said to be the decision makers for the Jews in judicial and civil matters."

"Yes, but not in things religious. The Jews have the peculiar notion that their god is the only true god and all other gods are false. Strange, and manifestly false, of course. How could the god of a people sprung from wandering, desert goatherds possibly be superior to all the gods? It is the delusion of a subject people," Pilate said.

"As I understand, it goes further than that. The Jews do not admit the existence of gods other than their own. Their god has chosen them, they say, of all people as his favored race. If you are not a Jew, then you are without a god, since the Jew god is the only god," Lucius said.

"Even if the Jew's god was the only god, I'd not have my foreskin chopped off to honor him," Pilate laughed.

"The Jews have a powerful idea," Kasha said. "Being the favored people of the most powerful of gods will surely protect you from all who oppose you."

Pilate laughed, "The most powerful? The Jews are crazy. Their god did not protect them from us. Nor did he save them from the Babylonians."

"The Babylonians are no longer a threat to the Jews. Or to Rome. Perhaps their god works according to his own plan?" Kasha said.

"Or, he is merely lucky," Pilate replied.

"Fortune plays by her own rules," Kasha said.

"As do we," Pilate said. "Now, forgive me. I must attend these people. I have asked Decimus to be your guide today. He knows the city well. The races begin soon. We have the biggest hippodrome east of Rome and the market is the largest this side of Alexandria. You will find much to amuse you. We will meet tonight for the feast in your honor. Farewell."

Invitations

That evening Lucius and Kasha attended the feast which was held in a large open air plaza bounded by walls and columns on three sides and the sea and shoreline rocks on the other. Guests were everywhere, reclining, eating, sitting in groups, some wandering about, talking and drinking. A group of musicians made low flute and scraping sounds in a corner. Few paid them heed.

"There is a member of the Jewish council here you should meet if you would know more about Judea," Pilate said. "He is an influential man and, mark you, no fool. He works with us, but is no friend to Rome. However, he can be counted on to support what is in the best interests of keeping the peace and the commerce flowing, even when it is not popular with his fellow Jews."

"Ah, there he is," Pilate said approaching a knot of men in animated conversation. "Joseph! Joseph, you must greet Lucius Quintus, recently from Rome, and trusted friend of our gracious Emperor Tiberius."

The conversation ceased as everyone turned toward them. An older man, well built and dressed simply, bearded, as were all Jews, and wearing a dark green turban stepped forward, extending an arm to Pilate who took it in his own and turned the man toward Lucius.

"Lucius Quintus, meet Joseph, son of Samuel, head of the Sanhedrin Greater Council of Jerusalem," Pilate said.

"Greetings to you," Lucius said.

"And to you," Joseph replied courteously. Indicating the two men with him he said, "These two are Mikhael and Judas, my friends and priests in our Temple."

"Have you come because of the unrest in Galilee?" Judas asked.

"Is there trouble in that region?" Lucius asked.

"The Galileans are a rude and troublesome sort," Mikhael said.

"Not always, old friend," Joseph said. "Those in Tiberias and Sepphoris are not so. True, many of them follow the Greek customs but most remain pious and observant Jews."

"However, you must admit that the farther north one travels into Galilee, the more rough and rude the people become," said Judas.

"Their ways are different. They live far from Jerusalem, closer to the gentile lands than we. It has always been thus. It is not the mark of inferior people," Joseph said.

"Ah, there you are wrong, I think," Mikhael spoke up. "For is not Galilee the seat of rebellion and violence? Is not it the home of Judas of Gamala and his sons?"

"Yes, but they are dead and no longer a threat," Pilate said.

"A threat?" Lucius said.

"A few years ago Judas of Gamala raised an insurrection against the census ordered by Quirinius. He declared that God was the Jews' only King and they would obey no Roman, Prefect or Emperor. After a few skirmishes, our legionnaires killed Judas and crucified two of his sons. One escaped, but he was later found and killed by the Pharisees. Is that not correct, Mikhael?" Pilate asked.

"It is, my lord," Mikhael said.

"Still, Galilee is not entirely pacified," Dimetrios said. "The 'sicarii' first appeared in Galilee, and they plague us yet today."

"Sicarii. Yes, the dagger-men. I have heard tales of them," Lucius said.

"They call themselves zealots, loosely meaning 'zealous for God'. They hate Romans and any of our people whom they believe to be sympathetic to Rome," Joseph said.

"They are impossible to identify," Pilate said. "They dress as any other person. They carry knives under their clothing and mark their victims within the crowds, in the markets or at the festivals, stabbing them, then fleeing in the confusion."

"Or they remain close by, part of the crowd, lamenting the slain. Oh, you may find the knives easily enough, they discard them quickly. Even though the dagger-men are spattered with blood, so too are many innocent bystanders. There is no way to tell who wielded the knives, unless someone talks. People dare not, else they suffer the same fate," Joseph said.

"I have been warned of them. No matter. Rome will not tolerate rebellion," Lucius said.

"Quite right," Pilate said. "Nail up their wives and children and see how long they persist."

"It is not just to make the innocent suffer for the wrongs of others," Lucius said.

"Just? Innocent? There is no justice for those who kill Roman citizens. There is only one response. Kill all who resist or offer the rebels succor," Pilate said.

Kasha spoke softly, "While it is just to kill someone who truly merits death, killing the innocent merely sows the seeds for a harvest of more enemies. It is not wise to create more reasons for people to hate you."

"Come, let us not dwell on banditry and death tonight," Lucius said. "Let us drink more of this excellent wine and talk of other things. Surely there are people of interest in this land who are not bandits or dagger-men?"

"Indeed, sir, there are many wise and learned men here in Caesarea and in Jerusalem," Mikhael said.

"Also in Tiberias and Sepphoris, let us not forget," a man standing nearby said. "Your pardon, sir, but we have not met. I am Jonathan son of Zebedee, and this is Benjamin, my cousin and partner in enterprise."

"Greetings to you both," Lucius said. "You have interests in trade?"

"Interests? Ha! They have fingers in many pies, most of them large and savory, neh?" Pilate said. "Olives, oil, spices from the Levant. Silks, slaves, and more than a few vineyards I understand. These two are richer than Croesus. Why, if they so choose, they could certainly pay us enough to take our troops elsewhere."

The two merchants smiled broadly at Pilate's little joke. "You give too much credit, sir," Benjamin said.

"But, if we Romans left who would there be to keep those damned sicarii from slitting their throats?" Pilate said. "Ah... your pardon. I have strayed again. Let there be an end to it tonight."

Joseph turned to Lucius and Kasha and said, "Lest you get the wrong impression of Judea, please accept my invitation to come to Jerusalem. Stay with me for a time so that I may acquaint you with our people and our city. The Temple is one of the wonders of the earth and it should not be missed. It will honor my family if you accept."

"Ah! An excellent suggestion!" Pilate said. "What say you, Lucius? Joseph keeps a fine table."

"Our thanks, Joseph son of Samuel. It is we who are honored. We gladly accept. We will be fortunate to have you as our host," Lucius said.

"Excellent. Excellent. It is settled then. Now, let us rejoin the women. I fear we must now pay for our overlong absence from them," Pilate said.

The following day Lucius and Kasha joined Pilate in his quarters.

"Welcome, welcome!" Pilate boomed. There was food and wine on the sideboard. Pilate was half drunk already. They spared each other a quick glance and took their couches near him.

"Quickly!" Pilate said slapping his hands together, "Our guests desire refreshment." The slaves scuttled about serving food and drink.

Pilate thoughtfully chewed an olive and spat the pit onto the floor.

"Now then, to business," he said. "How think you of our local guests last night? Entertaining, yes? They are not entirely pleased with the benefits of Roman presence."

"They did seem uneasy," Lucius said, "especially when the discussion turned to the sicarii and other rebels in the North. Are they a problem for us?"

"Rabble, nothing more. The Jews are no more fanatics when it comes to their customs and their gods than anyone whose lands we have taken. We deal with these things as they arise, nip them while they are mere sprouts, so they grow no larger. There were times, I will grant you, before I came, that there was trouble. But no longer. I have my sources. I am kept aware," Pilate said. He gulped a half cup of wine, wiped the excess from his beard with the edge of his tunic and dropped more olives into his mouth.

"The Emperor will be pleased that you maintain such control," Lucius said.

"Yes, the Emperor. Tell me, why is it that Tiberius has sent you here to me?" Pilate said looking askance at Lucius.

Lucius started to speak, but Pilate interrupted with a wave of his hand, "Never mind. I've read the message you brought from Tiberius. That is all well and good, but let us speak frankly. You are here to see that all remains quiet, that the grains flow from Egypt, that the tribute is collected and sent on to Rome without interference, and that the back door remain secure, neh?"

"Tiberius has no doubts of your allegiance and support. He feels that a closer understanding of Judea and the conditions under which you govern will enable him to be of even closer assistance to you. I am here to convey that message to you and to gain better understanding of your role and the challenges you face," Lucius said.

"Prettily done, Lucius Quintus," Pilate said, "but that is not the reason."

Neither Lucius or Kasha spoke.

"Sejanus!" Pilate said pounding his fist on the couch. "Sejanus, I say. He is the problem."

Lucius looked thoughtfully at Pilate. Then he spoke, "You must have heard rumor from someone who came with us from Rome."

"No one told me, nor have I spies in Rome. This is a secret easy to unravel. I know of the unease in Rome, of Sejanus' handling of the Guard and his disrespect of the Senate. I also know of his courtship of the Julii. Now, without warning, you are sent here by order of Tiberius to offer me unasked for aid. The reason for your presence was not difficult to divine.

"Tiberius will have no concern with Judea once Sejanus is dealt with. If he does not do this soon, there will be more than trouble, there will be death and war again among the great families. If civil war returns, this region will burn in flames, as will Rome. The fanatics here can't wait to drive us out. Every few years some crazed desert prophet whips the locals into a frenzy, then I have to send Marcus to kill them all.

"The last fanatic, the Egyptian he was called, assembled a great crowd on the hill opposite the walls of Jerusalem. There were perhaps a thousand of them trampling the olive groves while he preached magic to them," Pilate said.

"Magic? What kind of magic," Kasha asked.

"He claimed magical powers from his god, power to bring down the walls of the city. After he did this, he said his people were to storm the place, take the Temple where the Jews believe their god lives, and kill all the Romans. He would become their new King."

"What happened?"

"We killed most of the rabble and the rest fled, the Egyptian among them."

"He was not taken or killed?"

"So it appears. Perhaps he was. He was heard of no more, so either his magic helped him to escape, or a legionnaire skewered him on his pilum."

"Since then? Who is now inciting the people against us?" Lucius said.

"There are always the Jew prophets in the desert. Some are more popular than others, but they are always out there, railing against the priests in the Temple. The Jews can't agree amongst themselves on the nature and requirements of their one god. One of the desert wild men, a Galilean of course, has my interest presently. He is called John the Baptizer. He has so far been intent only in washing Jews with river water to purify them of their guilt or wrong doings or some such."

"Not recruiting an army?"

"Not unless you consider old men, women and children an army," Pilate laughed, waving his empty cup in the air. A slave moved quickly to refill it.

"Still, it would be wise to know more about this desert Jew. Have we no people watching this man, someone who can keep us informed?"

"No. I have not thought him to be enough of an irritant. But, you do have a point. Perhaps you would be willing to undertake the task. You could find this Baptizer, and while you are about it, see more of the country, get first hand information, which I am certain you wish to do. It would be a benefit to us both," Pilate said.

"Where is this Baptizer? Does he have a base?"

"I am told he wanders in the desert, dresses in skins and eats the raw flesh of wild animals. However that may be, he lives in a hard country and he does not stray far from water. He is working his pagan magic at the river called the Jordan which flows from the mountains in the north into a place they call the Sea of Salt. Sometimes, the Sea of Death."

"That is far?"

"It is three days from here to Jerusalem, two if you ride hard. From there, I suppose it would be another two or three days to the Salt Sea. He would be there, somewhere near the river. He should not be difficult to find."

"Then I will go in search of the Baptizer and learn what I can," Lucius said. "And, we will accept the Jew Joseph's offer of a visit. I will learn more of Jerusalem and the Jews there as well."

"Excellent! As I said Joseph cares little for us, but he is a wise Jew and knows that cooperation will gain him much more than opposition. When things are in his interest, he is very willing and has proved useful in dealing with their Council."

"When things are not in his interest?"

"Pressure works well," Pilate said.

The Road

A few days later Lucius and Kasha joined Joseph and a few other travelers journeying from Caesarea to Jerusalem. With them were Mikhael, the Temple priest and the two merchants, Jonathan and his cousin Benjamin. The remainder of the party was composed of these worthies' servants and four Egyptian traders and their camels laden with goods for the markets. Their journey began on the great coastal road that passed through Caesarea along the shore of the Middle Sea and on to Egypt. They took this road south, traveling slowly, keeping pace with the camels and the people on foot. Lucius and Kasha were mounted on horses. Jonathan and Benjamin rode a pair of fine mules, befitting their wealth and status. Joseph preferred a compact wagon pulled by an ox.

The party was three days traveling from Caesarea to Gezer, where the road from Jerusalem met the coastal road. There they found an inn for the night. The food was poor, the wine expensive and the beds lumpy. They turned east into the foothills the next morning and everyone's spirits rose. As they climbed higher the breeze off the sea cooled them and the party moved a bit faster. Near mid day they came to a place where the road topped a rise and curved into a valley defined by a line of trees bordering a small stream. Kasha, riding in the lead, pulled his horse up short and raised one arm. Lucius saw this and rode forward to him.

"You see something?" Lucius said.

"In the trees, near where the large gray rock lies," Kasha said.

Lucius thought he saw movement there, but he was not certain.

"What?" Lucius said.

"Bandits," Kasha said.

"I can make nothing out for certain, although…"

"Fix your eyes on the rock. Wait for movement."

Something glittered for a second in the trees and Lucius saw shadows moving deeper inside the grove.

"I see them."

"I make six, or seven. Two are mounted, the others are on foot."

"They are waiting for us to get near the trees, yes?"

"No longer. They know we have seen them," Kasha said.

"What now?"

"We wait."

"What is it? Is there trouble?" Benjamin said. He and Jonathan had ridden up beside Lucius and Kasha.

"Bandits," Lucius said.

"God save us," Jonathan said. "What will we do?"

"Return to the wagons," Kasha said.

The cousins looked at each other fearfully, turned their mounts and retreated.

"It will not be long," Kasha said and took his short, powerful bow from its protective cover and strung it quickly, using his thigh for leverage. He removed three arrows from the bow's case, notching one on the bow string and holding the other two in his left hand alongside the bow.

"I will kill the mounted ones. You take the others," he said to Lucius.

Two men rode from the trees into the open, followed by four men on foot. As they advanced, the men on foot spread out while the mounted bandits kept to the roadway. All had weapons, spears for the horsemen, swords, long knives, and clubs for the footmen. When they were about fifty yards away, Kasha turned his horse slightly to the right and quickly loosed the arrow strung on his bow. While it was still in flight he fitted another, drew and released it.

The first arrow struck the lead rider, piercing his chest just below the sternum and burying itself up to the fletching. The man looked with disbelief at the feathers protruding from his chest as the second arrow struck the other horseman in the right side of his neck just above the collar bone. This one, clutching the arrow in his neck, turned his horse and galloped madly toward the trees.

As Kasha released the first arrow, Lucius charged, his gladius out and held to the side, bearing down swiftly on the other bandits. They broke and ran. Lucius rode the slowest man down, slashing through his neck as he passed. The man went down, his club flying into the rocks.

Lucius reined in his horse. The remaining bandits were running hard for the safety of the trees. The man Kasha had hit with the first arrow still sat his horse. Lucius could see the iron arrowhead protruding through the back of the man's leather shirt then the man slowly toppled to the ground.

Kasha rode forward with Benjamin and Jonathan following a short distance behind. Kasha stopped and regarded the man on the ground, then swung down from his horse, drew his knife and quickly killed him with a thrust through the neck.

"You have killed a wounded man," Benjamin said. "He was defenseless."

"He was near death," Kasha said. "Better to reach the end quickly than to linger in agony."

"He is right, cousin. Nothing could be done, and he was a bandit. He would have murdered us had we been alone. You have our most grateful thanks!" Jonathan said.

"Your sentiments are worthy," Kasha said, "Death sometimes cannot be avoided, but it is rare for it to be a thing of thanksgiving. I will commend his soul to the gods now."

Kasha closed the dead man's eyes then stood and sang a slow and mournful song in a language that no one there understood.

When the party reached the trees, Kasha and Lucius went ahead to see that the way was clear. They found only the second rider, also dead, lying on the road just beyond the trees. They dragged his body aside and Kasha sent his soul on its way with another song. Leaving the bodies for the scavengers, the party moved on.

Near the end of the day the travelers topped the last hill west of Jerusalem. The ancient city spread before them. The late golden light washed the city walls in amber. White and red rooftops crowded within the walls, and tall square towers rose into the evening air. Smoke from many fires drifted lazily heavenward. Beyond, at the far end of the city, sprawled the Temple complex, glowing from recently cut stone, flowing with long colonnades bordering huge plazas and vast courtyards. In the midst of all this stood the Temple itself, a massive rectangular building, faced with finely cut marble, pierced by a single enormous wooden door flanked by tall stone columns that supported a gilt and decorated roof.

As the party descended toward the city gate, Lucius rode beside Joseph swaying on the wagon seat. "I was told that your Temple is one of the magnificent sights in the east. I can see that description does it justice. It can stand with any building in Rome."

"It is the second Temple to have stood on that place. The first was destroyed by the Babylonians after they defeated our people and took us into bondage. When we were finally released, many returned here, to our homeland and rebuilt the Temple," Joseph said.

"You are not finished, I see. There are many still at work on the outer buildings and walls," Lucius said.

"It required only nineteen years to rebuild the Temple itself. The former one was small, much smaller and not so magnificent. See," Joseph said pointing to the tallest building near the center of the vast complex, "the Temple building, and the other works you see, the outer courts and the walls, were begun by Herod. Mount Moria is not large enough to support the entire Temple complex so we have built up the ground around the mountain and leveled it as it is now," Joseph said.

"Your god must be pleased," Kasha said.

"Perhaps. Sadly, the Temple is without many of the elements that were housed in the old one. The Ark of the Covenant, the pot of mana that fed us in the desert, and Aaron's rod are no longer in our possession," Joseph said.

"Someday they may be returned," Lucius said.

"I do not think so, but one can hope," Joseph said. "Come, it grows late, let us enter the city. I greatly desire to see my family."

The traders and their camels turned off without a word of farewell. The rest of the party traveled the road alongside the walls and entered through one of the massive gates guarding the city that had existed in one form or another for over two thousand years.

Miriam

When they arrived at Joseph's house his family and servants were there to greet them. A young woman, not more than eighteen, with long black hair, gathered in intricate braids at her neck, ran to greet Joseph.

"Father!" she said embracing Joseph. "Welcome! I am so happy you have returned safely," she said. Then, seeing Lucius and Kasha standing just inside the doorway, "You have brought friends."

She looked Lucius directly in the eyes, frank and curious, with no hint of shyness or the coquetry he was accustomed to with young women. He was struck by her eyes, and by the overall look of her. Not beautiful, exactly, but someone lovely. Then something special grasped his heart and gave it a wrench. Kasha caught the look that passed between them. A slow smile spread across his normally impassive face.

"Friends and traveling companions, yes," Kasha said, "and most grateful to be welcomed. I am Kasha, of the house of Quintus," He bumped Lucius with his elbow as he bowed.

"Ah... Lucius Quintus," Lucius said giving a slight bow, "of Rome."

"Lucius and Master Kasha, I introduce my daughter Miriam," Joseph said, "and my sister, Deborah."

"You are both welcome," Deborah said. She was slim and graceful with dark hair piled high on her head accentuating her neck which was adorned with a necklace of gold links and lapis stones. She smiled broadly and her eyes were welcoming as she spoke. A few lines around them marked her as no longer a young woman but a mature and handsome one.

"Please, the servants will tend to your belongings. Follow me," she said. "We are prepared for guests and I am sure that you desire to refresh yourselves before we eat."

"Do you really live in Rome? Him too?" Miriam asked looking up at Kasha.

"Miriam, let our guests have time to rest and prepare themselves for questions," Joseph said.

Kasha laughed, "Yes, young daughter of Joseph, we both live in Rome when our duties do not take us elsewhere."

"Your duties have brought you to Jerusalem? Pity. I had hoped you were here for pleasure and relaxation. Our city has much to offer," Miriam said.

"We intend to partake of the sights and also the pleasures of Jerusalem. We intend to know it much better," Lucius said.

"Come, come, now," Joseph said to Miriam. "We can talk of this more at the evening meal. Sirs," he said to Lucius and Kasha, "we will call for you when it is prepared. For now, farewell."

Lucius and Kasha followed Deborah, and Joseph and Miriam went off, arm in arm, talking of his journey.

They gathered in a large room off the courtyard well lit by candles and lamps. The walls were tiled in colorful patterns, as was the floor. Long stone benches were built into the walls along three sides of the room and served as storage and sideboards for jars, pots, baskets and dried foods. In the center was a long narrow table made from fine cedar, inlaid with white stones in geometric patterns. The guests and family sat on sturdy, comfortable stools around the table. Lucius and Kasha were served first by Joseph.

"Is it your custom that the host serve his guests?" Lucius asked.

"It is my duty to see that you have all you need and you leave the table satisfied," Joseph said. "It is my honor to do so."

"Be watchful that Father does not reserve the best portion of the meat for himself," Miriam said with a laugh.

"Miriam, do not tease your father," Deborah said. "He is always the best host."

"I am sorry, Father. I know you would never do such a thing. I spoke only in jest," Miriam said.

"In that case, I will see that you get a sufficient quantity of this savory goat haunch instead of only bones," Joseph said smiling.

As they ate, Joseph was continually up, serving food, instructing the servants, calling for more from the kitchen and occasionally sitting to his own meal. Finally, after dishes of lamb stew, dates, olives, flat bread, lentils, green vegetables in an olive sauce, and the last of the savory goat, they rose from the table satisfied. The evening was warm, the heat of the day radiated from the walls and mixed with the cooler air settling into the courtyard where they gathered to take wine and talk. A servant girl offered round, thin pieces of baked bread coated with honey and toasted nuts.

"Tomorrow, we will take you through our city. There is much to see. It will require that you stay with us for some days," Joseph said.

"We are grateful. I would like to visit your Temple, if that is permitted?" Lucius said.

"You may see much of it, yes," Joseph said.

"It is really a bazaar. You may buy many things there, remembrances of the Temple, food, animals, jewelry…" Miriam said.

"You will give them the impression that the Temple is merely one enormous marketplace," Deborah said. "You may visit the Court of the Gentiles. The rest is open only to our people. All Jews may enter the Soreg, but within, there are places where only women, or men may go. The Court of the Priests that surrounds the Temple itself is solely for the priests."

"Inside the Temple, the tall one with white marble walls and gold topped columns? What is in there?"

"The Tabernacle which contains the Holy of Holies. In there reside the holy elements of our faith that remain to us. The others, of which we spoke, are, I fear, lost forever," Joseph said.

"I do not believe the gods live in only one thing or another," Kasha said. "They are capricious and come and go as they will, whether men wish it so or not. You believe your god lives here, in the Temple built for him?"

"We believe that when God comes on The Day of Atonement, when the High Priest sacrifices to God as atonement for our sins, God's presence is in the Temple, in the Holy of Holies," Joseph said. "But, does God live in the Temple? No."

"He comes, then, when he is called?"

"We do not call and God comes. He comes when he will. We are his chosen people. We have entered a covenant with God. That is why, on the Day of Atonement, God comes to the Temple, and we to him."

"Of all things here, I find this exceedingly strange," Lucius said, "that your people deny that any other gods exist but yours. I have traveled far in the service of Rome and nowhere, but here, do people have only one god," Lucius said.

"It is our way. God makes us who we are," Joseph said.

"Tomorrow, let us visit the Temple and you can see for yourselves," Miriam said.

In the following days, Joseph, often accompanied by Miriam and Deborah, took the two Romans through their city. The Temple complex was larger and more impressive than Lucius had anticipated. In and around it many people were coming and going, pilgrims, merchants, curious visitors from other lands. Priests were to be seen everywhere in their white linen robes and tall round hats, directing pilgrims, conducting tours for Jews who were permitted inside. Music and dancing and the smell of incense filled the courtyards and the open spaces.

They strolled the many streets that wound, up hill and down, through Jerusalem's markets, the vendors calling out, enticing them to bargain for their goods. Everything, it seemed, was for sale in Jerusalem, goods from around the world. Lucius found a fine, inlaid dagger from Spain which he bought for his father. He also found fine gifts for his sisters, and Kasha bought a large bolt of silk for Larissa.

One morning while Lucius and Kasha were walking with Miriam and Deborah, they entered a large area, shaped like a small plaza, thronged with people and lined with houses and shops. Suddenly, people screamed and the crowd drew back from two men on the ground, writhing from stab wounds, their blood rapidly spreading across the stones. Kasha and Lucius pushed the two women between them, and their swords flashed out at the ready. Quickly, the space around them cleared and they, along with the wounded men, were left in the middle of a circle of onlookers as a Roman guard detail roughly pushed through the crowd. Their leader, seeing Lucius and Kasha at the ready, strode up to them and saluted.

"Salve, Lucius Quintus and Master Kasha," he said. "We meet once again." The Centurion was the same man who had met them at the pier on their arrival in Caesarea.

"Salve, Decimus Lucullus," Lucius said sliding his gladius back into its sheath. The crowd had backed further away and was rapidly thinning.

"Another killing by the dagger wielding rebels. Did you see this happen?" Decimus asked.

"No, we heard screams and scuffling then saw those two on the ground," Lucius said.

One of the men still moved. The other was dead.

"Done for, that one," the Centurion said, "and the other soon will be. Nothing much to be done, the knife men will be well gone by now."

"We were told of these sicarii. Does this occur often?"

"Often enough to keep us alert. They kill Romans as well," Decimus said. "It was fortunate they didn't see you." Looking at Kasha he said, "Fortunate for them."

"Come," Lucius said to Miriam and Deborah, "it is time we returned. I will rest easier once we have you inside your own doors."

"Father, the zealots have struck again. We were nearby when it happened," Miriam said.

"Fools! Will they not understand that killing does nothing but beget more killing."

"I am told this happens frequently. Pilate does not yet consider them to be a serious threat. That could change if they are not somehow brought under control," Lucius said.

"I do not see how this can be done. The zealots do not care about peace. They live to fight Rome, to drive you and your Legions out of our land. They do not listen to us."

"Pilate calls them a rabble, an inconvenience, but should their numbers grow he will march against them. If he thinks they are building an army, he will move."

"There are not enough of them to make an army. More people go to hear the desert prophets than would ever join with the zealots."

"He told me of one such, a wild man who lives in the desert and goes to a river to wash the sins from your people. He is called the Baptizer."

"John," Miriam said. "You speak of John the Baptizer. We have heard tales of him. It is said he lives on honey and insects."

"Stories, my dear," Joseph said. "No one could live on that alone. He does baptize those who come to hear his rants. Some of them are willing."

"Rants?" Kasha said.

"He is another of the prophets. Crazy men who live alone, wandering from village to village, proclaiming that God is coming soon, that God will make all things right, will punish the wicked and drive the conquerors from our lands. God will establish his power here for all of his people," Joseph said shaking his head. "We have heard this from others before. Many times, yet God does not come and the world goes on as before."

"I have heard that John is different," Miriam said.

"Different? How?" Joseph said.

"I do not know. Many go to him so he must say something the people want to hear."

"I also would like to hear it. The message he brings to your people," Lucius said.

"You will not hear it here. You would have to journey south, near the great Salt Sea," Joseph said.

"Then, we will journey south," Lucius said.

"I will go too!" Miriam said.

"You will not!" Joseph countered.

"Why not? Are you fearful that I might hear something you will not like?" Miriam said.

"Miriam! Mind your tongue," Deborah said.

"John has nothing to say that either interests or concerns you," Joseph said.

"I am sorry, Father. But would you not profit by knowing what he is saying and what the people see in him? The Council could surely benefit from this."

"The Council pays little heed of these desert wanderers. Soon, he will disappear like the others."

"Knowledge of your enemies, or of those who may become your enemies, is always a good thing to have," Lucius said.

"Yes, and since Lucius and Master Kasha are going, I would be perfectly safe," Miriam said.

"Out of the question."

"Brother, do not be so hard set. You are a fair man and Miriam is a good daughter. I do not see why you should prohibit this," Deborah said.

"I cannot sanction my daughter going off on a journey with two men, regardless of how honorable they may be," Joseph replied, nodding toward Lucius and Kasha.

"She need not travel alone," Kasha said. "Deborah could accompany us. Honor, on all sides, would be upheld."

Joseph was silent. He looked at Deborah. 'No', his eyes said.

"How could we be more safe than in the company of Lucius Quintus, emissary of the great Tiberius, and Master Kasha, of the house of Quintus?" Deborah said.

"Deborah, I…" Joseph began.

"Father, please. It is only a short journey and I so wish to go," Miriam said going to his chair and kneeling beside him.

Joseph sat silent for a few moments longer, then said, "Very well. But no more adventures after you return. I agree to this only because both Lucius and Kasha will stand for your safety, and because Deborah will accompany you. You are young and youth would have its day. Mark me, I will be more strict in the future. You will afterwards remain here, in the city, at home where you belong."

"Yes, Father," she said kissing his cheek. "And I will obey."

The Baptist

John the Baptizer was standing in the Jordan's greenish, slowly moving water, talking in a clear but ragged voice. A large crowd was gathered at the ford on both sides of the river's banks. John did look the part of a wild man. He wore a crude leather shirt, the hair still clinging to it in patches. His own hair was black, long and unkempt. His eyes were wild. He spoke loudly, throwing his arms about, focused on his audience. God would come soon, maybe tomorrow. God will create his new kingdom on earth, destroy the Romans, the Pharisees, the Sadducees and all ungodly people.

Lucius and Miriam left Deborah and Kasha in the shade of a date seller's awning and moved closer to the crowd at the river's edge.

"He is not as ugly as I have been told," said Miriam.

A few people were slowly entering the river and wading out to where John stood shouting to the crowd.

"Oh? Are you perhaps interested in saving him from his lonely and destitute life?" Lucius asked.

"Don't be crude," she said. "I mean only that he is younger than I thought and not unpleasant to look upon."

"I see. A dirty, sun burnt wild man with long matted hair and beard, dressed in skins, is your idea of 'not unpleasant to look upon'," Lucius teased. Miriam ignored him.

"Who is that?" she said gesturing toward a group of men standing nearby.

"Those men? They are likely from Jerusalem or perhaps Caesarea. Priests or merchants, judging from their dress, come to see for themselves why your wild man is causing such a stir."

"No, not them. Him."

She pointed to a man standing somewhat apart from the crowd near the water's edge, listening to John. He was taller than the others, slim, with his hair worn long and beard cut short and dressed in a white tunic. He stood quietly, his arms folded across his chest, watching John closely.

"I do not know," Lucius said, "why do you ask?"

"He appears so intent. He hasn't moved since we arrived. Wait, he is going into the water."

The man waded into the river toward John. The other people in the water moved aside to let him pass. John put his hand on the man's shoulder and guided him a few steps further into the water then they began to talk. The man shook his head back and forth a few times and once gestured with his hands, pointing upstream. John hesitated for a long moment and then nodded in agreement. The man slipped out of his tunic, then John lowered him into the river and brought him back up again. He donned his tunic and slowly waded back to the river bank. The people in the water began moving toward John seeking their own baptism, but John, now silent, waved them away, waded downstream and disappeared beyond the river's bend.

"What was that about?" Miriam said.

"I do not know. Perhaps the man said something to displease the Baptizer."

The people were talking excitedly about what had just occurred. Some were angry, saying the other man had driven John away. A few dark looks were cast in his direction, but he paid them no heed. He stood quietly in his dripping tunic looking downriver to where John had gone.

"Let us go," Lucius said.

"Not yet. I want to talk with him," Miriam said and quickly walked to the dripping man.

"Sir...," she said and he turned and looked directly at her, and then at Lucius. There was something arresting in his gaze, something that both invited and challenged. The stranger's eyes were smoky gray, tinged with green. Lucius felt uneasy, as if the stranger had found a window left open to his thoughts.

"I am called Jesus," he said.

"And I, Miriam."

"And you?" he asked Lucius.

"I am Lucius Quintus, of Rome."

Jesus laughed. "Well, Lucius of Rome, God's peace be upon you."

"You also," said Miriam. "Sir, what did you say to the Baptizer that caused him to leave so suddenly?"

"Miriam, surely that is none of your concern, and an improper thing to ask," Lucius said.

"No," Jesus said, "it is a worthy question. I told him that Temple priests were here to see for themselves what he is doing. They mean to stop his baptism by water, especially here, in the Jordan. He replied, of course, that he is doing what God has called him to do and when God wants him to stop, He will let him know."

"Surely, he knows that he is being watched," Miriam said.

"Yes, child. He has known this for a long while."

"Why did he leave without blessing the others who came to him?" she asked.

Jesus smiled broadly. "You are quite curious and open with your mind, I see."

Miriam had that stubborn look Lucius had come to know well, her brows set just so and her body leaning forward into the questions.

"So I have been told," she said.

Jesus looked at Lucius, and Lucius could only shrug.

"John is unhappy," Jesus said. "We are kinsmen. He considers me to be his responsibility. When I told him I also wanted his baptism and his blessing, he did not want to give it. He fears for my safety, even though he thinks not of his own. I prevailed, as you saw. I do not know why he went away."

"You must be very persuasive," Lucius said.

"This is not the first time John and I have disagreed," Jesus smiled. "I also can be stubborn."

"If you are John's kinsman then you must know why he provokes the priests by purifying the people here, in the Jordan of all places? The Priests claim that authority from God and surrender it to no others," Miriam said.

A few passersby heard her question and stopped to listen.

"John is willful and stubborn. He believes God has chosen him, not the priests, to be His messenger. John burns with the Lord's message. When a man has a lamp, he does not keep it under a basket," Jesus said.

"Let your light shine too brightly and the Romans will come and take it away from you, and send you to God's kingdom before you are ready," one of the men standing near said.

"Better to live in the light than hide in the darkness," Jesus replied.

"Well enough for you to say," the man said. "We don't see your light shining."

He and the others with him laughed and walked away. Jesus turned and looked again in the direction where John had gone, then sighed.

"I am sorry for their rude behavior," Miriam said.

"No. They are right. I do have the light and it is time I must begin sharing it. Well met. You have brought light of your own and it has helped me see the way I must go."

"I don't understand what you mean," Lucius said.

"I hope we will meet again," Jesus said. "I must return to my Brothers at Khirbet Qumran. God's peace be upon you."

With that, Jesus lifted his hand in farewell, turned and walked into the bushes that crowded the river's banks.

"This Khirbet Qumran, is it nearby?" Lucius asked.

"Yes. It is there," Miriam said pointing to an area of green close upon a rocky escarpment in the far distance. "It is a place of the Essene Brotherhood. They live in celibacy and worship God in their own way, without need, they say, of the Temple."

"Celibates," Lucius said, "they must be a small and surly sect, having no wives or lovers."

"Why must Romans mock what they do not understand? Surely, even you must agree that there are many ways to worship God?"

"We worship all the gods in the ways most pleasing to them. You Jews insist on having only one god and cannot agree on the way in which he is to be honored. Now, which makes most sense to you?"

"You are skilled in the Greek arts of sophistry," Miriam said. "I will not debate this with you. Besides, it is not a matter of debate but of belief. It is a matter of the heart, not the mind."

"Then you stand accused by your own people."

"Meaning what?"

Lucius turned and pointed toward distant Qumran. "There. You said the brothers… what are they called?"

"Essenes."

"Yes, Essenes. You say they worship the same god as you, but they must believe in a different god or they would not live like outcasts in the desert when this same god lives and is worshiped in Jerusalem. Why is that?"

Miriam looked toward Khirbet Qumran. A number of people were walking along the dusty road toward that place. Miriam stood silently, watching, then said, "Let us go ask."

Qumran

Khirbet Qumran lay on a flat promontory beside the dry, forbidding escarpment bordering the western shore of the great Salt Sea. It was composed of a small, walled settlement dominated by a square three story tower. Date palms crowded and shaded the northern and eastern walls. Many more trees were visible inside the walls. Although its location and its surrounding wall, pierced by only a single gate, encouraged few visitors, a community had established itself adjacent to the settlement. Families lived in tents and ramshackle hovels made from rock and scavenged wood. They built cisterns to collect water when the runoff came down from the rocky heights after the short, vicious spring rainstorms.

Kasha halted the cart outside the gate and lifted Deborah easily from her place and swung her gently to the ground. Nearby, few Essene Brothers were talking with the people and others were reading from scrolls and debating with one another.

"Thank you, Kasha," she said.

"Let us find shade and refreshment," Kasha said.

Kasha and Deborah moved toward a food and wine seller's tent. Everyone stared at them while trying to appear not to. Miriam and Lucius walked to the shade of a date palm.

Two of the Brothers quickly disappeared through the gate into the settlement.

"I expect someone will come soon," Lucius said.

Directly three Brothers came out and walked to them.

"Greetings," said one, a short man, heavy and bearded with long hair curling down over his shoulders. "May God's peace be with you."

"And with you," Miriam replied.

"We seldom have Roman visitors," he said turning to Lucius. "I am Jacob, son of Aaron. We welcome you to our community." He held Lucius' gaze well, without sign of fear or apprehension. His companions though were not as composed. Their feet tended to shuffle and their eyes wandered. They were afraid.

"I thank you, Jacob son of Aaron. I am Lucius Quintus, emissary to Prefect Pilate in Caesarea, and what is more important, companion to my friend Miriam, daughter of Joseph, whose aunt also accompanies us." Lucius gestured toward Deborah who sat in the shade of the merchant's awning with a drink in her hand. Kasha stood near her, relaxed and watchful.

"The large black man?" Jacob said.

"He is with me," Lucius said.

"What brings you to us?" Jacob said.

Lucius looked at Miriam.

"My friend Lucius is curious about why we cannot come to agreement on how to worship God," she said, "and since I find it difficult to explain, I suggested we come here to ask."

"You have traveled from Caesarea to ask this?" Jacob said.

"No, we came from the river where we saw the Baptiser," she said.

"John," Jacob said turning to look toward the river. "We knew that he has returned and is causing trouble again."

"Trouble?" Lucius asked. "What sort of trouble?"

Jacob started to answer, hesitated, and said, "Please. Would you accompany me inside. This is a subject I must leave to the wisdom of others."

Deborah declared herself quite comfortable where she was, so Lucius and Miriam left her in Kasha's care and followed Jacob and his companions into Qumran. Just inside was built a square tower, pierced by sets of three windows on each side. They went through a second inner gate to a courtyard flanked by the living and working quarters of the Brothers. A narrow stone-lined channel carried water across one corner of the courtyard to a flour mill and storage area.

Jacob turned through another doorway and led them into the tower. They climbed narrow stairs to a room where a few Brothers were at writing benches set along each wall. The benches were built under the windows which provided light during the day. Lamps for nighttime use were hung on the walls above the writing benches, ink pots and papyrus scrolls. Jacob led them upward. As they neared the topmost landing, they heard voices coming from the room above.

"Please wait here a moment," Jacob said. Lucius and Miriam paused, listening. The voices from within were more distinct now, and one seemed familiar. Jacob went in, and the voices stopped. After a few moments, Jesus stepped through the door onto the landing. His face was flushed and his eyes seemed to be generating their own inner light. Seeing Miriam, he stopped and his face relaxed into a smile.

"Well met again," he said to Miriam, taking her hand. "You have followed me here?"

"Not exactly," she said, "but, in a way, I suppose that is true."

"Why have you come then?" Jesus said.

"I am curious about why the Essenes choose to live here near the Salt Sea away from the Temple in Jerusalem since I have been told that all Jews believe in the same God," Lucius said.

Jesus looked at Lucius curiously. "That is a matter of much debate among us. The reasons are complex and of little interest to Romans," he said.

"Could it not be that you have many gods, all similar, part of the same family, or perhaps one god with different natures?" Lucius said.

A voice from the doorway said, "But that is not the question. It is not a matter of the nature of God, but the nature of man who worships God according to how man understands Him." The speaker was tall and lean, with a full black beard and long hair tied back with a leather thong, his dress was the same as that of the Brothers except that his robe was adorned with a black cowl which hung loose down his back.

Jesus turned and smiled wryly at the tall man. "This is Caleb," he said extending his arm toward the man, "he is the Teacher for our brotherhood."

"Yours no longer if you persist in following that man," the Teacher said.

"He means John," Jesus said.

"Yes, I mean John. John the baptizer. John the rebel. John who would get us all massacred by the Romans," the Teacher said with some heat.

"Why would we wish to massacre anyone here?" Lucius asked.

"Your pardon, sir," the Teacher said. "I mean no disrespect to you, but as a Roman you will agree that sedition and rebellion are dealt with most severely."

"Indeed. How is this Baptizer creating rebellion by washing your people in water, for what I am given to understand, is the repentance of their sins?" Lucius said.

"My cousin is playing a dangerous game," Jesus said, "it is not merely water he baptizes with, but water flowing in the Jordan itself."

"And…?" Lucius said.

"You must understand our history," the Teacher said. "Generations ago when our people fled the Egyptians out of bondage, we journeyed long to reach the promised land and our freedom. When we crossed the Jordan, our journey was done and we were at last free. Now, to bring people to the Jordan and baptize them in its water is to declare them free, free from our masters once again."

"And Romans," Jesus said looking at Lucius, "are our masters now."

"I see no danger from the farmers, merchants, peasants and the poor I saw today at the river. They do not make an army or even a rebellious mob. They are simple people, come here out of curiosity and perhaps piety to see this man and hear what he says," Lucius responded.

"So far," Jesus said, "but more people are coming to John each day. His message is spreading among the villages and towns and even into Jerusalem, as witnessed by yourselves. If you know, Herod knows, and Herod is dangerous and ill tolerant of rebellion, or anything that smells like rebellion."

"Don't persist in being a fool," the Teacher said to Jesus. "John may be your cousin, but no good can come of what you propose. John is a marked man and so are his followers, those who carry his message to others."

"It is a good message," Jesus said.

"Yes, we all await the Kingdom but we are not enlisting an army of followers that may be a danger to Herod and Pilate. You know how they are," the Teacher said.

"Herod knows John. He will not believe John is anything more than a prophet, readying the faithful for the coming of God's righteousness. He is no threat. There are others like him and they suffer no harm from Herod," Jesus said.

"But they do not baptize in the Jordan. They do not announce the imminent arrival of God's rule and the punishment of the unrighteous and the nonbelievers. John does, and that will be an end to him," the Teacher said.

"He is right," Miriam said to Jesus, "I know he is. My father and the Council in Jerusalem know of John. They talk of him, and I think some fear him, fear that he will create trouble with the Romans. The Prefect has a short temper and little respect for our Law."

"Yes, that is possible. That is why he did not want to baptize me this morning," Jesus said.

"What? You were there today? Did he baptize you too?" said the Teacher.

"I would not let him refuse me this time," Jesus said.

"Jesus, I cannot allow you to remain with us now," the Teacher said.

"I know. I will be leaving today. I will miss you and the Brothers," Jesus said.

The two men embraced and and Jesus stepped away, sadness clouding those remarkable eyes, dimming their brilliance.

"Farewell, Teacher," he said.

"Farewell," Caleb said.

"Where will you go?" Miriam asked.

"I am returning to Galilee. I will carry the message there, where there is no Jordan and where it is far from Jerusalem and Caesarea, and Pilate," he said looking closely at Miriam and Lucius.

"Wherever I am, you are always welcome," he said. "Both of you."

Promise

Jesus left Qumran with only his staff and a water skin slung over one shoulder and his large travel bag over the other. He traveled north, near the river, for its water and the shade along the river's banks. He met other travelers occasionally, but kept mostly to himself. He needed time to think and to pray about what was happening to him. He was still not certain why he had sought his cousin at the river and pressed to be baptized. He and John had talked about this many times before, and always John found reasons why he should not enter into the Jordan like so many others. Finally, at the river, John had relented.

"You accept others, readily enough," Jesus had said standing beside John in the water, "why do you continue to refuse me? Am I not also worthy?"

"All who come are worthy in God's eyes. You are no less so."

"Then?"

John paused and looked at the others who were also in the water, waiting. He made a slight motion with his head, placed his hand on Jesus' shoulder and moved him a few steps away from the others.

"It is dangerous. You are my kin," John said. "I would have you safe from the priests and Romans. I promised your mother."

"And my father? Did he also beg your aid for my safety?"

John was silent, looking at Jesus.

"You gave that promise when I was a boy," Jesus said. "I am not a boy and you are no longer responsible for my life. I live as I choose and as I am called to live. As do you."

"Of all Mary's children, you are surely the most stubborn. You have always been so. Running off to Sepphoris, sneaking into the synagogues and hanging about with the Greeks. Worrying your parents no end. No wonder Joseph beat you when you bothered to come home."

"Then I ran away again."

"Joseph would have beaten you more had he not died. A good thing for you he did not have a long life."

"He was old when I was born," Jesus said. "I think he was born old."

"Still, one's father must be shown respect."

Jesus was silent.

"All right, we won't talk about that now. As your elder and your cousin, I urge you to speak with Mary about this. Get it settled in your soul. It is not good to dwell upon the past, and there is much you do not know."

Jesus looked at John, that stubborn light in his eyes.

"Promise me," John said.

"Baptize me," Jesus said.

The two men stood facing one another, neither willing to speak. Finally, John sighed and said, "Very well. I will baptize you now, but you must see your mother."

Jesus paused for a few breaths, then said, "I will. I will speak with her, as you wish."

"Good. Good," John said and helped Jesus remove his robe. He placed his hand behind Jesus' back. Jesus grasped his arm as John lowered him into the Jordan.

Sepphoris

Things happened swiftly to Jesus after that, the return to Qumran, the heated meeting with the Teacher, again seeing the Roman and the girl, Miriam. That had come as a surprise. He wondered why a Roman would be there, at Qumran, with a Jew, and such an impertinent and curious Jew at that. Something was odd there, and something special, he thought, as was his pleasure at seeing them again. That was not the last time they would meet. He felt certain of it.

Jesus continued north toward Galilee, accepting the hospitality of the country folk when it was offered. He called people to him at villages near flowing water and baptized with John's message. A few people came, most did not. Some waded in to be washed in the cold water, but the others stood nearby watching and listening, then, talking among themselves, went back to their work or their homes.

In this way he journeyed until he came to the city of Sepphoris, built on a hill only three miles from his birthplace in Nazareth. He went into the town, through the markets and into an area of smaller houses and apartments in the northern part of the city. This part of Sepphoris had changed little. He remembered it well. As he approached the house where he had spent many youthful days, he saw Ariston sitting on the stoop. He had known Ariston since Klietos had taken him in off the streets, a ragged orphan, begging for food.

"God's peace, Ariston," Jesus said as he approached.

The young man looked up then laughed, jumped up and grasped Jesus by both arms.

"Jesus! It is so good to see you! An unexpected surprise!" he said.

"Unexpected, indeed," Jesus said grasping Ariston's arms in his own. "Look at you. No longer a stripling but grown into manhood. I have been away long."

"We had news that you were living with the Essene Brotherhood near the Salt Sea. We did not expect to see you here in Sepphoris again. Klietos threatened to seek you out if you did not return. Of course, he would never do so, but he still thunders and threatens from time to time."

"Ha! I would expect no less from the old man. How does he these days?"

"Not so well. He tires easily and seems often to dwell in a world of his own. Sometimes I must badger him to eat, and he sleeps little enough. I think he is at times in pain, but of course he will not admit to it."

"He is old, Ariston. His body is failing and he is now concerned with what will become of him after he departs this life."

Ariston paused and looked toward the doorway.

"I fear for him. You have your Jewish God, but Klietos has no god to turn to. He has only questions, always questions."

"Even the faithful have questions. God is not easy to understand. Many of our wisest men have different understandings of the will of God and the meaning of our lives. Klietos is not different in that way, even though he accepts no god as his own, and perhaps no gods at all. Still, he seeks to know, as we all do."

"Come, let us go in," Ariston said.

Jesus followed him, stooping as he went through the door. The room was spacious with a fireplace and hearth set into the far wall, flanked by a square wooden table set with two chairs on one side and a low bed on the other. A stool was drawn close to the bed where the old man lay propped up on cushions. He appeared to be asleep, his hands folded across his stomach, chin down, breathing rhythmically.

"You bring a visitor," Klietos said softly, eyes still closed. "Come closer."

Jesus and Ariston walked to the bed.

"A traveler," Klietos said. "I smell the country. Grass. Dust. Animals. Someone not from Sepphoris I think."

"I see your senses have not failed you, old man," Jesus said.

Klietos opened his eyes and looked up at him. A slow smile spread across his face and he reached out a frail hand toward Jesus, the tendons and veins showing clearly through his brown and mottled skin. Jesus moved to the stool and took Klietos' hand in his own. It was warm and thin and full of bones.

"It is good to see you again. I hoped you would come before Charon ferried me across the river," Klietos said.

"It is good to see you. I knew God would not release you before we met again."

"Pah! What has your god to do with it? I am a Greek, not a Jew."

"As I well know," laughed Jesus. "You have reminded me many times."

"Not that it did much good. Where have you been these past years? We heard rumor that you were living with those exiles by the Salt Sea, a community of the ones who are at war with your Temple priests in Jerusalem. The... now what do they term themselves?"

"Essenes."

"Yes, that's it. The 'essenoi'. Bookish lot, I'm told. Those by the Salt Sea especially, living off by themselves in the desert. No water. No women. Pah! Not such a life for a man."

"They serve God, not man," Jesus said. "The choice of how to do this is their own."

"Were you there? One of them?" Ariston asked.

"For a time. For a time. I was never one of the Brothers, although in the beginning I felt that God had called me to them. There are good men there, godly men who seek a pure path to Him. But, as it happened, their path is not mine."

"So, wasted years, eh?" Klietos said. "Better you had remained here and pestered me with questions as you once did."

"Not all was lost. I studied the torah for many hours. I have learned to write."

"A worthy accomplishment, indeed. Do you write Greek or that common tongue everyone speaks here?"

"Neither. I can write fairly well in Hebrew. The Aramaic I have yet to learn."

"Then you must learn to write and read Greek," Klietos said sitting up and swinging his legs off the bed. "Hand me my staff, boy."

Ariston gave him a long cedar staff and the old man used it to stand upright. Jesus and Ariston knew better than to help without being asked. Klietos shuffled to a trunk stowed at the foot of the bed, flipped the lid open with his staff and pointed inside.

"If you learn Greek, I have these for you. Many scrolls. The thoughts and conversations of the old ones, the Greek thinkers of many years past. They also have pondered the questions that you and I are struggling with today. I can't say they have all the answers, no, but they dug deep and their words can help us light the way."

"I do not think so," Jesus said. "I have other tasks before me now. I want to tell you about my cousin."

"Which one? You have many."

"John. The one who lives in the desert and baptizes in the Jordan."

"This is unwelcome news. Still… Ariston, go buy food and wine. We will eat while we talk about your cousin, the Baptizer," Klietos said.

While Ariston was away they sat at the table.

"Have you been home? Seen your mother?" Klietos asked.

"No. Nor do I intend to. There is nothing for me there. You know that."

"You must see your mother. She worries about you. She does not know if you are alive or dead."

"You know I have no wish to return to Nazareth."

"Yes, so you have said. I remember when your father came here and took you home after you ran away. Beat you too. Threatened to beat me, but he knew that he could not."

"I got your beating and mine," Jesus said. "Even though he was old, he was strong." He looked up at Klietos. "He is dead now. My cousin told me."

"Ah! That is unfortunate, unfortunate for you. I am sorry,."

"I care not."

"You should. You care whether you admit to it or not. All children care when their parents die even when there was little love between them. Wait too long and you will not be able to heal the wounds that have marked you."

149

Jesus sat quietly for a moment, then stood and walked to the door and leaned outside.

"Where is that boy?" Jesus said to no one in particular.

After the three had eaten and as the light faded to evening, they sat by the fire drinking wine and talking.

"I made John baptize me in the Jordan," Jesus said.

"You made him?" Ariston said.

"In a way. I persisted and eventually he relented."

Klietos laughed. "John stood no chance with you. Once you set your mind to a thing, you are the most stubborn man I have known. This, as I have told you, is not always a good thing. A man must know when it is time to relent and seek another path. Men are not infallible. Nor are the gods."

"Yours perhaps," Jesus said. "If God shows me the way, I cannot but follow."

"You are certain that it is your God who has spoken to you thus?"

"It is not through words that God speaks. I know in my heart what God says, or would say were he speaking as a man. I have no doubt of his message to me."

"What was the message that sent you to John in the Jordan?"

"John heard it too. The time is coming, soon, when God will set things to right in this world. This world is his, his creation, and when we stray too far from his intentions for us, and are oppressed by others, by nonbelievers, he will bring righteousness to the earth. He will bring his kingdom and rule with might and power and justice," Jesus said. His fists were clenched and he looked directly into Klietos' eyes.

"You have been too long in the desert with the 'essenoi'. You have changed, and not for the better."

"I am the same Jesus you have always known."

"No. You are not. You have grown to manhood but I see others have shaped your growth in ways I would not have wished."

"You would have me be a Greek like you? I am not and never will be. I am a Jew and I live as such, keeping our Law and worshiping God."

"Which version of the Law do you keep? The Law of the Temple, the Pharisee? The Law of the Sadducee or that of the 'essenoi'? How do all these different Laws come from only one God? Can't he make up his mind?"

"It is men whose minds are unclear. Men understand the Laws of God in the ways that seem best to them. Some interpret them solely for their profit. These are not righteous men. When God brings his Kingdom, they will suffer along with the Romans and the rest."

"Romans! Romans are pigs. There is your real problem. Someone needs to do something about them and I don't mean waiting around for a heavenly army to come to the rescue. The Romans are a true plague upon the earth. If your god has any justice in his soul, he will drive them from the earth into the darkest corners of Sheol," Klietos said. "They are your problem too. Attend me closely," Klietos said.

"This cousin of yours is walking on very dangerous ground. Baptism. Jewish rituals. Ha! The Romans care not a piss in a pot for that. They think you are all crazy anyway for insisting on only one god when it is obvious that the divine powers are many and varied. Look around! Everything you see on the earth, it is not possible for one god, let alone two or three to make all this and tend to it years on end. An entire household of gods would be needed for that. But... that is not my point.

"In the Romans' eyes John is not merely washing Jews in a muddy stream. He is building an army, an army that may come together to overthrow the Roman yoke. And Herod too."

"John builds no army," Jesus said. "He has no camp, no town to house them; they have no weapons. He lives in caves and depends upon others for food and drink."

"So you say. If I were Pilate and Herod I would be most interested in a growing number of people who were reborn into freedom in the Jordan by a crazy prophet. Herod, if no one else, is in danger because of this."

"John said as much to me. That was why he refused to baptize me."

"He was certainly right in that. Mark my words, if Herod is smart, and we know he is crafty and sly, he will put a stop to John's work before the Romans decide to send a legion into the desert to kill him and everyone he has baptized."

"John is my cousin, he is stubborn and will not stop the work God has given him to do."

"He will," Klietos said. "When Herod or the Romans will it so, he will stop."

Jesus remained in Sepphoris for six days, talking with Klietos and Ariston, walking the streets of the city, listening to, and sometimes debating with the Greek ascetics on the streets and the Rabbis in the synagogue. Much had changed since Jesus had last seen it. The new theatre was complete enough for plays to be held and the three of them attended in the evenings when they could. On the sixth day, after

Jesus had celebrated Passover with Klietos' Jewish neighbors, Klietos bade Jesus sit at the table.

"It is time to talk about Nazareth," Klietos said.

Jesus sat with his hands folded on the table and said nothing.

"Nazareth," Klietos said.

"I do not wish to return to Nazareth."

"I know."

Jesus remained silent for a time, then looked up at Klietos. "I am troubled. There are many paths open to me now, but I do not see the way. My cousin is right. It is time to speak out. Living in the desert, scribbling commentaries on the old books, teaching against the priests and the Sadducee, that accomplishes nothing. The Priests stay behind their walls in the Temple, or in their great houses and call upon the Law, but they do not obey it. It is on their tongues but not in their hearts."

"It has always been thus, and others before you have not been able to make it different. Can you?"

"No, not me. God will make it different. John says the time is drawing near when God will smite the unrighteous and return the land to his people. John is God's messenger, as am I now. That is why John baptized me. John does God's will."

"Now, since you pestered John into dunking you into the river, you are now also God's messenger?"

Jesus did not answer but sat, eyes locked to Klietos', brows drawn together, lips firm and unsmiling. Klietos knew that look. There would be no arguing Jesus out of anything when he retreated into himself like that.

"Never mind," Klietos said reaching out to touch Jesus' hand. "You will find your path, do not worry. With time and thought, prayer as you would say, it will come. No need to be rash."

Jesus relaxed and placed his hand on that of Klietos. Looking into the fire in the hearth, he said, "Yes, old friend. Your words are true. I must have time to think and pray and listen to what God will tell me. Tomorrow I shall go."

"You may stay as long as you will. We can talk, you can pray and we will see what comes."

"No, I will go into the country where I can find quiet and time for prayer."

"While you are praying, see what your god says about a son's duty to his mother."

Light

Lucius, Miriam, Deborah and Kasha left Qumran on the same day that Jesus departed, pausing for a while by the river where they had first met him. John did not appear again, although there were people waiting and hoping for his return. They found poor lodgings in a nearby town then continued their journey to Jericho and on to Jerusalem without incident.

Lucius and Kasha remained with Joseph and his family for many days. Members of the Council came to call and see this new Roman who appeared ever more friendly with Joseph and his family.

"It is the girl, young Miriam, who has caught his fancy," some said. They were close to the mark. Lucius and Miriam, always in the company of Deborah, were often seen in the city streets, looking through the shops and bazaars, walking the outer Temple grounds, Miriam pointing out various places and histories to Lucius, visiting Joseph's vineyards and farms nearby or privately sitting in a quiet corner of the garden talking together.

One evening Joseph, returned home from the Council meeting in the Temple and found them talking by the fountain.

"A beautiful evening, is it not?" Joseph said.

"Greetings, Joseph," Lucius said, "indeed it is."

Joseph gave Miriam a brief kiss and reclined on a couch next to them. Hanna brought him wine in a silver cup. He drank and said, "Do you recall that Essene fellow you met in the spring, the one baptized by that wild man John near Jericho?"

"Jesus," Miriam said, "yes, of course. A most remarkable man."

"Remarkable? I suppose so. He is beginning to make a name for himself. The Council was discussing him today," Joseph said.

"If he has drawn the attention of your Council, he must have become someone of importance. Is he now in Jerusalem?" Lucius asked.

"No, no, he's not here. Somewhere in Galilee I hear. Two of our priests have returned from Capernaum and bring news that he has acquired a following in the country there."

"What sort of following?"

"Oh, nothing to concern you, my friend. Or Rome, for that matter. He wanders about the countryside through the villages and farms, baptizing some in the manner of John, and teaching what he learned from the Baptist. 'God is coming. Prepare yourselves. All will be well.' That sort of thing. We've heard it all before."

"Such things are of little consequence to us," Lucius said, "unless he begins to stir the people to acts of violence."

"I think not. He teaches and ministers to the sick. A healer too, some will say. He does not remain in one place long enough to acquire a solid following. The ones who do follow him must tramp from village to farm and provide for themselves along the way."

"In that case, your Council need not worry."

"True, but the priests, the Pharisees are not happy. If they had let well enough alone…" Joseph sighed and took another sip. "They merely create their own troubles."

"How so?" Miriam asked.

"This Jesus will often stop and speak in the synagogues. He teaches his own interpretations of the Law, nothing extreme I understand, but troublesome to those priests and Pharisees who are more traditional. Too often they find it impossible not to challenge him."

"Father, our people have always argued the Law. Regard the Pharisees and the Essenes. They will never be reconciled."

"True enough," Joseph said, "but the two seldom meet where the people can hear their arguments. Not so with Jesus. The scribes and the Pharisees challenge him in the synagogues and in the villages before the people but he is able to best them. The man understands the Law and he argues like a Greek. Such encounters end with the people laughing at the priests, calling them fools."

"Why does he remain in the North? He could come here and argue with the Temple priests," Miriam said.

"I hope not. There would be more trouble if he came to Jerusalem. No, I think he remains there because Galilee is his home. He is from Nazareth I am told," Joseph said, "a small village near Sepphoris."

"It is little wonder that he is well versed in argument," Lucius said, "for I have heard that Sepphoris is now more Roman and Greek than Hebrew."

"That is true. There are many Greeks, and Romans also, skilled in the arts of rhetoric who live in Sepphoris. As the city continues to be rebuilt, I expect more will come," Joseph said and got up from his seat. "I will leave you now. Deborah and I must discuss the household account. It is not a subject I wish to spend more time with than necessary. However..."

After he had gone, Miriam said, "I wonder if he has found his light?"

"Light?"

"Yes, you remember, at the river, where we met, he spoke to us about finding his light, his purpose?"

"Something like living in the light, not the darkness?"

"Yes, that was it. I believe he has found it, his purpose, his light."

"That may be. As for me, I also I have found my light," Lucius said.

"Oh, and what might that be?"

"It is here, with me now."

Miriam looked all about them. "I see nothing," she said.

"It may not be possible for the light to see itself."

"Lucius, I…"

"You need not speak. I believe you know my feelings, even though I have said nothing until now. Let us continue as we are, friends, and perhaps more than friends. I wish you to know me better. No, speak now and you may say something regretful in haste. Take time to consider my words. Kasha and I will be leaving the city tomorrow. We will be travelers for a time, visiting other cities and towns, learning what we may."

"When will you return?"

"I do not know. The season for travel is good, the roads are open and there is much to see. I will send word to you, and Joseph and Deborah of course, when I can. Be well, Miriam."

"And you, Lucius," she said.

Klietos

Jesus was more confident now. He had traveled the country north and east of Galilee's great lake, baptizing where he could and speaking the message of the coming kingdom, John's message. A few people from the villages and farms came to listen and a few of them consented to be baptized. Increasingly, the poor and destitute came, brought by the expectation of help for their suffering and illnesses. He accepted them all, and healed those he could, often giving hope where there had been none. As word of his message and deeds spread he was invited to stay with the prosperous and influential families, but he usually accepted invitations from the poor, staying especially families whom he had helped.

Now, he and five followers who had attached themselves to him, pestered him with questions, bought or begged food along the way, had come to Cana. They sat on stone benches in the shade of the synagogue discussing the Law, eating bread and broiled fish brought to them by women in the village. Two priests, coming out of the synagogue saw them and began to reproach them.

"It is the Sabbath, yet you sit here, by the synagogue, eating and drinking?" the elder priest said.

"We have enough to share," Jesus said.

"Do not mock me. You know what you do here is against the Law," the priest said.

"The Law. Sabbath," Jesus said looking around at his companions. "Magdalene, were you made for the Sabbath?"

"I... what do you mean, Teacher?" she said.

"No, she was not," Jesus said standing and taking a step toward the priests, who instinctively backed away, "and neither were you. None of us here was made for the Sabbath. The Sabbath was made for the sons of men, not men for the Sabbath."

"Who are you to speak so?" the young priest said stepping in front of the older man to confront Jesus. "You have no authority here, you are not a Teacher of the Law who is known to us."

"I need no authority from you, my authority comes from the Father."

"The father? You are speaking of God?" the older priest said.

"His will be done."

"I know who this one is," the young priest said. "He is one of the baptizers, a follower of John. Another crazy one. Come, let us leave them to their food and their wine!"

"Yes, you should go. Go and prepare yourselves for the one who will be coming. John eats no bread and drinks no wine, yet you mock him. We come here eating and drinking and you say, 'gluttons', 'drunkards'. Yet, wisdom can be found in all of her children. Even you."

"Gluttons and drunkards do not enter the kingdom of heaven," the old priest said. "Only the righteous, the followers of the Law."

"I will tell you who will enter God's kingdom," Jesus said pointing to a group of children playing in the street. "Those. Those who are as children will enter."

"You see," the younger priest said, "he is crazy. Like John."

"Hold, Aaron," the old priest said, "let us seek the answer to this riddle the crazy prophet poses. So, tell if you can, how a grown man may become like a child?"

Jesus smiled. "You do not know? By being reborn in the water and the spirit."

"Enough of this, Benjamin," Aaron said tugging at his robe, "He is but another of the baptizer's people. Pay him no heed."

The two priests turned and walked away, Aaron turning to look back as they went.

"The priests will never accept your authority, Teacher," Samuel said.

"Perhaps, but that is not my concern," Jesus said. "There are many others who need to hear and to trust in the coming of the kingdom. The Father will send a son of man to separate the wheat from the chaff with fire and power. Then, they will listen although it be too late."

"When will this be?" a bystander who had heard the conversation with the two priests said.

"Soon," Jesus said.

"How soon?" the man said.

"A wise man will secure his house, put locks on his doors and windows, prepare himself, arm himself against the thief who will come in the night. The wise man does not know when the thief will come, but, being wise, stays ready."

"God's kingdom will come as a thief?" the man said.

Jesus looked at Samuel, shook his head and sighed.

Then, another voice, a familiar voice said, "Jesus. I have found you."

Jesus turned. Ariston stood before him.

"Ariston!" Jesus said clapping his hands on the youth's shoulders. "Ariston. It is good to see you, my friend."

Ariston did not smile. He looked into Jesus' eyes and said, "It is Klietos. He is very ill. He is dying. Will you come? He asks for you."

Jesus and Ariston departed quickly leaving his protesting followers behind. Sepphoris was a hard two day's journey, and they stopped only to rest briefly overnight. They arrived in the morning of the third day and went directly to Klietos' house. The old man was obviously fading, shriveled almost to bone and sinew. The wife of his Jewish neighbor was sitting by his bedside when they arrived.

"Ah, it is good you came," she said getting up to meet them at the doorway. "I do not think he will last this day through," she said quietly. "I will be just outside. He has been expecting you."

Jesus and Ariston moved quietly to the old man's bedside and Jesus knelt down and took one of his hands. Kleitos turned his head on the pillow and opened his eyes. They were bloodshot and the pupils two black holes.

"Yes… I knew you would come. I have been waiting…. Waiting…" he coughed faintly and closed his eyes again.

"We are here now," Jesus said. "Are you in pain?"

"No longer," Klietos said his voice weak, barely above a whisper. "I am with the boatman now. It is not far to the other shore."

Jesus kissed the frail hand. "I know it is your time, but, still, I would have you wait for a while longer. There is much I have to tell you."

Klietos' eyes opened and he looked up at Ariston, then at Jesus. "You both are sons to me. I am better for it. I cannot stay. Ariston, all I have is yours. Jesus, I have one thing for you only."

"Tell me," Jesus said.

"My last request. Go to your mother. As you promised."

"I will go. After your soul has departed, I will go to Nazareth and see her."

Klietos face moved into a fleeting smile and Jesus thought he felt a slight pressure on his hand. Then Klietos said, "Now, children, I...." and his breath slid out of his mouth and he moved no more.

Klietos had no family or relatives in Sepphoris. Jesus and Ariston prepared his corpse for burial according to the Greek custom. His body was washed and dressed in his best robes and laid out for all to pay their respects. Many people came, for the old man was well known and many mourned his passing, forgiving, for the most part, his keen wit and sharp tongue. The following day they moved him to a burying place outside the city walls where they laid him to rest with a few of his treasured possessions.

Jesus and Ariston spent the night talking, remembering Klietos and their times with him. Jesus prayed to his God and Ariston to his. The next day, Jesus bid farewell and set off to fulfill the old man's last request.

Family

The journey from Sepphoris to Nazareth is short. Walking down the hill from Sepphoris, Jesus could see Nazareth on its own hill to the east, the white buildings spilling down toward the road connecting the two towns. There was much traffic, most of it going from Nazareth to Sepphoris. Shopkeepers, stone workers, wine sellers, laborers off to another day's work rebuilding the city and caring for its inhabitants.

Jesus walked slowly, thinking of Nazareth as he once knew it, of his father Joseph, a strange and silent man with whom he had never been close. He thought of his brothers and sisters, especially James who would now be head of the family. James, always serious, like his father. Devout and unquestioning in faith or authority. Temperamental and unforgiving. Even though Jesus was eldest, James never accepted his own position as the second son. Joseph didn't help matters by always favoring James, using James' behavior to instruct Jesus, driving a wedge between the brothers. Joses and Simon tended to side with James in most things, but the youngest brother, Judas, was Jesus' favorite. He did not really know the twins, Jessica and Sarah. They were only three years old when Jesus left Nazareth for the last time.

Lost in his memories, Jesus entered the outskirts of Nazareth and made his way through the familiar streets to his childhood home. It stood at the top of a gentle rise, five small white buildings surrounding a cramped irregularly shaped courtyard housing a covered well. Set between two of the buildings was a short wall pierced by a wooden gate. Jesus pulled the latch string and quietly entered through the gate into the courtyard. A young woman was drawing water from the well. She was dressed simply in homespun robes, and her long, dark hair was tied up with a scrap of red cloth. She was exceedingly beautiful.

"Greetings," Jesus said softly.

The young woman paused with the well rope in both hands to look at him. He smiled and made a slight bow.

"Would you be Sarah or Jessica?"

"How is it you know my name, and that of my sister?" she said.

"It was only a guess, but I think a good one. I am your brother."

She looked at him closely, the rope slid swiftly through her hands, and the bucket splashed back into the well.

"Mother!" she called, still looking at him. "Mother, there is someone here."

"What is it?" a woman's voice said from an open doorway. "I am busy with my bread. What is it?"

"You must come, Mother. There is someone here," the young woman repeated more loudly.

"Seventeen years and she still does not know how to treat a visitor. Must I do everything..." the voice came out of the doorway along with the speaker, a short, plump woman, the gray in her hair complimenting the white flour on her hands and apron. Seeing Jesus she stopped short.

"Jesus?" she said. "It is you. Yes,... I know you."

She began to cry silently, tears making tracks down one floured cheek.

"Yes, mother. It is me and I have come to see you. And you too," he said looking at the girl.

"This is Jessica, your sister," Mary said. "Jessica, greet your brother, then go find your sister. And find James and the others. Tell them Jesus is here."

Jessica ran quickly to Jesus and gave him a tentative kiss on his cheek. "Welcome home brother," she said and dashed through the gate, paused to look back at him then ran into the street.

"Where have you been? Why did you not send word to me these many years? I have worried for you since you left. I have been afraid," she said as she wiped the tears on her apron.

Jesus' heart sank, but he said nothing.

Mary dropped the apron from her eyes and came to him, taking both of his hands in hers.

"I have missed you. I am glad you have come."

"As am I," he said, "and I am sorry to have given you such grief. It is not you, no, not you. I think of you always."

He bent down and they embraced for a long moment without speaking. Then Mary pushed him gently upright and said, "Let us go into the house before Jessica returns with the others. Tell me where you have been."

They had not talked long when the sounds of others coming through the gate reached them.

"Please. Do not quarrel. Your brother loves you even though he does not know how to show it," Mary said.

"You see with a mother's eyes," Jesus began when the door opened and a tall, dark man, bearded and almost gaunt, stepped through and stopped. He removed a wide straw hat and stepped aside as the others pushed past him, looking directly at Jesus all the while.

"This is your brother Judas and your sister Sarah," Jessica said to Jesus, pulling forward a young, fair haired man and a young woman.

Sarah came forward and knelt by Jesus's side and said, "I do not remember you, brother, although Jessica says that you must be him." She was in appearance very much like her sister Jessica, slim, curling hair, wide eyes. Her smile revealed a little gap between her front teeth which enhanced rather than detracted from her beauty.

Jesus took one of her hands and smiled at her, then at the young Judas who had moved nearer the tall man who remained by the doorway clutching his straw hat.

"Yes, it is true," he said. " I am your brother. I am sorry to have been away for so long. Look how much I have missed. You are a woman now."

"And still unmarried," said the tall man to Jesus, his voice dark and rich.

"Greetings to you, brother," Jesus said shortly.

"James, that is no way to greet your brother," Mary said moving between them. "Besides, Jessica and Sarah have many suitors and it is their right to choose whom they will."

"They are far too independent of mind for this family. A trait shared by their older brother," James said looking at Jesus.

Jesus, still holding Sarah's hand, sighed and looked back at James. "I did not come to argue. I have been away long. I came to see mother, and my sisters and brothers. Nothing more."

James started to speak, but remained silent.

"Where are Joses and Simon?" Mary said. "They should be here too."

"They are in Sepphoris, working to put bread on this table, as they should be," James said. "Have you by any chance brought bread for the table?" he asked Jesus.

"I bring bread for the spirit, without which, bread for the body is of no use," Jesus said.

"If I had any doubt that you are my elder brother, now I am certain of it. Farewell, Mother," James said and, stooping, went through the door into the little courtyard.

Mary followed, calling, "James... James... wait."

The young Judas stood by the door, watching quietly. Jesus said, "Greetings, little brother." Judas shuffled his feet and gave a shy smile, but remained where he stood.

Jessica came and stood beside her sister.

"Why is it James does not like you?" she asked.

"Why do you think this is so?" Jesus said.

"He says you deserted the family," Sarah said. "I have heard him speak of it before."

"I suppose he is right, in a way. I ran away often when I was near your age. Joseph was very angry at me. I think James took much of Joseph's anger for his own."

"James says that even though Father beat you, you were stubborn, like us," she giggled, looking at her sister, "and you would not obey but would sneak off again to be with that gentile in Sepphoris."

"And you never came back," Jessica said.

"Why did you run away?" Judas said from his position by the door. "Did you hate us?"

"I have never hated you, any of you. Never. Even James," Jesus said. "I thought I hated Joseph, Father... but I think now I did not hate him so much as I feared him. I thought he hated me since I was so different from him, and from James. Now, I am not so certain."

"That you are different?" Judas said.

"No. That he hated me. I think maybe he was somehow afraid too," Jesus said.

"Afraid of what?" Jessica said.

"That we were so different," Jesus said. "That..."

The door burst open and Mary rushed into the room.

"James is upset, and surprised that you are here. He promised to return tomorrow and greet you more properly," she said.

"Come, Jessica, Sarah, let us prepare food. We are all hungry. We can talk more while we eat. Judas, show your brother where he may wash and see to clean bed things for him. Hurry now, it will soon be evening, and there is much to do," Mary said shooing them out of the house.

James returned early the next day. Jesus was talking with Judas and Sarah by the well.

"Greetings, brother,' Jesus said, "God's peace be with you."

"People have come to Nazareth, two women, three men, asking for you. They say you are their teacher," James said.

"They wish to learn more of God's plan for his people."

"You know God's plan? God has chosen you as his messenger?"

"Like John, I must do what God calls me to do. Why are you so angry, brother?"

"John!" James almost spat the word, "John is yet another blight upon our family, and now you, a disciple of that raving troublemaker. Why come you here, to plague us in our own village? Why not follow your hairy master where he dunks fools into the river and calls out to God for help?"

Sarah whispered to Judas, "Go, bring Mother. Quickly."

"Yes, your mother, the peacemaker will protect you as always," James said.

"No, Judas. Wait," Jesus said.

The youth stopped, looking uncertainly at Sarah, who reached out and took his hand.

"James, I did not come here to fight with you. I came only to see my family. I did not come to stay and whether you will or no, God calls me to take his message to others. John has his way, I have mine. Cannot we part in peace?"

"Peace? All was at peace until your return. Even when you were young you were always in trouble. Fighting with father, running away to that Greek, playing wild in Sepphoris with Mordecai, plaguing the elders with your constant questions and speculations. What have you brought this time? A ragged bunch of nobodies who follow you from village to farm, begging food and a place to lay your heads. Teaching against the Temple. Yes, I have heard this, and washing fools in the waters in the manner of your cousin," James said. Having blurted this out, he stood silent, his gaze fixed on Jesus.

"Who needs to hear God's words more, those who go daily to the temple, take the best seats in the synagogues, have servants and slaves to labor for them, or those who have nothing, less than nothing? The few who follow me do so of their own will. It is the Father's choosing, not mine."

"The Father? Why say you, 'the Father'? Was not Joseph the father to you, as to the rest of us?"

"Was he? Of all of us, why did he not treat me as a son?"

"So, now you deny Joseph, and call God your father. Do you deny me? Do you also deny Sarah and Judas. Mother?"

"No, I do not deny that all of us are from the same mother, that we are all brothers and sisters. But, now my family are those who obey the words of the Father. Those who follow me are my family."

"Then we have nothing more to say to each other. Go to your family of followers. They seek you in the market," James said turned and walked through the gate without a backward glance.

Jesus watched him go. He said to Sarah and Judas, "James has always been angry with me. I am sorry you witnessed that. He is right. I must leave now. Tell mother goodbye. I am happy that we were together for a time, but I have much to do."

He picked up his traveling wallet and slung it over his shoulder.

"God's peace be with you both," he said and left them there by the well.

The Cliff

He found Magdalene and the others in the market surrounded by a crowd of villagers. Voices were raised, tempers were high.

"Of course we know him," said one of the village men, better dressed than the others. He stood close to Magdalene, leaning forward, hands on his hips, his voice lecturing and sarcastic.

"Knew him when he was a pup. Anyone could tell then he was trouble. Disrespected his father. Same with the priests, always going on with questions, why not this? Why not that? His mind confused by that Greek, no doubt. And, I'll wager he hasn't changed. What's he here for?"

"His friend, the Greek as you call him, died. In Sepphoris. We were there. They said Jesus had come here, to Nazareth. Have you seen him?" Magdalene said.

"I am here," Jesus said.

The crowd surrounding Magdalene and the four others grew silent and turned toward Jesus.

"It is the miracle worker," one of the villagers said, "the Baptizer's apprentice. Come to wash us clean of our sins? You'll have to make a river flow through here first."

The crowd laughed. Magdalene and the others moved to Jesus' side.

"No, he is here because his Greek died. Spent more time with the gentile than he did here, with his own family," the well dressed man said.

"A special Greek friend, was he?" the man said with a sneer.

"Do not mock what you cannot understand. I have not come to banter words with a soft merchant, dressed in flowing robes, smelling of nard and oil. A camel has a better chance of passing through the eye of a needle than you have of entering God's kingdom," Jesus said.

"Who are you to tell us who is righteous and who is not?" another said.

"Jesus, we should go now," Magdalene said pulling on his sleeve.

"Mark me well," Jesus said ignoring Magdalene's insistent tugging, "every one of you who acknowledges me, the Father will acknowledge, but deny me and you will be denied when the son of man comes."

"Deny you? We will do more than that," the well dressed man said. "Let us show you how we deal with a blasphemer in Nazareth!"

The crowd surged forward, pushing Magdalene and his followers aside, seized Jesus and began dragging him down the street.

"To the cliff!"

"Yes, death to the false prophet!"

"Throw him off!"

As they marched Jesus through the village, the disturbance grew, drawing more people as they went. Most did not know the mob had Jesus, but took up the cry nonetheless. Kill the blasphemer.

Just on the outskirts of Nazareth is a rocky promontory, overgrown with stunted trees, shrubs and boulders. It drops steeply away from its summit. A fall from there was almost always fatal. The scene had witnessed many executions, the condemned being flung onto the rocks below. The mob pushed and shoved Jesus up the slope to the top then two men bodily dragged him to the edge. Caught up in what was about to happen, the mob screamed and jostled for a better view.

"Hold there!" a voice boomed out.

Two men on horseback forced their way through the mob. One of them, a large black man, slid off his horse, and landed cat like on his feet. The steel blur of his sword flashed out and stopped with its tip lodged into the neck of one of the men holding Jesus. The man froze, wide eyed, as a trickle of blood oozed down his neck and into his tunic.

Kasha looked at Jesus and raised one eyebrow.

"No," Jesus said, "let him live."

Kasha withdrew his sword, wiped the blood from the blade on the man's tunic and said, "As you wish, Teacher."

Lucius wheeled his horse, and shouted, "Disburse! Now! All of you, or by the gods I will kill every one of you!" he said touching the horse with his heels, moving forward and raising his gladius high above his head.

"Go!" he bellowed and they went, stumbling and running, some glancing back fearful of the Roman on the big horse and the black man with the sword. When Lucius was certain that they were all put to flight, he turned back to the others. Jesus was sitting on a rock, Magdalene kneeling beside him and those of his followers who had swallowed their fear were huddled apart, watching Kasha uncertainly.

"Teacher, are you hurt?" Magdalene asked, touching his wounds gently.

"Cut and bruised, no more," Jesus wearily said.

"Can you stand?" Kasha said helping Jesus up with a hand under his arm.

"I am all right. I can walk," Jesus said. "You, both of you, how came you here? How did you find me?"

"We came looking for you, Teacher," Kasha said, "and it is good that we did. The gods favor you."

"If it is God's will that I die, there is nothing that you, or your gods can do. I believe that your coming here this day is proof that God wishes me to live," Jesus said.

"I do not know what your god means for you, but I do know that if we had not stopped on the chance that you were here, you would have met your god on this day," Lucius said.

"We heard the disturbance as we rode into town. People in the market told us you were in trouble. The rest you know," Kasha said.

"I cannot stay here. There is no welcome or honor for a prophet in his own town," Jesus said.

"None for you it appears," Lucius said. "What about those?" he said gesturing toward the four who were standing silently by.

"My friends. They have chosen to follow me," Jesus said.

"Where will they be following you now?" Lucius asked.

Jesus looked at them, then at Magdalene who had moved close to him, supporting him with one arm. He put one arm over her shoulders and said to her, "Where should we go now?"

"Wherever you choose. I will go with you always," Magdalene said tightening her arm around his waist.

"Of all my companions, you, Mary of Magdala, I hold the closest," Jesus said. "Let us journey to Capernaum, by the great lake. I would rest there and pray to the Father to show me the way I must go. Come," Jesus said to the others, "let us shake the dust of this place from our feet and return here no more."

Bruised and battered, Jesus could not walk far, so Lucius put him up on his horse and walked with the others. They traveled slowly taking three days on the road to Capernaum. Jesus was walking by the time they reached the outskirts of the city.

"We are here," Lucius said. "What will you do now?"

"We will go into the city. I have friends there. We will be all right," Jesus said.

"My friend, I counsel you to be cautious. I do not understand the hostility you bring out in your people. There may be no one to save you another time," Lucius said.

"I must do what God calls me to do. I will not deny God, and he will not deny me."

"You Jews can be the most stubborn of people, and I have seen many stubborn people."

"Yes, that is one of our enduring qualities," Jesus smiled.

"And, it is one of your worst dangers," Kasha said, "for Romans too are stubborn, more stubborn than your people."

"Why would this be a danger?" Magdalene said.

"The Romans are stronger, and they show no mercy to their enemies."

The Seven Springs

Tiberius moved against Sejanus after sending Lucius and Kasha to keep watch over Antioch's Roman Governor. Tiberius condemned Sejanus to death by his order to the Senate. Sejanus was immediately seized and strangled on the Senate floor, then his body was flung down the steps into the street below. All of Rome waited for the blood bath that would surely follow. However, over the following months, Sejanus' friends and conspirators were quietly executed, and Rome slowly relaxed and turned to other pursuits.

Lucius and Kasha remained in Antioch over the winter and returned to Judea in the spring. After a brief stay in Caesarea they traveled on to Jerusalem.

Lucius was greeted at Joseph's by Hanna, one of the house servants. She brought him to the garden and went to tell Joseph. Lucius was standing by the fountain when he came down the stairs.

"Lucius Quintus, may God's peace be with you," Joseph said.

"Greetings, Joseph. It is good to see you again."

"Welcome," Joseph said gripping Lucius' arm in friendship. "Come, let us take refreshment and talk. You have been away long."

"Yes, Antioch is far, and a most entertaining city, but I prefer Jerusalem."

Hanna brought wine and dishes of food.

"The grapes were good last year. Although this is new wine, I find it excellent already. A few years will improve it, yes? Although I am not certain there will be much left," Joseph said.

"Yes, it is very good," Lucius said. "Tell me, are Deborah and Miriam well?"

"Before they left, yes," Joseph said, "but I cannot say presently."

"Gone? They are not in the city?" Lucius said.

"Alas, no. My daughter and my sister... there are times when I do not understand them. They have gone to follow that Galilean prophet, the one you met at the river last year. Oh, I opposed them, you can be certain of that. There was no peace in this house for days, but, in the end, I relented."

"When? How long have they been gone?"

"I am not a weak man, but I fear I am too tolerant with my daughter. Since Sarah died, I have not had the heart to discipline her as I should."

"When did you last have word of them? Are they safe?"

"I had a letter from a merchant who came from Capernaum perhaps ten, no I think more, twelve days ago. Deborah entrusted it to him. They are well enough. Deborah took gold with her to pay for food and good lodging. Not that it has been useful. The Galilean spends little time in the larger towns, always moving from place to place, sleeping with strangers or alone in the country. Not a pleasant life for two women I suppose, but I sent Jacob, one of my slaves, to accompany them," Joseph said.

"Does Jesus have many followers now?"

"Jesus? Oh, you mean the Galilean. Yes, he has become quite the sensation among the country people. He is drawing larger crowds who come to hear him teach and many who are ill come to seek healing. I am told he is a healer as well as a country prophet."

"I cannot say I am pleased to hear this. Not that he is unpopular among your people, but that Miriam has chosen to become one of his followers."

"Nor I. There is talk in the Council. It is bad enough that my daughter and sister are among this man's followers, but more so that he is creating problems with the priests. I have counseled the priests and the scribes to ignore him, not to debate him or seek him out. They do not listen. He is crafty, like one of those Greek philosophers, turning arguments against them, making them play the fool. Ignore him, I say, and he will soon enough overstep and be punished, or fade away like those who have gone before."

"Is there nothing more you can do?"

"I have sent my advice to the councils outside Jerusalem. It is up to them to deal with the man as they feel they must."

"I meant, is there nothing you can do to bring Miriam and Deborah home?"

Joseph looked down at the floor, and took a long drink from his wine cup. "Persuasion has not worked. Threats, well, I do not wish to thunder and threaten and push my daughter away from me. Pleading does not become me, although I have resorted to that, and, as you see, without result."

"Perhaps I can try."

"My friend, Lucius. I would be forever in your debt. I do not expect Miriam to change her mind. She will suspect that I have sent you to bring her home."

"I will go," Lucius said, "for myself. To see that she and Deborah are well and safe, not to bring back, but to assure you of their well being."

"For this you have my deepest thanks. I believe God has brought you back to us for this purpose," Joseph said. "A weight has been lifted, praise God."

"We will leave tomorrow, early. Your last message came from Capernaum, by the great lake in Galilee?"

"Yes, Deborah said they are often in that city. It would be a good place to begin."

"That is where we will start," Lucius said. "Capernaum."

Jesus and his band of followers were not in Capernaum, but north of it near the shore of the lake at a place called by the Greeks, 'Heptapegon', or Seven Springs. These springs emerge from the surrounding hills, coming together at that place before emptying into the lake. Jesus and his people had been in this area for days, teaching and working with the sick and ill that came in from the surrounding villages and towns. Each day the crowds grew larger until, this day, the slopes around the Seven Springs were crowded with old men and women, children, beggars, farmers, the curious and the sick.

It was early in the hot afternoon. Jesus was standing on a rock near the Springs. He had been speaking for hours. His voice was hoarse but was still powerful and carried to most of his listeners.

"He needs rest," Magdalene said. "He can't keep this up much longer. Soon he will not be able to speak."

"I am worried about the children," Miriam said. "There are so many and they have had nothing to eat all day. The sick are suffering too. We must do something."

"What have we to give them?" Elizabeth said.

"Not much," Miriam said. "We have a few loaves of bread, some broiled fish, perhaps five or six. A few olives and a meager amount of wine."

"Not nearly enough," Magdalene said.

"We must get more," Deborah said. "Come, bring some of the others and we will go into the village and buy what we can."

Within an hour, two boats appeared on the lake, beaching quietly near the Springs and men and women began unloading baskets of bread, fish, olives, dates and a few rounds of cheese. These were carried near the rock where Jesus was still speaking.

"Jesus, we have food for the people," Miriam said. "The children and old ones must be very hungry."

Jesus smiled at her and the other women who were beginning to distribute the food, then he turned to the men around him and said, "Break the bread and divide the fish and other food stuffs among the people."

"Where did all this come from?" they said. But Jesus was speaking again and did not answer. The people listened to him while the children played and his followers passed out food to the multitude.

Capernaum

Lucius and Kasha traveled east from Jerusalem, crossed the Jordan and took the good road north to the great lake in Galilee. They took passage in a cargo vessel to Magdala where they hired horses. Riding along the lake shore they arrived in Capernaum late in the afternoon. They rode into the marketplace where Lucius stopped a passerby who was carrying a large basket slung over his shoulder.

"Greetings, friend. We are seeking a man, Jesus, son of Joseph of Nazareth," Lucius said.

The man paused and looked at them closely.

"Roman, from the look of you. Him?" he said looking at Kasha. "He Roman too?"

"Roman, and not Roman," Kasha said smiling.

The man pondered this for a moment then said, "There are many here called Jesus, but I know of none from Nazareth."

"Our thanks and good day," Lucius said moving his horse forward. The man turned and watched them, shifted his load and spat into the street. At a vendor's stall they found someone who knew.

"Yes, I know of him," the merchant said. "Strange eyes. Always preaching about God's kingdom. Going to rid us of the Romans and set things to rights."

Looking warily at Lucius, he forced a smile and said, "No disrespect, sir."

"We Romans are here, and here we will remain. It is no disrespect to not love those who have conquered you. But it would be wise to be more careful of your tongue with others."

"As for me, I care not," the man said, "business is good, as you see. Fighting. War. Phaw!.. What good have they ever done but for the victors? For the rest, for us, what? Misery and death, I tell you. Both bad for business."

"Where will we find him?" Kasha interrupted.

"Find him? Ah, him… I have heard he is often at the synagogue. Some come to listen, but most come for the healing."

"He is known here as a healer?"

"I have heard it told that he has healed many. Some remain well. Some do not. After all, that is the way of it, is it not?" the man said.

"The way of it?" Kasha said.

"Life," the man said. "We all must make our way the best we can, but at the end, we all must leave it."

"All we have is the journey. Attend it well," Kasha said. "Which way to the synagogue?"

As they approached, the streets grew more narrow and crowded. They dismounted and walked their horses among the people. On the synagog's wide front portico, Jesus stood surrounded by a modest group of people, holding the arm of a frail woman, speaking closely to her ear. Those nearby strained forward to listen. The old woman nodded and Jesus kissed her on the forehead, then she was gently lead away. As Lucius and Kasha came near, Jesus saw them and raised a hand in greeting.

"Hail, Lucius. Hail, Kasha," he said. The others turned and two stocky men stepped in front of Jesus. The larger of them glared at Kasha.

"Cephas, there is no need for alarm," Jesus said placing one hand on the man's shoulder. "These men are friends."

Peter moved aside slowly, keeping a wary eye on Kasha.

"You have need of protection now?" Lucius asked.

They embraced and Jesus said softly to Kasha, "Cephas means well, and he does not know you or he would be more fearful."

"It is of no consequence, Teacher," Kasha said, "Cephas has little to fear from me if he is one of your followers."

Jesus smiled. "His name is Peter, but I call him Cephas, which means "rock" in our language. He is stubborn and hard, and his thoughts move slowly. We must keep that in mind. Come, let us walk. It grows late and I am hungry."

"I will go ahead, Teacher, and see to our food," Peter said.

"We will be along directly," Jesus said.

Peter and the others departed. Jesus led Lucius and Kasha to a garden adjacent to the synagogue where they sat on stone benches among green shrubs and lavender flowers watching the townspeople come and go.

"Why have you come seeking me?" Jesus said. "You have been in Jerusalem?"

"We have," Lucius said. "Joseph desires news of Miriam and Deborah and we have come on his behalf. He misses them greatly and he is concerned for their safety. He heard of your troubles with the Pharisee priests. They do not like you."

"Ha! Nor I them," Jesus said. "God needs no mediators, no gatekeepers to stand between him and his people. The priests care little for the problems of others, the sick, the destitute. They are blinded by their interpretation of the law and their authority. God's laws are simple and meant to bring one closer to his kingdom, not to line the purses of the Pharisee and the Sadducee."

"Even so, they are in control. You are not. Your temple belongs to them and most of your people don't seem to mind following their rule, obeying the Law, as you put it. The people go to the Temple to pay respects to your god without protest. Why continue to oppose the Priests? It only creates more trouble for you."

"The Pharisees come to me. They seek me out to question me, to trick me and mock me before the people. So far, this has not gone well for them," Jesus smiled as he said this and those sitting nearby also smiled and nodded their heads in agreement.

"This is what I mean. You humiliate and embarrass them in front of the people. This only makes them more angry and determined against you. Do you not see where this is going? Do you not remember what happened with John?"

"That was Herod's doing. Herod will not brook rebellion, however small. I spoke with John about this the day you and I met, at the river, remember?"

"I remember," Lucius said. "And, like you, he refused to listen."

"I am not baptizing in the river. I am not collecting an army. I have no place to lay my head or call my own. People do not come to me, I go to them. It is not the same."

"In your mind, perhaps, but the result is the same. The Pharisee and Sadducee have Pilate's ear. We were sent here to keep Pilate in check and to do what we can to keep the peace. You, my friend, are not helping."

Jesus looked at Lucius for some moments then said, "You must give to Caesar what he commands, and so must

I give to God what is His. Let us hope Caesar and God do not come to cross purposes. Let us talk more after we sup. I have not eaten since morning and my mouth waters at the thought of fish and bread. Come, let us join the others and eat!"

They walked a short way to a small, roundish stone house where Peter, his wife and her mother were waiting. They followed Jesus inside and took seats where they could. Three women came in bearing platters of grilled fish and bowls of vegetables, olives and dates. Miriam was with them, carrying bread in a basket. She saw Lucius and Kasha, smiled, then went about the room distributing small loaves. When she came to them Kasha said, "It is good to see you again, child."

"It is good to see you as well, Master Kasha," she said touching him on the arm, then looking at Lucius she said, "My father ordered you to come here, to take me back to Jerusalem?"

"Ordered? No, he asked that we come so that we might bring him news of you. We agreed only to this. We were not sent."

"We would have come, regardless, young daughter," Kasha said, "because we care for you, and your friends."

"You see, Miriam, you are not the sole reason for our friends' visit. But, I think you are the most important reason for one of them," Jesus said looking at Lucius.

Both Miriam and Lucius turned and looked at Jesus. He smiled broadly at them, then quickly became occupied with his fish. Those sitting near him were smiling too.

Miriam took a small loaf and dropped it into Lucius' bowl, spilling fish and onions onto the table and his lap.

"Men," she snorted, "thick headed and dull witted and…"

She turned and hurried from the room.

"Miriam, do I not get bread?" Jesus laughingly called after her, and the men chuckled. A loaf came flying from the door and Jesus deftly caught it before it bounced off his head.

Decision

After dinner the men gathered in the garden beside the house, drinking wine and talking. Jesus kept silent, deep in thought and they gave him room.

"Passover will be here soon," one of the men said. "We have already begun preparations."

"Teacher, will you stay here with us to celebrate Passover?" Peter asked.

Jesus didn't answer. He sat on a stone bench, leaning forward, his elbows on his knees and his head bowed, looking at the ground between his sandals.

"Jesus? Will you take Passover here, in this house?" Peter repeated.

Jesus looked up slowly, eyes blinking, then focused on Peter.

"Passover. Yes,… Passover. It is time now."

He straightened, rolling his shoulders and head, working out stiffness. "I will celebrate Passover, but not here. I will join the pilgrims for Passover in Jerusalem."

A tall red haired man dressed in a worn brown tunic rose quickly and said, "No! Teacher... you must not do this. It is too dangerous."

"Andrew is right. Jerusalem at Passover is no place for you now," Peter interjected. "The scribes, the Pharisees, they will be after you, and they will have you in their city. It is not a good idea."

"They had me in Jerusalem before and, as you see, I am still with you. I have no need to fear them. Besides, the Romans will be keeping order in Jerusalem, yes?" Jesus looked at Lucius. "With our friend Lucius present, Pilate will be even more cautious to keep the peace. Am I not right?"

"Yes, Pilate will be on his guard. He understands the need to keep the peace, but that is no guarantee that your safety will be his concern. To him, you are only one among many potential troublemakers," Lucius said.

"Ah, but I am no troublemaker. Pilate cares little for our arguments about God."

"True as far as it goes," Lucius said, "but do not forget that Pilate is a devious and dangerous man. You would be in danger should he perceive you as a threat."

"But, friend Lucius, how could I, an unlettered nobody from Galilee be a threat to the Prefect of Judea?"

"Surely one would have to ask that of the Prefect himself," Kasha said. "Let us hope you will not have to."

Lucius slipped quietly away from the conversation in the garden and went in search of Miriam. He found her inside the house sitting with Deborah and the other women near the hearth.

"Miriam," he said, "I bring greetings from your father, and to you, Deborah, from your brother."

"Greetings is it? Or a summons?" Miriam snapped.

"Miriam, you are too hasty," Deborah said. "You have forgotten your manners."

"I am sorry, Lucius," Miriam said, "that was rude. Forgive me."

"Your father cares for you, as do we."

Deborah looked at the two of them, then rising she said, "I have things to attend to. It is good you are here, Lucius. It has been too long since we have seen you. Come," she said to the other women. They mumbled greetings to

Lucius and quickly left the room. Lucius drew a stool close to Miriam.

"Your father is worried about you, about your safety, and seeks reassurance that you are well and not in danger," he said.

"Danger? Why would I be in danger? We travel the country with Jesus. He helps people. He heals many who are sick and we feed those we can. He brings God's message to people who have lost hope. They love him. They would never harm him, nor we who follow him. How could I be in danger?"

"Things are not a simple as you wish to think, or as Jesus believes. Your father told me that his reputation grows in Jerusalem and it is known he is a kinsman of John. Herod thought John enough of a threat to have him killed."

"Jesus does not speak out against Herod or the Romans. He no longer calls on God to come and destroy the Romans as John did."

"Perhaps, but your father's friends speak ill of Jesus and say he is breaking your laws, and that he is a threat against your god."

"Impossible! They don't know what they are saying."

"Perhaps. I know they are quite serious. Your father is worried."

"I don't care. If Jesus is going to Jerusalem, I too will go with him."

"No. You may choose to go to Jerusalem, but you cannot accompany me," Jesus said.

"How long have you been listening?"

"Long enough," Jesus said. He moved to the hearth and sat down with them.

"Teacher, you cannot go to Jerusalem alone," Miriam said.

"I will not be alone, but you, dear Miriam, must return to your father."

"Do not ask this of me."

"I do, though. You must obey me in this."

"But why?"

"Because Lucius is right. I have many enemies in Jerusalem."

"Then why go? Why tempt them? Stay here in Galilee and continue your teaching. Help those who need you," Miriam said.

"It will soon be Passover and every Jew should be in Jerusalem at least once to celebrate it," Jesus said "There will be many people there who should hear what God has in store for them. As someone once said to me, if you have a light, you don't keep it covered under a basket."

"Miriam is right," Lucius said. "There is no need for you to go now. Pilate and his men will be on guard against any disturbance. So would I, if I were Prefect. Thousands of pilgrims crowding into the city, camped outside the walls, filling the villages in the hills round about. Jerusalem could be a tinderbox awaiting a spark. You do not want to be seen as that spark."

"I will be careful and I am not interested in riots or rebellions. God will move to take care of his people. He does not need me for that. Besides, Lucius, argument and discussion are good. You have seen us at the synagogue, discussing the Law. We are a passionate people and sometimes express ourselves with vigor, and yes, argument. There are different ways to understand God."

"I've seen a mob of your 'passionate' people ready to throw you to your death from a cliff."

Jesus looked at Lucius for a long moment, then said, "Sometimes people lose control and passion overcomes reason."

"And sometimes friends are not there to help," Lucius said.

The next morning as they were preparing to depart, Jesus came to them in the courtyard next to the house. A mule had been bought to carry Miriam and Deborah's baggage. Kasha was lashing the last of the bags to the pack saddle. Lucius was strapping his spare gladius to the front pommels of his saddle.

"So, you are ready to depart?" Jesus said.

Lucius said nothing.

"You are expecting trouble on the road?" Jesus asked, slowly drawing Lucius' sword from its travel sheath and turning it in the sunlight.

"One must always expect trouble, though it seldom comes. When it does, it is wise to be prepared," Kasha said.

"The one who made this must be a master at his work," Jesus said turning the sword in his hands. "It is a pity that men must still depend upon weapons such as these."

"Yes, but until men no longer turn to violence, such tools are necessary if we are not to be totally ruled by such men," Kasha replied.

"There are many who say the Romans are a people of violence and conquest, living by the sword," Jesus said putting the gladius carefully back into its sheath.

"I cannot deny that we can be a violent people, even among ourselves. But we also are a people of laws, and of art and commerce. We make war, and conquer, but we also bring laws and peace. We build roads and towns. We are often less cruel than those we subdue. There has been more peace among your own people since we came than in all the time before. You no longer kill and fight each other for possession of your Temple and the right to serve your god," Lucius said.

"No, you have taken that right of decision from us and now make it yourselves for the benefit of Rome."

"From what you say to your people, I think you do not care so much for your Temple priests and the Sadducee, the power brokers, in Jerusalem. What difference, then, does it make who controls the Temple?"

"I believe the day will come when God will bring his judgement here and those who have done wrong will pay and those who have lived as the Law demands will reap the rewards of his just and righteous rule. Until then, we must strive to see that such a kingdom is already present here, now. All men must do is to live it. Swords and violence and cruelty are not necessary if men would but forsake them and live as God meant life to be lived."

"Teacher, you speak as someone new to this world, as someone who has no knowledge of men and their ways," Kasha said. "In these matters, I know better. You have not seen what we have seen, the gods be praised, for if you had, you would know what evil men are capable of. Still, you are no fool. Men are as they are and will never be as you wish. If your god is the most powerful god, surely he would kill all the evil ones, remove suffering and woe from the world, and begin anew with only love and peace for all his children. If he is the most powerful god, and does not do this, then he must love the world as it is."

"It is not for men to delve the purposes of God," Jesus said.

"If men do not, then who will?" Kasha said, "If we are the mere playthings of a devious and cruel god, I have no interest in such a one. Life alone is hard enough. We do not need such a god to make it harder still."

Miriam and Deborah came into the courtyard ready for travel. Miriam walked directly to Jesus and put her hands on his arm. "You must be careful and do nothing foolish in Jerusalem," she said.

"When have you known me to be foolish? Careless occasionally I grant you, but foolish?"

"You know what I mean, and do not jest," Miriam said. "For you, Jerusalem is a dangerous place. I fear for you. Do not tease me."

"My dear Miriam," Jesus said taking both her hands in his, "I do not tease you. I cherish your feelings and I have no desire to bring harm to myself or to others. I will be cautious, as you wish. I do not forget that I also have the support of friends."

Jesus looked at Kasha and Lucius as he said this. Kasha said nothing.

"We will watch after him as much as we are able," Lucius said, "but he is master of his fate, as we all are, and he will do what he must."

He placed his hand on Jesus' shoulder and said, "He is no fool. Careless at times, perhaps, but he knows what he must do."

"Men," she said pulling her hands away from Jesus, "men are impossible. You care for nothing but preparing the people for the time when God will come to save us. You do not know when, or where or how that will come to pass. We are all supposed to just wait and live as if it had already happened, but it hasn't. Why should it? Nothing changes except for the worse."

"And you," she said pushing Lucius away with both hands, "you bring peace at the point of a sword. You bring laws, your laws. You bring your gods to battle with our God. Why are you here? Why don't you all just go and leave us in peace?"

Deborah stood near Kasha, listening. She stepped forward and took Miriam's arm.

"It is all right, child. Such questions have no answers," she said and moved her gently toward the cart that awaited them in the street. "Come. It is time we go home. Your father is waiting."

Miriam offered no other protest but went along quietly with Deborah. When she looked back at the men, her eyes were shining bright with tears.

Jesus turned to Lucius and Kasha and said, "Watch over her well. We will cross the lake and take the eastern road to Jerusalem. Many Galileans will travel that way so we will have much company. We will lodge in Bethany. Look for the house of the Essenes where the sick are cared for. They will know where to find us."

"No harm will come to her," Kasha said, "while she is with us."

"And you, friend, take care," Lucius said.

"God's will be done," Jesus said then turned and walked back into the house.

Kasha looked at Lucius and said, "I remember he once said that when a blind man leads another blind man, they will both fall into a hole."

"He says a great many things," Lucius replied.

Hope and Fear

"How fares my daughter today?" Joseph asked.

"She is well enough, if that is what you mean," Deborah replied.

They were taking the morning meal in the upper courtyard of the house. They were alone. Miriam had not made an appearance since arriving home two days before. Lucius and Kasha had stayed only briefly before making their excuses and leaving to find Pilate who had moved his Passover headquarters to Herod's Palace in Jerusalem.

"Here," she said passing a bowl to Joseph, "taste the olives and new cheese. They are particularly good this year."

"Olives and cheese! What care I for olives and cheese? My daughter returns from Galilee, from that magician she is following everywhere. She skulks in her rooms, refuses to come down, to talk… Ha! I have more troubles than the quality of my foods."

"You worry over much. Such things will pass. Young girls often become fascinated with men of whom their fathers disapprove."

"A nobody. A wandering peasant with no family. A Galilean. What can she possibly see in him? I have heard he practices magic. Perhaps he cast a spell over her. Yes, he has somehow bewitched her I think," Joseph said. "I forbid it. I absolutely forbid her to see this wandering fanatic again, and that's an end to it."

"Tell me, brother, when has forbidding Miriam something ever stopped her from getting what she wanted?"

"No more. I'll have no more of this. Horses, clothes, jewels, those are one thing, this passion for an unwashed, wandering tramp is another. I will not have it."

"He is neither unwashed nor a tramp and you had better understand that if nothing else. Some think him a holy man who cures the sick. I have seen him too, remember. He is a good man and he believes he is chosen to do God's work. If you will but use your mind you will see that this infatuation will run its course. When it is finally done, you might still have a daughter who does not shun your company."

"How might that happen?" Joseph asked.

"His mind is set on things other than Miriam the daughter of Joseph. He believes he has the ear of God. He has no time for family and children. Besides, his eye is always on another who travels with him. He regards Miriam as a friend, a follower of his teachings and a supporter. Nothing more."

"Miriam does not see this?"

"She sees, but does not wish to believe."

"So you say."

"I am a woman. I understand these things."

"Perhaps. But you cannot foretell the future. You think these things are true, but you do not know. Things happen. He could change his mind. Something must be done."

Deborah rose from the table and touched Joseph affectionately on his shoulder. "Then, do so if you must, brother, but take care that Miriam does not blame you for it. She, like her father, is not quick to forgive. And, Lucius Quintus is here."

"Quintus? Did he say why he has come?"

"I rather think he is here to see Miriam. Oh, you as well, I am sure, but his main interest is with Miriam."

"Interest... Yes, I feel he is showing entirely too much interest in Miriam as of late." Joseph said. "First it is the wandering cynic from Galilee. Next it is a Roman aristocrat. Romans, whose feet are firmly planted on our necks. That girl is impossible! How did this happen?"

"A woman's heart does cares not about such things. Nor does a young man's. You should know this. You were young once, even though you often deny it."

"The heart has nothing to do with this. It is not proper, nor is it according to our laws and customs. She does this to spite me."

"She does this because she must. This is not about you, brother."

"It is about our family, our people."

"Yes, but... No, this is not the time. We will continue this talk later. Now, Lucius is waiting," Deborah said and left him there, returning shortly with Lucius.

"Here, brother, is one of our conquerors, come to pay his respects," she said and walked away.

"Conquerors? Have I missed something?" Lucius said.

"Yes, you have. But no matter. It is a private amusement Deborah and I share. No disrespect intended."

"I have grown accustomed to Deborah's views. She is very outspoken for a woman."

"Your Roman women, they are different at home?"

"No, not so different. They are often more open with their thoughts than are men. More private in their expression of them, perhaps, but no less... original?"

"Original? Stubborn I say. What brings you here, Lucius?"

"I come on a personal matter. As you know, I have passed much time in the company of your sister and your daughter. I wish you to know that I have developed great affection for Miriam, and I wish to marry her. I have not spoken about this with her, I have come first to ask your approval."

"Lucius Quintus of Rome, were you one of us, one of God's people, I would be most encouraging and gratified. But, you are not. Conqueror. Yes, that is what we call you. Friend, I think, to me and my family, but also conqueror and ruler over our people, here by conquest, and remaining by power. I cannot give my blessing to such an arrangement."

"Surely, such a connection between our families, you as head of the Council, and my family, one of the important families in Rome, would serve you well."

"With a few of my people, yes. For the others, having my daughter wed to a non-Jew, a Roman, they would oppose me at every turn. Life, my friend, would be more difficult for us both. Children? What about children? Jews raised as Romans? Or would they remain here, to be reared as our faith demands?"

"There are many Jews who are also citizens of Rome."

"Do they not also worship the Emperor Tiberius, and Augustus, and others as gods? You do not accept the God of our people. How is this possible, to be a Jew and a Roman? I do not understand this."

Lucius was silent for a moment before saying, "I do not know about such things. I cannot foretell the future. I can only know what I know now, and that is I intend to ask Miriam to marry. If she is willing, we will deal with the these things as we must."

"I see that I cannot dissuade you. But I ask that you delay. Do not speak with her now. Allow me to think on this. Let us both think on it and talk more. I do not wish to lose my daughter."

"I understand. I will agree if you will not speak against me until you and I have talked again."

"Very well."

"I too will hold my silence. Then, with your approval, I would like to see her now."

"There is one other thing," Joseph said. "The matter of this Jesus from Nazareth."

"There is that."

"I am concerned. Miriam is young and impressionable and has acquired an unseemly attachment to this wandering… this self-styled prophet. I am told his family does not accept him yet my daughter follows him and refuses to obey me. Tell me, is she, ah.. are they…?"

"No. There is nothing between them except for friendship. Whatever power he holds over others he also holds over her. But Jesus has a constant companion, one Mary of Magdala, called Magdalene, who accompanies him everywhere. She is seldom from his side. They may be married, I do not know. He and Magdalene are affectionate. He dotes upon her and frequently kisses her on the mouth as if they were husband and wife, but I do not know if this is so. I suspect not, for a few of his followers are jealous of this woman and do not like her. Miriam, though, is faultless," Lucius said.

"I would have her home, not following this man. Nothing good can come of it."

"Your daughter is strong willed. You could order her to stay home. Put guards on the door."

"I could. I am her father, but that would, in the end, drive her further from me, not closer. No, I must find another way."

"Perhaps I can help. While Jesus is here in Jerusalem. I will keep watch and discourage anything that may prove unseemly or dangerous to Miriam. I will protect her. You have the bond of Lucius Quintus."

Joseph stood taller, straightened his shoulders.

"I am exceedingly grateful, Lucius Quintus. Exceedingly," he said clasping both of Lucius' hands in his.

"After Passover, when this person has gone back to the country from whence he came, we will talk more about you and Miriam. Yes. After Passover will be a better time."

"As you wish. Now, I would like to see Miriam."

Choices

Joseph called for his stick and robe, left his house and passed into the crowds, walking slowly among the vendor stalls and shops, stopping now and then to inspect some cloth, a string of pearls or jewels, a leather worker's belts and sandals. Near the Temple he paused for a bowl of dates and cup of wine. A troop of Roman soldiers made their way easily through the throng which parted quickly for their passage. One of the Romans looked briefly at Joseph as they passed, his eyes flat, without human interest, taking in Joseph quickly, evaluating him as nothing to be feared or dealt with, then passing on to others in the crowd.

Joseph paid for his dates and wine, troubled by the look the Roman had given him. He began walking through the city. His feet took him up the long west ramp into the Temple grounds. As he moved among the throng in the main outer court, going nowhere in particular, he was greeted by a familiar voice.

"Joseph, old friend, good day to you," Mikhael the Temple Priest said.

Joseph stopped suddenly, startled to see Mikhael standing directly front of him.

"Oh. Forgive me. I did not see you," Joseph said.

"What is the matter? You look troubled."

"Do I? Yes, I suppose I do. It is nothing."

"Nothing, eh? Joseph, head of the Council, moping about aimlessly through the Temple grounds. I'd say it is more than nothing. Come, sit. Tell me all," Mikhael said taking Joseph by the arm and steering him to a nearby bench in the shade.

"Trouble with the Romans?" Mikhael offered.

"The Romans... No, not the Romans. More of a personal matter."

"Are you unwell?"

"Yes... I mean no. I am well. I am concerned about Miriam."

"Ah, daughters. You should not fret yourself, Joseph. I have been blessed with four daughters, as you know, and I can attest to the trials they put you through."

"So you have said but this, I think, is different."

"Tell me. It can not be as bad as you may believe. Young women can be headstrong and foolish. This is why they should be married to a strong and upright man as soon as they are of age. Nothing like a firm husband to bring a young girl in check."

"Would that she was interested in such a man."

"Oh, she has developed an interest in someone, perhaps, not so suitable?"

Joseph looked about, studying the people talking, walking and milling around them. He sat up straight and turned to look directly at Mikhael.

"My friend, I do value your counsel but you must promise me that what I tell you will go no further. It is a family matter and I do not wish it to become common gossip."

"I see. As you have trusted me in the past, you can also trust me now. I would do nothing to harm you or your family. Tell me how I can help."

"Very well. Miriam has developed an attraction to a Galilean, a homeless wanderer, living off the charity of others. I have forbidden her to see him but I now have received word that he is in Jerusalem. I fear that she may join him here. I must find a way to keep her from his influence without driving her from me."

"Ah, I see. That is a problem. You do not wish to confine her to your house, then?"

"I do wish it, but I do not wish to lose the affections of my only child. I need to find another way, but I do not see how this can be done."

"Have you talked with this Galilean? Perhaps he could be reasoned with, or bought off?"

"I have not. I have no wish to meet him. From what I have been told of this man, money, land, and possessions do not interest him. I do not think he will be swayed by any offers I can make."

"Then you must find another way. Who is this man? What is he called?"

"Jesus, son of Joseph."

Mikhael smiled.

"Yes, I know the irony of it," Joseph said. "He is from Nazareth, a small village near Sepphoris, most likely where he learned his debating skills. He is very good at debate I am told."

"I know of this man," Mikhael said. "He has been a thorn in our side for some time now. Unfortunately, our less competent Brothers have fared badly in public argument with him. He is here, now, in Jerusalem you say?"

"He may be in the Temple, now. He would be difficult to find in the crowds but I am told he spends much time here debating with those who will, and teaching his ideas of the Law to his followers."

"Good. Good. Here in our Temple, you say."

"Why is this good?"

"Because of Passover, old friend. Passover and the Romans. Debates are one thing, but disturbing the peace and stirring up the crowds, especially during Passover, is quite another. Since this Jesus attracts controversy, it would be an easy matter to turn a debate into something more, enough to attract the attention of the Romans. You are on good terms with the Prefect, are you not?" Mikhael said.

"We have an understanding."

"Then, suggest to Pilate that when this Jesus comes before a magistrate, he be banned from Jerusalem. That will solve your immediate problem. Let the Romans take your daughter's wrath."

"You can arrange for such an incident to occur?"

"Think no more upon it, old friend. It can be easily done."

"Very well. I will speak with the Prefect. I think this might be best. Yes, it is a good plan."

The two men embraced and Mikhael said, "I will make the arrangements. Take care to be elsewhere but the Temple tomorrow."

"I will. Mikhael, you have my thanks. You have eased my worries but my mind will not be totally at rest until this Galilean is out of our lives for good."

"Leave it to me," Mikhael said, " I know how to handle people of this sort."

Opportunity

"Prefect, that Jew on the Council, ah... Joseph I think, the one who always wears the turban, he is here asking to see you," Marcus said.

"What does he want?" Pilate asked.

"He says it is a private matter."

"Private... This could prove interesting. Bring him and then leave us," Pilate said. He crossed to a large table and poured two goblets of wine. As Joseph entered, Pilate turned and offered one to him.

"My thanks, Prefect."

"Pontius. Let us talk as friends."

Marcus quietly closed the door behind him.

"Tell me, friend, how can I assist you?" Pilate said.

"Marcus told you this is a private matter."

"He did."

"I, ah, I do not quite know how to begin," Joseph said. He took a gulp of wine and looked away from Pilate.

"Ah, a matter of some delicacy I see. The best course is the direct one. Tell me what is on your mind," Pilate said taking his ease on a couch and motioning Joseph to another. Joseph sat and leaned back on his cushions.

"It concerns my daughter, Miriam. You have met her."

"Miriam. Yes, I do remember her. Dark hair, tall, very pretty. Go on."

"She is... strong willed. I spoil her too much, but since my wife died... She is my only child, and I am often too lenient."

"As a good father should be. Within the limits of propriety, of course."

"Yes, but I have gone too far. She is following an itinerant prophet, a Galilean who moves about the countryside stirring up the poor and the malcontent."

"He has a number of followers, this wandering holy man?"

"Holy man? I do not call him holy. He flaunts our Laws and consorts with beggars and thieves. His close disciples are all unlettered and ignorant, fishermen, laborers, the homeless. Holy? I think not."

"How did your daughter come to be one of this man's followers? What is he called?"

"Jesus. Of Nazareth, son of a Joseph I believe."

"Son of Joseph? Strange irony, is it not?" Pilate said smiling.

Joseph did not answer, but took a thoughtful sip of his wine.

"He is related to the Baptizer but we did not begin to hear of him until after the Baptizer's death," Joseph said.

"So your daughter is enamored with this new baptizer? Is that it?"

"Yes, you could put it that way, but this new one is no longer baptizing. I believe John's death has turned him away from that practice," Joseph said. "I have been told that he brought a dead man back to life. I do not believe this, of course. No one but God can overcome death, and he most assuredly is not God. Were he to claim such, he would be subject to death by the Law of our people. He is not that foolish."

"How can I help you?"

"If my daughter merely supported this man with food, lodging and the necessities, as others of his followers do, I would not be concerned, but I fear a connection, a growing affection for this man, and I cannot permit it. It is possible this Jesus may try to use Miriam's affections to influence me, and, through me, the Council. He is here, in Jerusalem, for Passover."

"You have nothing to fear from this wandering Jew. I have men from the Tenth Legion in Jerusalem and I intend that your Passover festival be peaceful. Any disturbances will be quickly dealt with, I assure you."

"He is no threat to Rome, or to the Council for that matter. We have dealt with the likes of him and his Essene friends for many years now. No, I am only concerned with my daughter and how I may distance her from this man."

"Should you wish it so, it can be easily arranged."

Joseph looked closely at Pilate who sat quietly, inspecting the contents of his wine cup before looking up at Joseph and smiling.

"Nothing need be connected to you or your people, of course," Pilate said. "It would be a matter only among friends."

"Is it possible he could be removed from the city? Banned from Jerusalem?"

"He could be, shall we say, permanently relocated. The details need not concern you."

Joseph sat quietly for a long moment, his eyes locked to Pilate's, then he looked away.

"I, ah, I could not condone. I could not agree to anything that would transgress our laws. I..." he stammered.

"I believe you have misunderstood. I have no wish to transgress your laws, except, of course, where they conflict with ours. That need not happen. More wine?" Pilate rose to refill their cups.

"I am relieved. If the man could be merely removed from Jerusalem, banned from returning, that would serve my purpose."

"Do not concern yourself. I will have my people watch this Jesus, son of Joseph, closely. Should anything transpire that might be of interest to you, I will inform you immediately. We will watch and wait only. With Lucius Quintus here, I do not wish any trouble that might cause him concern."

After Joseph left, Marcus quietly entered the room and closed the door.

"Trouble?" he said.

"No, I think not. Opportunity? Perhaps."

"Oh?"

"I may have found a means to bind Joseph and the Council more closely to our purposes. And, as an unexpected benefit, perhaps a lever to use with our friend Lucius Quintus."

"You, my lord, do possess a fine and devious mind," Marcus said helping himself to a cup of wine and a handful of olives.

"Tell me, how would Lucius, a Roman noble, and Joseph, a Jew, be connected?"

"Love," Pilate said. "Isn't love a beautiful thing?"

"Ah, the girl, Miriam."

"Indeed. Now, Marcus I have a task for you. You will set your people in Jerusalem to finding this Jesus from Nazareth and reporting on his movements. Being a Jew, he will undoubtedly come into the city for their religious rituals. From what I hear, he loves to argue with the Temple priests concerning their strange religious practices, and he often gets the better of them. This is good for our purposes."

"What are our purposes?"

"To eliminate the prophet," Pilate said. "To do it in such a way as to bind Joseph and the Council more tightly to us. Find him and provoke him, good Marcus. Provoke the prophet into breaking the peace, creating a riot, killing a priest... I care not, but we must help him behave in such a way that we can remove him from the board and, if necessary, put the blame on our good friend Joseph."

"Joseph, head of the Council, neh?"

Pilate smiled and took another pull at his wine. "You understand me well."

"My lord, I shall move at once," Marcus said.

House of Misery

The village of Bethany, meaning "House of Misery", lay a mile beyond Jerusalem on the main road from Jericho, on the southeastern slope of the Mount of Olives. The village was originally settled by people from Galilee and had become a lodging place for pilgrims coming to Jerusalem who could not afford lodging in the city itself.

Bethany was where those who were sick, injured or destitute could be cared for out of sight of the city in keeping with Jewish law. The town was also home to a small population of lepers. With the help of Herod the Great, the Essenes had established a large hospice there. This place was crowded every year at Passover with people suffering from their long journey to Jerusalem.

Those who were well and could afford it, stayed in Bethpage, located on the top of the Mount with a marvelous view of the city. The sick, poor and destitute had Bethany.

Jesus and his band followed the traditional route, crossing the great lake at Capernaum, then traveling the eastern side of the River Jordan, crossing near Jericho on the main east-west road to Jerusalem. Although not as direct as the southern road out of Capernaum, it avoided Samaria and any unpleasant conflicts between Judeans and Samaritans. The group walked into Bethany late in the day and went to the house of Lazarus and his sisters. Martha, the eldest sister, was in the courtyard when they arrived.

"Martha, it is good to see you again," Jesus said.

Martha looked up from her washing, then drying her hands on her outer robe, crossed quickly to him and embraced him, kissing him on both cheeks and held him at arm's length.

"Jesus, the wandering son of man from Nazareth! Welcome, welcome!" She looked closely at him, noting the wrinkles around his eyes and the flecks of gray at the edges of his beard.

"You have come a long way? You seem... tired," she said.

"It has been a long journey, but, now I am here," he said.

"You have brought friends with you I see," Martha said looking over his shoulder at the people standing in the gateway and in the street outside.

Jesus gestured to Magdalene who came quickly forward.

"A few. Some follow because they are curious, some because they love me. This is the one who loves me the most," he said taking Mary under his arm. "Martha, you remember my beloved companion, Mary of Magdala. We call her Magdalene."

Magdalene smiled up at him and Jesus leaned down and kissed her on the mouth. Martha too smiled, and took Magdalene by the hand saying, "You must be special, indeed. I do not recall him lavishing such affection on you before."

"No, things are changed since we were with you last. Many things have changed," Magdalene said.

"So I have heard. Jesus, your name is on the lips of many here of late. Is it true that you are still healing the sick and living with the poor, that you have no house of your own? Are you still at odds with the scribes and the Pharisees? Why are you..." Martha blurted.

"Peace!" Jesus said smiling at her. "I cannot answer all of your questions in a rush, and besides, we are tired and I wish to see the others. They will have their questions too."

Martha laughed, "Forgive me. I am happy to see you, and have forgotten my courtesies. Lazarus! Mary! Jesus of Nazareth is here to see us!" she bellowed.

"That should bring them running."

It did. The door into the courtyard burst open and a tall, slender youth dashed out, followed by a short, portly young woman. The youth ran up to Jesus and threw his arms around him, almost bowling them both over. Martha reached out to steady them, "Easy, brother. Greet him but don't break any bones while you are about it," she said.

The youth released Jesus, but grasped one of his hands and held it. He was very slender, with pale skin and dark hair, worn long, his beard thin and sparse.

"Jesus. It is you. I am so happy you have come again. I think of you every day," he said.

"As you should, since he saved you from the tomb," Martha said.

"It was not I who saved you, Lazarus. God saved you. I merely was his messenger. If you had not believed what God said to you, you would surely have died. But you live. The thanks must go to God, and also to yourself," Jesus said.

"Without you, if you had not come…"

"But I did come when I heard you were sick. They said you were already dead, but I did not believe it. See, you recovered. You live and owe your thanks to God, not to me."

"Enough, enough," Martha said. "See, sister Mary is waiting to greet you, Jesus. Let us spare time for her."

Jesus and Mary embraced as did she and Magdalene.

"You have come for Passover?" Lazarus asked.

"Yes, it is time I celebrated Passover in the Holy City."

"Stay with us," Martha said. "There is no room in Jerusalem, and your reputation precedes you, which is not altogether a good thing."

Jesus laughed, "Indeed, with some, it is not. They are mostly men of small mind and limited interest."

"Come then, let us eat and talk of your discussions with these men of small minds," Martha said.

Jesus and Magdalene went with the sisters and Lazarus into their house. His other followers left to seek their own dinner and beds in the town. After the meal, Lazarus and his sisters collected the remaining bread and soup for the poor and the sick. They, along with Jesus and Magdalene went among those the Essenes were caring for the sick and needy, feeding those who were unable to feed themselves. Jesus talked with many that night and laid his hands on some who were in dire need of prayer and God's help.

"There are many here today," Jesus said.

"We always have the poor and the sick with us, but their numbers swell at Passover," said Jonathan, one of the Essene brothers.

"Yes, I am certain that the poor will be with us always, until God's Kingdom does come," Jesus said, "but we must do what we can to live righteously now. If we follow the law and God's teaching we can bring forth the Kingdom, which is already here but men do not see it."

"I do not agree, brother," Jonathan said. "Look around. This is not God's Kingdom. It is a world afflicted with pain and sores and death."

"If the Father were here, now, there would indeed be an end to all this. He made the earth as it is and so what is here now is also the Kingdom. It is ours to make for good or ill as we will. If men were more disposed to the good, there would be far less suffering in the world," Jesus said.

"You may be right, brother, but when you have seen and dealt with as much suffering as we have here, you will be always ready for God to set things right."

"I think when the Father comes, your place will be assured."

"Would that it be soon."

"It will be," Jesus said. "Now, I yearn to see the Temple again. It has been too long. Tomorrow we go to Jerusalem."

The Watcher

"Who are you, that you say these things to us?" shouted a stout priest, his face red and his finger pointing accusingly at Jesus.

"Yea, yea!" shouted his fellows. "You have no authority here. Nonsense and drivel. Who can make sense of your babble?"

"You do not know who I am, but I know you. You have stolen the keys of worship and keep them for yourselves!" Jesus responded.

The group of men and women with him drew closer around him.

"You are like the rich man who had much money. He was pleased with himself and said 'Tomorrow, I will buy more grain for my storehouse. I will go to the market for new wine. I will buy new horses for my sons.' That night he died. If you have ears to hear, you better listen!"

"Easy enough for you to say," the stout priest responded, "clearly you have never had a pot to piss in. What would you know about rich men?"

"Enough to know that when God's Kingdom comes, and it will come soon, your golden piss pot will not help you to enter there. Your riches will not make you worthy. Adam came first from God and his wealth did not make him worthy or he would not have died," Jesus replied.

"So you say," one of the priests replied, "but who are you? What gives you the authority to lecture us about God?"

"Answer a question and I will tell you," Jesus said. "From where did John the Baptizer get his authority?"

Jesus' supporters were growing more vocal now.

"Yes, priest, tell us that?"

"Aye, explain that to us!"

The priests looked at one another and drew together for a whispered conference. The crowd that had gathered to hear, waited. Among them was a short, sharp-nosed man wearing a black turban. His name was Jazred and he had been circulating through the Temple all morning, searching for someone. He said to the men standing by him, "Who is that man arguing with the Priests?"

"Arguing? Getting the better of it, I say," one of the men said. "Got 'em again. If the priests say John got his power from God, they'll have to admit he was a holy one, one of God's messengers. If they say he got his power from the people, well, there's plenty of folks here to believe John was from God, and that won't go well with the priests."

"Aye, he's got them again, he has. He is that Galilean, the one from Nazareth who has been giving the Pharisees fits. Serves 'em right, too. Pious bastards," said another man, taller, roughly dressed and stooped from an injury. A long scar ran across his left cheek and what would have been the bottom of his ear, had it still been attached.

"What's it to you? You know him?" the scarred man said looking hard at Jazred.

"It is nothing, friend. I don't know him. Merely curious. You don't see this often, not here in the Temple you don't," Jazred said.

"True," the scarred man's companion said, "but the Nazarene doesn't seem to care. Giving 'em what-for, that one is. Got protection too. Can't be that outspoken lest someone has your back."

Jazred stood on his toes, straining for a better view. "Who? I see no one."

"The big fellow, greenish robe, long beard, just behind the Nazarene. That would be the one they call Cephas, rock-head. Not too bright, but he is devoted to the Nazarene and would just as soon knock heads as not," the scarred man said. "Best give him a wide berth, eh?"

"You should know," the second man said.

"Caught me unawares, he did. Won't happen a second time, I can tell you," the scarred man glared.

Jazred quietly slipped away, pausing to get a good look at Jesus who had evidently said something that pleased the crowd, for they were laughing and nudging one another. He left the Temple, and went directly to the tavern where he found Samuel in his usual place behind the counter dispensing wine and food and keeping watch over his customers.

Jazred stepped up to the counter and Samuel leaned close, "Well," he said, "you have news?"

"Aye, and good news at that. He is in the Temple, giving better than he gets from the priests. I saw him good," Jazred said.

"Very well. Take Esau and Malak with you and point him out. They will set their watch boys on him," Samuel said.

"Right. What about my pay?" Jazred said.

"You'll get what's owed you after we know for sure he's our man, and when the watch on him is locked down. Marcus wants to know where he is at all times. Then you'll get your money, but now, take the boys and get them on him before he leaves," Samuel said, "or I'll be taking it out of your hide."

Warnings

It was late in the day when Jesus and his tired followers began their trek back to Bethany. They paused on the tall hill of the olive groves to take in the view of the Temple bathed in the light of the lowering sun. The red tile roofs glowed and here and there torches and lamps were being lit. The workers at the olive presses were gathering their possessions and heading for their homes. As the sun slid below the hills, the tired band resumed their walk to Bethany, food and rest.

After eating, they removed the tables that had been pushed together to accommodate their number, and talked about the events of the day. Jesus and Magdalene reclined together on a large couch and the rest took their places as best they could.

"I don't like it that you stir the crowd so," Magdalene said. "The priests scare me."

"Don't fret, little woman," Peter said, "I'll let no harm come to him."

"You'll not be so brave after the temple police crack your thick head with their clubs," Martha called from across the room.

"Let 'em try. There are more of us than there are of them," Peter shot back. "You're a woman. What do women know about such things?"

"You see, it is not wise, annoying the priests like you do. It is dangerous," Magdalene continued, ignoring Peter.

"We always argue, the priests and I. You've seen it many times. They may be angry, but they will not be quick to break the peace," Jesus said.

"Perhaps not," Judas spoke up. "Afterwards, I remained to see what they would do."

"What did you see, little man?" Peter sneered.

"It is what I heard that matters. The priests were still talking after you left. I was behind one of the pillars so they didn't make me out. What I heard was not good," Judas said.

"Well, go on, what was it?" Andrew asked.

"They want to goad you into more arguments tomorrow, find something that will anger you. I think they want to provoke you into doing something rash so they can put their police on you," Judas said.

"That will be difficult for them," Jesus laughed. "They are the ones who always come away angry, not me."

"No, I think it is different this time. I think they are plotting something to make you lose your temper. They are angry," Judas said. "It would be wise to stay away from the Temple tomorrow."

"That's what they would like. I did not come here to stay away, to be silent when God calls me to speak. They are fools and have lost their way. It is God's will that I shine my light upon the path to the kingdom. I can do no less."

"If it is trouble they want, we'll be ready for them, right?" Peter snapped, looking around the room at the others. "Right?"

Andrew stood and said to Jesus, "If you return tomorrow, I will go with you, but I have foreboding in my heart. Jerusalem will be here tomorrow and the next day and the next. It is best to wait until after Passover when the crowds are smaller and most of the Romans have gone."

"No," Jesus said, "the time is now. It will soon be Passover and I wish us to celebrate in Jerusalem."

Unnoticed by the others, Magdalene slipped off the couch and quietly made her way outside. A deep foreboding welled within her and she was afraid. Soon, another figure joined her in the courtyard.

"You are troubled," Martha said.

"I fear for him. He is more stubborn now, blind almost to what is happening around him. He thinks God speaks to him in his head."

"Perhaps God does," Martha said. "He has a strange power. I have seen it."

"As have I. Yet, he is but a man. I have seen him full of sorrow at the plight of others, and I have seen him turn in anger at a simple request from a stranger. He cannot foretell what will happen, none of us can, but I fear he is in danger here."

"I fear this too. He has enemies and this is their place, their ground. Here they are most dangerous."

"He will not leave."

"I know. He is not strong enough to resist should the priests move against him."

"Then, we must find more strength, in case it is needed."

"How can we do this, two women alone?"

"I know someone," Magdalene said, "someone who can help. We must go into the city first thing in the morning."

Arrangements

Lucius arose early, ate hurriedly and left Kasha to his meditations in the garden to make his way through the streets to Joseph's house. The hundreds of stalls and stores were opening as he walked along. Young boys were dashing everywhere with crates and baskets of bread, dates, baked delicacies and produce for the stalls. Merchants were hanging colorfully dyed cloths, scarves, tunics, hats and other merchandise and setting up trays holding hundreds of items in their many compartments - beads, glassware, figurines, religious icons, incense, rings, bracelets, inlaid boxes, games, and all manner of goods that daily flowed into the city, especially now, at Passover.

He stopped to buy a delicate teak box, heavily inlaid with silver, containing cones of a heady incense. He also bought a set of finely engraved silver cups. He had the seller wrap them in silk kerchiefs, and resumed his walk through the noisy streets.

"Lucius Quintus, a good day to you," Deborah said greeting him at her door. "Please, enter."

"Yes, a good day. Greetings to you and may the gods favor this house and all in it."

"You come bearing gifts," she said eyeing the wrapped bundles under his arm.

"I do. This," he said handing her the larger bundle, "is for you. And this other is for…"

"Miriam. Of course," Deborah said taking the bundle in both hands. "I will tender my thanks now." She leaned forward and kissed Lucius on the cheek.

"I believe Miriam will want to thank you herself. Come, make your ease in the garden and I will fetch her."

As they walked, Deborah said, "I know your feelings toward my niece. Joseph may say I am a silly woman, but I understand and approve, Lucius Quintus. You are not one of our people, but, when the heart calls, that is of little consequence, especially to the young."

"I..." Lucius began.

"You need not speak in your defense. I believe that Miriam also feels affection for you, but she is young and still under her father's influence, though it may not appear so at times. Joseph? Joseph is stubborn and he is traditional and does not like Romans. Don't misunderstand. He values your friendship and considers you a friend, especially a friend of the family, but to welcome you into the family, that is quite another matter."

"I thank you for your honest speaking," Lucius said, "and I am of the same mind. If Miriam were to accept me as a suitor I would have a long campaign to win Joseph's approval."

"Exceedingly long."

"Still, there is another impediment," Lucius said. "Jesus, the Galilean."

"I have seen no sign of affection for Miriam that he does not hold for others of his women followers, except for Mary the Magdalene. Miriam sees this. She knows where his affections lie, but, like many young women who are pierced with love, she sees, but does not believe."

"It is as I feared," Lucius said sitting heavily on a couch in the garden.

"What? A Roman, a soldier in his Emperor's service, giving up so quickly?" Deborah said smiling down at him.

"Why must this be so difficult?"

"Because it is important. Because it is life, your life, Lucius Quintus, and sometimes life is hard."

"Schooled by a Jewess. Life holds many wonders," Lucius said smiling at her in return.

"Then, let the schooling continue. I will go fetch Miriam and you many continue with your lessons," Deborah said and went off to find her.

With Magdalene's help, asking for directions along the way, the two women found the house of Joseph, head of the Sanhedrin Great Council. Hanna called to Deborah who recognized Magdalene at once and brought them inside.

"Magdalene, you are most welcome. Who do you bring with you?" Deborah said.

"This is my friend Martha, brother of Lazarus in Bethany. We need your help," Magdalene said. "It is about Jesus."

After hearing their story, Deborah said, "Come, there are others who need to hear this." She led them into the garden where Lucius and Miriam were talking.

"Your pardon," Deborah said, "but you must hear what these women have to say."

"Magdalene!" Miriam said and ran to greet her. "It is so good to see you. Welcome to our home. But, what is it? You are troubled."

"This is my friend Martha," Magdalene said. Before Lucius could greet her, Magdalene plunged ahead. "There will be trouble. With Jesus. In the Temple. We are fearful that something will happen today."

"Trouble?" Lucius said. "What kind of trouble? How do you know this?"

"We don't know it, but we think something is going to happen," Martha said.

"What is it? What is going to happen?" Miriam said. "It is all right. You can speak. There is no one here but us. Joseph is with his council at the Temple."

Magdalene and Martha told them of what had happened the night before, of the rumors that a plot was made to involve Jesus in a disturbance so the Priests could arrest him.

"Does he know of this?" Lucius said.

"Yes, but he does not care, or believe it. Or both," Martha said.

"He believes God will protect him. He told me so," Magdalene said.

"That may be," Lucius said, "but still, now is the time for caution. It is not wise to tempt the gods."

"What can we do?" Magdalene said.

"I will go to the Temple and find Jesus and his friends. If someone attempts to create trouble, I will deal with it. Magdalene, you must go to Herod's palace and find Kasha. Tell him what you told me and ask him to come to the Temple. I will need his help," Lucius said.

"We may," Miriam said.

Everyone looked at her.

"I am going with you," Miriam said to Lucius.

"No, you are not," Lucius said. "It will be too dangerous."

"I am not afraid."

"I would be afraid for you. I cannot protect both you and Jesus at the same time," Lucius said.

"I will go with her," Martha said. "She is one of his followers and should not be kept from him, especially if there might be trouble. Her father is head of the Council. I do not think any harm will come to her. We will stay well back."

Lucius looked at Deborah who slightly raised one eyebrow. He sighed. "Very well, but stay away from the crowd. If anything happens you must leave, quickly."

"We will," Miriam said.

The Denarius

It did not take Lucius and the women long to find Jesus. He was in the center of a Temple crowd near the money tables where pilgrims exchanged their money for shekels and to buy the Paschal lambs for the Passover meals. As they drew near, the crowd broke into spirited laughter. Lucius found a place beside nearby pillars for Miriam and Martha to stand, then moved into the crowd until he could watch Jesus and still see the two women.

A red-faced priest, short, well dressed with long curling hair and beard was speaking heatedly at Jesus who stood by calmly, smiling at the man.

"Stories that play to the crowd are one thing," the priest said, "but here, in the Temple, I question your authority to criticize the Law."

"You may question. Again," Jesus said and some in the crowd chuckled.

"Very well. Tell us then, being a teacher and a follower of the Law, is it lawful that we pay tribute to Caesar?" the priest said holding up a silver denarius for the crowd to see.

One of the men near Lucius whispered, "They've boxed him in now. If he says yes, he's a Roman collaborator. No, and he's a Roman enemy."

"No," whispered his companion, "its a question of the Law, you fool. The Law prohibits graven images, and whose face is carved on that coin? Tiberius, that's who, and the Romans hold that he is a god. That's the real problem, false gods. You can't pay tribute to a false god."

"Let me have that coin," Jesus said to the priest who stepped forward and handed it to him. Jesus turned it in his fingers, then held it close to the priest's face.

"Whose image is on this?" Jesus asked loudly for all to hear.

"Tiberius Caesar, of course," the priest said laughing. "Not yours!"

The crowd laughed.

"Caesar..." Jesus said holding the coin high, turning it for the crowd to see. He flipped it high in the air toward the priest.

"Then give to Caesar what belongs to him, and give to God what is his," Jesus said.

Some in the crowd laughed, others were silent, puzzling this out.

"That is the answer!" one of the money changers shouted to the crowd. "Denarii, shekels, gold, what difference does it make. The Romans demand their tribute, and the Temple wants its tax. Bring us your coins, whoever is carved upon them, and we will exchange them for you."

"And rob us blind, too!" someone in the crowd shouted.

A big man dressed in a cheap tunic stepped out from behind the tables. His arms were heavy with muscle and his hands were scarred.

"Still, that's no answer," he growled, his voice rough. He smelled of garlic, sweat and wine. "What is it, little man from Galilee? Do we give tribute to a Roman boy-lover who calls himself a god?"

"To call yourself a god does not make you God," Jesus replied.

"Are you simple minded?" the big man said stepping into the open, closer to Jesus. "I asked you a question. Pay, or not? Which is it? Come on, I ain't got all day."

Lucius began moving closer. Peter, who had been standing behind Jesus in the throng pushed through on the other side.

"Friend, there is no need to be rude. The question has been asked and answered. If you want me to explain it to you, just ask," Jesus said.

"Piss off, peasant. I don't need a country bastard explaining nothing to me," the man said taking a step toward Jesus. Before Lucius could get clear, Peter stepped between them.

"Get out of my way," the man said moving to shove Peter aside, but Peter struck him in the face with a wild blow of his fist.

As the man staggered back, Lucius reached Jesus, spun him around and pushed him into the crowd.

"We are leaving. Now!" Lucius hissed as Jesus turned to look back. "Move! It is too dangerous for you here."

The big man had stumbled, but not gone down. He straightened to face Peter and spat a bloody stream into the sand at his feet.

"Surprised me with that one. Now, it's my turn," he said drawing a short knife from under his tunic. Peter backed away, putting the money changers and their tables between them.

The man called out to the crowd, "You all seen it. I was attacked."

He moved toward Peter, his knife held low and ready. The money changers fled and Peter kicked over the tables, blocking the man's advance, and backed further away.

"You are a big man for such a little knife," a voice called out from the crowd. The man turned toward the sound.

"I should perhaps not kill you with this," Kasha said stepping forward, raising his gladius. "It would be more fitting that I use this."

He sheathed his sword and drew a curved dagger from his belt. The man looked at Peter, then back to Kasha. Fear and uncertainty were on his face and in his eyes. He backed away a step.

"You can run or you can remain and die. Which do you choose?" Kasha said.

The man hesitated only a moment, then turned and disappeared into the crowd.

Peter's eyes were wide and his hands were trembling.

"Come," Kasha said. "We must leave now."

Jazred, watching from the porch nearby, moved quickly. Marcus would want to know, and Marcus might be generous in his thanks.

Kasha and Peter caught up with Lucius, Jesus and the women outside the Jericho gate. The rest of Jesus' followers were there too, talking excitedly about what had happened. Together they took the road down the hill and up the other side to Bethany and the house of Lazarus.

"I will watch the gate," Kasha said. "The young Teacher is shaken. He will be more willing to listen to reason now."

"I will go and speak with him," Lucius said.

"It is best he leave this place. The Temple priests will not let this go without repayment," Kasha said.

"He should return to Galilee. They will not follow him there. They will be satisfied if he is no longer in the city," Lucius said. "I will speak with him."

Inside, others were speaking to Jesus, urging him to leave Bethany, or at the least, not return to the city during Passover. He sat moodily at a table, eating a portion of broiled fish, bread and olives that someone had brought to him. Peter was flaming with anger.

"I should have killed him myself for what he said to you," he said to Jesus. "I would have, if that black heathen hadn't interfered."

"He would have cut you from brisket to belly if not for Kasha. If I had not brought him, you would be dead," Magdalene said. "You were scared enough then. No use talking big now."

"Be silent, woman! What do women know about death or fear? I fear no man," Peter said.

"Cephas, your pride has the better of you. It is no shame to fear death. You need not have acted so hastily," Jesus said. "I could have handled him. I have seen his like before."

"You could not have handled him alone," Lucius said.

"Ah, Lucius. You have my thanks for your help," Jesus said. "I could have done so if Cephas had not gotten between us. There was no need for violence."

Peter started to object, but Lucius cut in, "No, you are wrong. Peter is right. Violence was the object from the start. Do you not see it? That man was there solely to provoke you into violence or to make you run, a coward before the people. He is no priest, no money changer or temple man. He does others' bidding for hire. He was there at the command of another, to provoke you, to create an incident so that the priests could take action against you."

"Who would do this? The priests? They do not like me but I do not think they would resort to this. If they had reason to arrest me, they would have done so before now."

"They have nothing with which to charge you. You have not broken the Law. You did not do so today, even though they attempted to trap you with the denarii," Andrew said. "You are too smart for them and they hate you for it. Don't you see, when you debate with them you make mockery of their attempts to best you. You create more enemies with the Priests, and you become more popular with the people. When you were in Galilee you were not a threat to them."

"Yes, no one here takes prophets there seriously," Lazarus said. "Bring your teachings here, to Jerusalem, and that is a different thing."

"Listen to what they are saying to you, Jesus," Magdalene said. "You are in danger here, more so now than ever. You cannot stay."

Jesus was silent for a moment, then said, "Lucius, what of the Romans? Will they take notice?"

"Notice, certainly. Not much transpires in Jerusalem, especially at Passover, that escapes the notice of Pilate and his men. His function is to keep the peace and he will do what is necessary. He is not in the Emperor's best graces. Look around you. Your friends are here and they are all telling you the same thing. It is time to go."

Jesus looked at the familiar faces gathered around him. All looked back at him, unsmiling, many nodding in agreement. No one spoke.

"I must have time to think and to pray," Jesus said and walked out into the garden. Magdalene went with him.

Lucius turned to Martha and Lazarus and said, "What more can we do?"

"Find his mother and bring her here," Martha said. "We have word that she is coming here to be with him."

"Where would I find her? It is days to Nazareth and back."

"She will be close, somewhere on the Jericho road. All Galilean pilgrims take the east road through Jericho to Bethany. She will be somewhere on that road," Lazarus said.

"You know her, do you not?" Martha said.

"No, I have never seen her," Lucius said.

"I will come. Two pairs of eyes are better than one," Miriam said.

"No. Not this time. I want you here with Kasha. Lazarus, can you come?"

"I will pack some food and we can start now."

"Good. I will ask Kasha to remain here and keep watch."

Spider's Web

Mikhael found Joseph in the inner court of the Temple, speaking with men of the Council. When they were done, Mikhael approached Joseph privately.

"We must talk," Mikhael said.

"Yes?"

"Not here. Come," Mikhael said leading Joseph away from the others. They left the Temple and found a nearby wine shop. They sat in a back corner.

"There was a fight in the Temple today, with this Jesus and his followers," Mikhael said.

"A fight? What do you mean?"

"A fight. Money changers' tables upset, weapons were drawn, but there was no blood spilled, fortunately, if you don't consider a broken nose to be blood drawn."

"Jesus did this? In the Temple?" Joseph said astonished.

"No, it was not him. Someone else began it."

"Weapons drawn, in the Temple! Mikhael, you have gone too far! I wished only to create a disturbance, not a…"

"Keep your voice down. This was not our doing. A stranger began it, a street ruffian by the looks of him. He was not sent by us, I assure you."

"Why? Was it a private matter?"

"My people do not think so. I am told the Nazarene was not at fault. The ruffian provoked the fight," Mikhael said. "But it did not end well for him."

Mikhael related what happened and both men were silent, considering what this meant.

"So, there is someone else who does not want the Nazarene speaking in the Temple," Mikhael said. "Does this suggest anything to you?"

Joseph sipped his wine looking at Mikhael. "No, only that he must have other enemies. What of the Romans?"

"I do not know. Everyone involved left before the guards arrived. The Romans broke up the crowd and went away again," Mikhael said. "Should the Nazarene return, I think it will bode ill for him."

"He is too smart for that. He knows now that he is a marked man. We will see no more of him in Jerusalem."

After they parted at the wine shop, Joseph went directly to Herod's Palace.

"I must speak with Pilate," Joseph said, "it is a matter of urgency."

"The Prefect is not available at present," Marcus said.

"Where is he?"

Marcus merely looked at Joseph and did not answer.

"Begging your pardon, but can you tell me when I can see him?"

"That will depend on the Prefect. If you care to state your business, I will see that he is informed."

"Tell him that it involves the Galilean of whom we earlier spoke. It is most urgent."

"Very well. I will tell him. Good day," Marcus said motioning to the soldier who had accompanied Joseph.

"Follow me," the legionnaire said leading Joseph from the room.

Marcus found Pilate in the baths, reclining in the company of two beautiful youths who were hanging on his words. Marcus stopped at the entrance and waited. Pilate finished his story and the boys laughed with what seemed to Marcus to be too much enthusiasm. Pilate said, "Leave us." The youths quickly vanished.

"Come, sit, take some wine," Pilate said indicating a couch near him. Marcus took a cup and rolled onto the couch. It was still warm from the young body that had rested there before.

"Beautiful, are they not, with the bloom still upon them?" Pilate asked.

"Don't care for boys," Marcus said. "They act like girls, so why not have the real thing?"

"Perhaps you lack a certain refinement in taste?"

"Or I just don't care for boys."

"Ah, well. Pity. Now, what brings you to me?"

"Joseph the Jew."

"Back so soon?"

"He has learned about the disturbance with the Galilean in their Temple. Wants to speak with you about it," Marcus said.

"You told him what?"

"That you aren't available."

"That is all?"

"What more does he need to know?"

"Indeed. Then, let us proceed. I want to act quickly before this Jew can change his mind, and before our friend Lucius gets involved. Yes, it will be more difficult if Lucius Quintus gets his nose in this business.

"Send a detail to find this Galilean, bring him before one of the magistrates as soon as possible then take him out and crucify him. No delays, mark you. Get it done quickly."

236

Under the Olive Trees

The evening was clear and balmy. The group at Lazarus' home had finished the evening meal which had been dominated by much drinking and heated discussion of the day's events. Jesus, grown weary of the constant arguments, had disappeared with Magdalene.

"He cannot stay, I tell you," Andrew said. "We must leave this place, return to Galilee where we will be among friends."

He took another gulp of wine and glared at Peter.

"I do not fear the Romans or the priests, and neither does Jesus," Peter said slurring his words.

"Ha! You should fear them you rock-head. Almost got yourself gutted proper today," John said.

"Had it not been for the big black fellow you'd be dead for certain," Andrew said. "Your own doing, too."

"Where were you? Cowering behind the women?" Peter growled. He drained his cup and looked menacingly at Andrew.

"You weren't the only one ready to protect him. I was there too," Andrew said slamming his wine cup down and standing to face Peter.

"Kasha," Miriam whispered, "I am scared. Will they fight?"

"Do not worry, little Daughter," Kasha said. "If it comes to that, I will ask that they refrain."

Miriam looked at Kasha and smiled. Kasha returned her smile as Jesus spoke from the doorway.

"Brothers, why are you fighting? You have let this turn you against one another. Have you forgotten yet again what I have taught you? Love one another, as you would have yourselves be loved."

"Master, how can you love someone who accuses you of cowardice?" Andrew said.

"What difference should that make to you. You know yourself. If another does not know you, should that be a reason for you to not treat him as your brother? If someone wrongs you is it just that you wrong him in return? Where will it end?

"Come, all of you. Put down your wine cups and follow me," he said and walked out the door.

Most of them did so. He led them to the hill overlooking the lights of the city and the Temple. They gathered in the groves near the great olive press and stood silently, thinking about the day and what the morrow might bring. Peter and most of the others lay beneath the gnarled olive trees, tired from the stress of the day and too much wine. Jesus, with Magdalene, Miriam, Kasha and a few others drew apart to pray and talk quietly.

The Roman guard detail guided by Jazred found Peter and the others asleep under the olive trees. The soldiers prodded them awake with blows from their javelin shafts and heavy sandaled feet. Judas, who had been lying apart from the others, quietly slipped away into the darkness.

"Stand them up and bring them into the light," the Centurion charged with the detail said to his men.

The soldiers got everyone to their feet and moved them into the light of the torches and lanterns.

"Is the Galilean here?" rasped the Centurion.

"I don't see him," Jazred said. "He's not among this rabble."

"Over here!" a voice shouted from a short way down the hill. "Over here! I've found more of them."

A detachment of soldiers appeared, lanterns swaying, herding a smaller group. They were pushed into the circle of light along with the others.

"I followed this one," a soldier said thrusting Judas forward. "Slipped away to warn them."

"How about this lot?" the Centurion said to Jazred.

"Hold those lanterns a bit higher," Jazred said taking a closer look at the newcomers. "That's him. The tall one with no hat, next to the finely dressed woman. That's him."

"You're certain? No mistake now, or it'll go bad with you," the Centurion said motioning for Jesus to be brought forward.

"Certain of it. He's the one you want," Jazred said.

Peter gave a yell and cut at Jazred with a short knife. Jazred reeled backwards, clutching his ear, blood streaming down his neck and hand. Before anyone could react, Kasha had Peter on the ground, his foot on Peter's neck, his arm twisted painfully aloft. Kasha's sword was in his other hand, the blade glowing like bronze blood in the lamplight. The Centurion took a step forward, unsheathing his own gladius. No one spoke.

"Centurion," Kasha said in Latin. "I am Kasha of the house of Quintus of Rome. This one," he gave another twist to Peter's arm and Peter grunted in pain, "had too much wine and does not understand that you are Roman soldiers with orders to obey. Fortunately, he has only injured a Jew."

The Centurion looked at Jazred, now whimpering, holding a bloody rag to his head.

"True. One of the priest's servants. He is of little concern. You are the companion of Lucius Quintus are you not?" the Centurion asked.

"I am," Kasha replied.

The Centurion looked at Kasha for a long moment then sheathed his gladius. He said to Peter. "The gods have been good to you this night."

"Come, we are finished here," the Centurion said. The guard detail formed up with Jesus in its center and marched away into the darkness.

Kasha released Peter and turned to Miriam. "Are you all right, little daughter?"

"Where are they taking him? What are they going to do?" Miriam said clutching Kasha's arm.

"They are taking him to the Antonia Fortress, where prisoners are held until judgement is rendered upon them," Kasha said.

"They will kill him tonight," Magdalene said. She was on her knees, tears streaking her face. "They will kill him."

"No, they will not kill him. Not tonight," Kasha replied.

"They came all this way to find him and take him. Why won't they just kill him and be done with it?" Andrew asked.

"Because they are Romans," Kasha said.

"What difference does that make?" Miriam said.

"Romans have laws," Kasha said. "Someone sent the soldiers after him. Someone has a reason and will not want him killed outright or they would have done so. Regardless, the time is short. We must find Lucius."

"I will go," Andrew said.

"And I," John spoke up.

"Take this," Kasha said handing Andrew a leather bag heavy with coins. "Get horses and ride fast. Tell him what you saw, and that he must get to Pilate quickly. He will know what to do."

The two men ran back to Bethany.

"What can I do?" Miriam asked.

"Go home, child. Be with Deborah and your father tonight. I will take you."

"You will come for me tomorrow? I must see him."

"I will come."

"Magdalene, please, get up," Miriam said gently helping her to her feet.

"I don't know what to do," Magdalene said. "Tell me what to do."

"You will come home with me, and we will pray together for his safety," Miriam said.

Kasha took them, one under each arm, and slowly walked them down the hill toward Jerusalem.

Galba

Tertius Galba was sleeping off a good night. Drinking, gaming, and sport with the women at the Persian's. It was good that he had won plenty of denarii earlier because he had spent liberally all evening and staggered back to the Fortress with an empty purse. It was still dark when some fool began hammering on his door.

"Go away, you drunken bastard!" he yelled from his foul bed.

The hammering continued.

"By the gods, leave off that racket or I'll cut your ball sack off and stuff it up your arse!"

Bang! Bang! Bang! The hammering continued.

Galba heaved himself out of bed, staggering for a moment as his head spun and pain surged through the little that remained of his frontal lobes. "Fix you, you son of a whore," he muttered, grabbing his worn gladius from the table as he lurched to the door. He yanked open the door to be met by the butt of a javelin that rammed him in the chest and sent him sprawling back into his room.

"Get a light going," someone said.

Soldiers pushed through the door. Lanterns illuminated Galba sitting on the floor where the javelin's blow had driven him. Marcus stepped forward and sniffed.

"The gods! But you do stink," he said. "Bring him outside where I can breathe."

Galba was summarily hoisted from the floor and thrust outside. Light was beginning to paint the eastern sky. Marcus was waiting impatiently, one arm leaning across his horse's saddle.

"You are Tertius Galba, Centurion, keeper of the prisoners here?" Marcus asked in a bored voice.

Galba didn't know who this perfumed Roman was but he was certain he was someone to be obeyed.

"Aye, your lordship, that would be Galba," he said.

"You can read?"

"Aye, your honor, that I can."

"Show him," Marcus said and one of the soldiers handed Galba a scroll.

"I will save you the trouble," Marcus said. "Work it out on your own time later. You will gather the group of prisoners brought before you this morning and take all of the men to the execution grounds and crucify them without delay. As to the others, do with them what you will. Do you understand?"

"Aye, your honor. Ah, without delay. Right away. Soon as possible," Galba stammered.

"One of my men will remain with you and report to me when this is carried out. Do this speedily and I will see you rewarded," Marcus said swinging up on his horse.

"Aye, your honor, as quickly as may be," Galba said.

"See that you do," Marcus said turned his horse and rode away, leaving one legionnaire behind. Galba looked closely at the man, smiled and said, "Young soldier, what might your name be?"

"No concern of yours," the soldier said. "Get dressed and get down to the lock up. You heard him, no time to lose." He shifted the javelin until the point was directed at Galba's midsection. "Understand?"

"Aye, Galba understands."

While the bored soldier waited outside, Galba went into his room to make ready. He splashed cold water over his head and face, donned his faded red tunic and cinched it tight with an old belt around his middle. After slipping on his nailed boots and tightening the lacing, he donned a leather segmented skirt, which protected his upper legs, then slung his gladius over his left shoulder. Retrieving his helmet, with the transverse crest signifying his rank, he pulled it on, picked up his cudgel and announced to no one in particular, "Now, Galba is ready."

It was a short walk through the Fortress to the prisoners' cells. The night's haul was small. Fifteen prisoners were crammed into a single cell, eight men, three boys and four women. Three of the men and one of the women were still drunk, but all were awake.

"All right, bring 'em out in the courtyard," Galba growled at the jailers.

The prisoners were roughly herded outside into the growing light of the day. The last stars were fading. Somewhere a cock crowed and goats bleated.

"By the gods," Galba muttered, "would that I was back in Spain. It's going to be another hot one, it is."

The prisoners were gathered in a rough knot before him, surrounded by the guard detail. The boys were scared and the women nervous. One of the men was crying but two of them looked at Galba with more anger than fear.

"Let's get on with it," Galba said. "You three, boys, there, step forward."

The three boys shuffled uncertainly toward him then stopped. They were all of an age, probably eight to ten years, and had been caught together, stealing food from a merchant's stall.

Galba belched, and said loudly, his voice growling menacingly, "Find you here again, and it won't go easy on you. Understand?"

The three mumbled, "Yes," and "Aye, sir" and "We're sorry, sir."

Galba said to one of the guards. "Give 'em a taste of your stick on their way out." Turning to the boys he said, "Now, run. Get out and don't let me see you here again!"

The boys immediately broke for the gate with the guard hard on their heels switching them across the backs of their legs as they ran. He stopped when they shot through the gate into the streets, then walked back, grinning, his long stick swishing against the ground.

"These women, what are they here for, then?" Galba said.

"These three for fighting in the market over some chickens," one of the soldiers said, "and the other wench for robbing Varro. 'Course, Varro was drunk at the time."

"Those three, give 'em ten lashes and send 'em on their way. The other one, she stays with the men."

"Those two men, the ones in front there, they was taken fighting in…" the guard began, pointing his pilum at two of the prisoners.

"Don't matter. They are all going up on the trees this morning," Galba said.

At this, the woman staggered, but one of the prisoners grabbed her and kept her from falling. The men looked blankly at Galba except for Jesus who stood, supporting the fainting woman. He looked over his shoulder toward the gate.

"What are you waiting for? Get 'em moving," Galba said.

The whips cracked and the ragged collection of prisoners were driven out the gate and through the city streets toward their meeting with death.

The Warrant

As the morning's condemned were whipped through the streets of Jerusalem, Lucius and Lazarus rode into Bethany with Jesus' mother Mary and her companion, Salome. They had found her not far outside the town and hired one of the pilgrims traveling in her group to bear her quickly in his cart. Mary, Lazarus' sister met them in the street.

"We must hurry," she said. "The Romans came for Jesus last night."

"So quickly and at night," Lucius said, "this is evil news. Where are the men, his companions?"

"They have fled," the younger Mary said, "and have gone into hiding."

"Where have they taken my son?" Mary said.

"They will have him prisoner in the Fortress, the big one next to the Temple," Lucius said. "You must stay here. There is little you can do now. I will go to Pilate and secure his release."

"No, I will not stay away while my son is in danger. I will go to him. He must know that I am here," Mary said.

"You can do nothing," Lucius said. "You will not like what you see."

"I will go," Mary said, "and if you cannot accompany me, I will go alone."

"I will go with you," the young Mary said. "The two Marys will go."

"As you will," Lucius said, "I must be quick. Go to the Fortress and wait there for me. I will come once I have seen Pilate."

He wheeled his horse and galloped through the town toward Jerusalem.

Miriam, Salome, Magdalene and Kasha had left Joseph's house for the Fortress. They were pushing through the Passover crowd when they heard yells and the crack of whips as the condemned were driven into view. The crowd gave way as they passed, two of the soldiers plying whips, the rest cursing and shoving the prisoners with the butts of their javelins. Jesus was supporting a woman as they ran.

"Jesus! Jesus, over here!" Magdalene shouted, but he gave no sign that he heard.

"Where are they taking him?" Salome cried.

"They'll be going to the Place of the Skull, young matron," an old woman said. "They're all dead now, they are."

"No! They cannot!" Magdalene sobbed. "They cannot…"

Kasha took them aside and said forcefully, "Something is amiss. Listen. You must follow them and watch what they do. You know this Place of the Skull? You know where it is?"

"Yes, yes… I have seen it," Miriam said. "It is a terrible place of suffering and death, where the Romans crucify the condemned. It is outside the walls, by the Damascus road, for all to see."

"We must hurry. You and Salome take Magdeline and go there. I will find Lucius and we will do what we can."

"How can you find Lucius? He has gone to find Jesus's mother," Miriam said.

"He will have news of what happened and he will go to Pilate. Only Pilate will be able to act, and Lucius knows this. He will go to Pilate and so will I," Kasha said. "Now, go. Do not get involved or invite the attention of the soldiers."

The women hurried off following the soldiers. Kasha went west, through the streets to Herod's Palace.

Marcus was sitting with Pilate as the Prefect picked his way through his breakfast.

"Bring more wine, and bread! This lot is stale," Pilate croaked, flinging the platter of bread across the room.

"And fish, broiled fish," Marcus said reaching for his wine cup. "Arising early gives me an appetite."

"How is our little drama with friend Joseph the Jew playing out? Is the hook set?" Pilate asked.

"Will be this morning. We have the Galilean. Took him last night outside the city. Good thing, as otherwise he would be nowhere to be found today."

"Well done," Pilate said helping himself to a fresh loaf and a slab of broiled fish. "And now?"

"Justice is swift, particularly swift in this case. Our Galilean fish will be up on his tree very soon. You should be able to bring the other Jew fish to the net this evening."

"Pardon, my lord, Lucius Quintus is here asking for you. Says it is urgent," one of the palace guards reported. "Send him up?"

"No. Do not send him up. I will tell you when," Pilate said shortly. "You will go and tell Lucius Quintus that I am not available but will be with him soon. When he tells you again of the urgency of his need, have him remain where he is and report back here to me. Understand?"

"Aye, Prefect," the guard said and turned to go.

"One more thing," Pilate said.

"Yes, my lord."

"Take your time."

The soldier paused for a moment, smiled, and walked slowly from the room.

"This is unexpected," Marcus said.

"Not really. Our Lucius is a resourceful man. And, he is in love. I suspect he wishes to rescue his fair maid's wooly prophet and worm his way further into her affections. He is playing the long game, our Lucius."

The Skull

The soldiers drove the condemned up a stony hill next to the Damascus road. Nothing grew there. Every living plant had long ago been ground into the earth by thousands of bare feet and the nailed boots of Roman soldiers. If blood had been able to enrich the ground, a ghastly garden would have covered the hill, but there was nothing, only bare earth, rocks and blood-stained wooden crosses lying piled among the stones. Crowning the hill were more crosses, standing erect, leaning from the weight of the bodies nailed and bound to their cross pieces. Hundreds of crows flapped and croaked, feeding on the dead and dying. Carrion dogs skulked along the fringe, waiting for the soldiers to leave.

The newly condemned looked about, dazed from the the whips and blows they had suffered along the way. Jesus, on his knees, as were the others, looked about, unbelieving.

"All right, break's over, get to work," Galba said. "You know what to do."

Most of the poor victims who were already up on their crosses paid no heed. Some were unconscious, a few babbled incoherently or begged for death. One, a large man nailed and tied to his cross, his nude body covered with blood and fresh scabs, raised his head, seeing the newcomers, and laughed, a bubbling raw croak, "Welcome to hell."

The soldiers set about their work. Each of the prisoners was forced to select a cross from the pile and drag it to one of the many holes that had been dug into the earth and rock.

The soldiers then stripped and cut away the prisoners' clothing and stretched them out on the wooden beams. One soldier pushed a two wheeled handcart from cross to cross, dispensing long iron nails and hammers. All the victims screamed as their hands, arms and feet were nailed to the wood. The soldiers tied ropes to the ends of the cross beams and hauled each one upright until it and its human cargo slid with a jarring thump into the hole that had been dug to receive it. Working quickly, the soldiers had everyone suspended from their crosses in short order.

"All right. Well done, lads, now form up and we're off. Who can use a drink, eh?" Galba said.

The soldiers moved into a ragged formation, and leaving four of their number behind to stand watch over the dying men and women, marched down the hill talking and joking past a group of onlookers. Miriam, Salome and Magdalene averted their faces as the soldiers went by.

"We must go to him," Magdalene said starting up the hill.

"No! Stay back. The soldiers will not permit you to approach him," Miriam said. She held Magdalene by the arm, resisting her pull with both hands.

"Please, I must go," Magdalene said looking at Jesus who hung, head down, unmoving. "He is dead, he is not moving, let me go…"

"He is alive. See, he breathes. Look at his ribs. He breathes," Miriam said. "You cannot go to him. The soldiers allow no interference. You could be hurt."

"I care not," Magdalene cried. "They are killing him."

"Yes, but Lucius will soon come. It takes a long time to die on the tree," Miriam said.

Miriam held her fast and soon she stopped resisting. Miriam searched the faces of the other people gathered on the hill. Peter, Andrew, Judas, John were not there. None of the men were there. Only the women. The men were still in hiding. She held Magdalene close and waited for Lucius and Kasha to come.

Death

Lucius was pacing back and forth in the entry courtyard when Kasha arrived.

"Pilate is here?" Kasha said.

"Somewhere. They have gone to tell him I am here."

"Has he kept you waiting before?"

Lucius paused in his pacing and said, "No, he has not."

"He is playing at some game."

The guard who had gone to Pilate returned and said, "The Prefect is busy but will see you soon."

"We will find the Prefect ourselves," Kasha said then moving almost too fast for Lucius to see, struck the guard with the back of his left fist. The guard dropped silently to the floor.

"Come, help me move him," Kasha said to Lucius. "It will be best if he is not found soon."

The two dragged him out of sight into a dark corner then went to find Pilate. As they approached his quarters one of the door guards slipped inside. Pilate and Marcus were sitting at a long table, studying a map.

"Prefect, Lucius Quintus and his black shadow are approaching," the guard said.

"Are they now?" Pilate said. "Impetuous, but not surprising. Keep him out until I send for him, understand?"

"Aye, Prefect," the guard said and hurried from the room, closing the door behind him.

"Change in plan?" asked Marcus.

"Merely an adjustment. We will move things along faster. Now, before I admit our friend Lucius, you must be off to see that this Jew is dead."

"He will be dead soon, along with the others," Marcus replied.

"Ah, but that may not be soon enough. Lucius has come to rescue the Jew, to ask me to take him down from his cross and perhaps revive him. His lady love would surely be in his debt for that, don't you think?"

"Indeed. So, this is why he has come so quickly."

"I will keep them here while the necessary document is being prepared. You will go immediately to the execution ground and ensure that when Lucius and his African arrive, they will find only a dead Jew. Understand?"

"Aye, Prefect," Marcus smiled, "I will see to it with my own hand."

"Be quick."

Marcus hurried out through a side door. Pilate walked to the main doors and opened them himself.

"Lucius Quintus! Master Kasha! Welcome! I must apologize that I have kept you waiting. Important business. I trust you understand. Enter," Pilate said stepping back into the room.

"Pontius, we come on urgent business. My apologies for coming directly to the point, but we need your assistance," Lucius said.

"Certainly."

"There is a Jewish man, a friend, who was taken last night by the Antonia guard and sent to be executed this morning. He was involved in a disturbance in the Temple yesterday, but he is blameless. I was there. I saw it. We come to ask that he be released," Lucius said.

"This man is a friend of yours? And yours too, Master Kasha?"

"He is, Prefect," Kasha said, "and a worthy man. No threat to Rome or to the Jews."

"Well, then, we must have him released," Pilate said motioning to a graying man dressed in a simple tunic. "Falco, you will prepare the necessary document. Quickly, now."

"Yes, Prefect. I will fetch the scrolls immediately," Falco said and dashed from the room.

"Who is this Jew? Falco will need to put his name into the release," Pilate said.

"He is called Jesus, the son of a Joseph from Nazareth," Lucius said.

"Nazareth? Near to here?" Pilate said as Falco appeared with a portable writing desk, scrolls and ink.

"Very near Sepphoris," Lucius said.

"A charming place, Sepphoris," Pilate said, "but too many Greeks for my taste. An argumentative race. Think too much of themselves."

"Pontius, the release. We are in need of haste," Lucius said.

"Falco, ask what you need and get on with it. Quickly now," Pilate said turning to Lucius. "Yes, you must act quickly, but I fear you will be too late."

"Too late? They were taken to the place of execution only this morning. If they get him down quickly, the doctors will still have a chance..."

"If he still lives, yes, but I have given orders for all the crucified to be mercifully killed today."

"Today? Why?"

"Tomorrow will be the day of Passover for the Jews, and it will also be their Sabbath holy day," Kasha said. "Their law prohibits burial on that day."

"Master Kasha, you are a continual surprise," Pilate said. "It is in the best interest of a peaceful Passover celebration that those crucified not be left to hang on their crosses during the Jew's holy festival day."

"It is done," Falco said.

Pilate scrawled his name across the document, Falco rolled it and secured it with hot wax and pressed Pilate's seal into it. Pilate snatched it from him and flipped it to Lucius.

"Off with you! You must hurry," Pilate said as Lucius and Kasha dashed from the room.

"Well, well. It is turning out to be a good morning indeed," Pilate chortled, rubbing his hands together and smiling. "I believe it is time for the baths."

As Lucius and Kasha began their frantic run through the crowded streets of Jerusalem, Jesus' mother Mary, accompanied by the young Mary, came out of the Damascus gate and hurried to the hill crowned with the dead and dying. Seeing them approach, Miriam and Salome went to help them up the final rise. The women stood together, watching Jesus on his cross.

Marcus and a mounted troop of soldiers left Herod's Palace though a hidden gate and rode directly across country to the hill of execution. Even as they dismounted, Lucius and Kasha were fighting their way past the vendor stalls and stores, through the Passover crowd.

Marcus approached the captain of the guards overseeing the dying prisoners. "Which one is the Galilean, the one taken last night?" he said.

"Don't know about no Galilean, sir, but that one there, he's the one we grabbed last night in the olive groves. We marked him special," the guard said pointing to Jesus. A crude wooden sign was nailed to the cross above his head.

"Marked? How so?"

"Among this lot, he's the King, he is," the guard said pointing to the poor wretches hanging on their crosses. The other soldiers laughed. "Galba said 'He's special, this one. Make sure he's hung up proper.' So the boys made that sign. Says, 'King of the Jews'."

"That is all very well, but can you say for certain he is the one taken last night outside the walls? Think carefully, soldier."

"Not for absolute certain, sir, but there's only three that could be him. The rest are too old or too young."

Marcus took the guard's pilum and walked up to Jesus on his cross. He thrust the long iron shaft into Jesus' right side just below the ribs, driving the point up through the heart. Jesus stiffened against the ropes and nails, his head jerked back and up and he screamed, "My power!... Why have you forsaken me?" then his body went limp and sagged heavily, his head rolled forward and collapsed, his chin against his chest.

"What was that he said?" one of the soldiers asked.

"How should I know?" Marcus said. "I don't speak their abominable tongue."

Marcus, withdrew the pilum then, with it, quickly killed the other two men the guard had pointed out.

Marcus tossed the pilum to the guard and said, "Kill the rest."

He mounted his horse and watched while the soldiers spread out across the hill, thrusting their javelins into each of the hanging victims. When all of them were dead, Marcus and his troop rode back to Jerusalem.

Shortly after they were gone, Lucius and Kasha ran out of the gate and up the hill. Miriam and Magdalene stepped out in the road.

"He is dead, Lucius," Miriam said. "They have killed him."

"I have a release from Pilate," Lucius said. "He is strong. He has not been on the cross very long, and…"

"No! You do not understand. He is dead. They are all dead. We saw it. Roman soldiers came, more soldiers on horses. One of them stabbed him with those spears they carry. Stabbed Jesus and everyone else. Everyone. They are all dead," she sobbed.

Kasha was standing before Jesus' cross. Blood had spilled from the wound in Jesus side and soaked the ground around it, but it no longer flowed. Kasha looked at Lucius and shook his head.

"We were not in time," he said.

Miriam turned and went to Salome, who cradled his mother Mary in her arms. Magdalene stood apart, staring off into the distance, not looking at Jesus' body.

The captain of the guard approached, saluted and said to Lucius, "Greetings, Lucius Quintus."

Lucius looked at the guard and said, "You killed them all?"

"Aye, they are all dead. Orders. It was good fortune for them. Being hung on a tree for days isn't the way I'd want to go."

"The scroll," Kasha said to Lucius, extending his hand.

"What good is it now?"

"Do you know what they do with the bodies?"

"We dump them in a pit, and cover them with lime," the guard said.

"Criminals cannot be buried with their families, and when you are crucified, you become a criminal," Kasha said. "Pilate released Jesus to us. It does not say alive."

Lucius handed the scroll to Kasha who showed the guard the intact seal and gave it to him. The guard broke the seal and read. He shook his head, smiled and said, "Don't know why you would want a corpse, but orders is orders. You there, Graccus, get the King down from his tree and be quick about it."

Soldiers picked up two long wooden poles, forked at the end, and moved to Jesus' cross. They raised the poles, one on each side of the cross, setting the forks under the crossbeam. Then, two men to a pole, they pushed upward, levering the butt of the cross out of its hole. It crashed to the ground. One of the soldiers moved in and cut the rope lashings around Jesus' forearms while two others drew the nails from his arms and feet with a long pry bars, working against a block of wood. When they were done, the guard rolled the scroll into a cylinder and said, "I'll keep this."

The women laid their shawls and robes on the ground next to Jesus' body. Lucius and Kasha helped them roll his body onto a long robe and covered it with the cloths.

"We must get him off this hill," Lucius said.

"I will hire a cart," Kasha said and went down the path toward the city gate. He soon returned with a horse and a two-wheeled cart. They carried Jesus' body to the cart, bending the legs so that it would fit inside. Silently, they made their way down the hill past the other onlookers. When they reached the bottom, they stopped.

"Where are we going?" Lucius asked.

Tomb

It was past noon and the day had grown hot. People passing by saw the bloody robes in the cart and looked at them strangely.

"We cannot remain here," Lucius said.

"Let us go to Bethany, to Lazarus," Kasha said.

"It is far, and besides, we have no family there," Mary, his mother said. "No one would take the body of a criminal into their home. Tomorrow is Sabbath."

"We will put him in our family tomb," Miriam said.

"No, child. Your father would never permit it," Mary replied. "He should be taken home, to Nazareth."

"Nazareth is too far. He must not be unburied at sundown. You know this," Magdalene said.

"My father is not here to say yea or nay. We cannot leave him in this cart. We will place him in the tomb and then I will talk with my Father. It is a newly cut tomb, no one is buried there. My mother lies in another. After the proper ceremonies, he can be taken to Nazareth," Miriam said.

"Well spoken, young daughter," Kasha said. "This is the best choice before us. What say you, Lucius?"

"I see no other way. Let us go to the tomb," he said.

They took a road around the city walls to Joseph's family tomb which had been cut into a lush garden watered by a stone faceted ditch. Stone chips from the tomb's cuttings were still scattered about. A large circular stone, resting in a trough cut into the rock blocked the entrance.

"Let us move this stone," Kasha said.

He and Lucius put their shoulders into it and strained hard. The stone moved slightly in its track but they could not force it to roll further. A few curious people had followed them into the garden. Two men came forward to help. With their added strength, they rolled the stone from the doorway, revealing a rectangular opening into the darkness. One of the men placed a smaller stone beneath it, to prevent it from rolling back and sealing the tomb.

Lucius and Kasha lifted Jesus' body and carried it into the tomb. They placed it on a rock shelf cut for that purpose. The women also entered and arranged the cloths so that his body was completely covered. Mary began a keening prayer and was joined by the other women. Lucius and Kasha backed slowly away and out of the tomb.

"You have our thanks," Kasha said to the two men standing nearby.

"Who was he, this man with a Roman and a foreigner as part of his burial party?" one of them asked.

"He was a friend," Lucius replied.

"And a wise man who cared for others," Kasha added.

"May he rest peacefully, then," the man said. They walked back to their companions and they all slowly departed, talking quietly among themselves.

After a while the women emerged into the sunlight.

"We will return to Bethany," Mary, Lazarus' sister said. "His mother needs rest and food."

"I will accompany you there. We will hire another cart for the journey. It will not do for his mother to ride in the same one that brought her son to this place," Kasha said.

"I will go with Miriam," Lucius said.

Miriam looked at him but said nothing.

"You must return home now," Lucius said. "Staying here will accomplish nothing and your father will be concerned by your absence. Come, I will walk with you."

They returned to the city gate where Kasha went to find another cart and Miriam and Lucius began the long walk to Joseph's house.

Confession

"Where have you been, child?" Deborah said. "Your father is very concerned. I am afraid he may have the Temple police searching for you."

"Jesus is dead," Miriam said.

"What? Jesus, dead?"

"Killed. Killed by the Romans this very morning."

"Lucius, what do you know of this?" Deborah asked, taking Miriam by the arm and leading them both inside the house.

"They crucified him this morning. We were too late."

"Too late for what?"

"To save him," Miriam said. "Lucius went to Pilate who ordered Jesus taken down, but before Lucius and Kasha arrived, he was dead. All of the condemned were killed by the soldiers. It was horrible…"

"Come child, sit," Deborah said leading her to a couch and easing her onto it, sat beside her. "Hanna! Quick, bring water and wine."

"Tell me everything."

As Lucius was talking, Joseph entered the room.

"Miriam! You are returned. Where have you been all this day? How often have I told you that you are not to go off through the city alone? It is too dangerous, not to mention unseemly…" Joseph spluttered.

"Brother! Be silent. A moment. Give her a moment. Cannot you see? She is distraught," Deborah said.

"Are you all right?" Joseph said going to her. "Are you injured? Has something happened?"

"He is dead. They have killed him. That is what happened," Miriam said.

"Who? Who was killed?"

"Jesus, the Galilean," Deborah said.

"Now you will no longer have to worry, father. He is dead and I am home. I have nowhere to go now," Miriam said.

"How did this happen?" Joseph said turning to Lucius.

"He was arrested last night, near Bethany."

"Arrested by whom? I should have been told."

"By soldiers from the Fortress. Your people had no hand in this."

"But, the Prefect, he…" Joseph said then stopped, turning away from them.

Lucius stood. "The Prefect? Pilate. What has he to do with this?"

"It is nothing. I do not know," Joseph said.

"Father, what is it? You know something. I can tell you are keeping something from me," Miriam said.

"It is nothing, child. Pilate… he should have sent word if any of our people were taken, that is all," Joseph said.

"Why would Pilate be interested in common criminals swept up by the Fortress guard?" Lucius asked.

"It is Passover. We have an agreement, Pilate and I, that, well, that when… if there is a danger to the peace that concerns our people, he will inform me, and I will, ah, do what I can."

"You met with Pilate about this? When?" Lucius demanded.

Everyone was now looking closely at Joseph. He could not meet their eyes. He strode to the table and gulped a cup of wine.

"You told him about Jesus. You told him about me," Miriam said.

Joseph's shoulders slumped and he took a step toward Miriam who was now standing beside Lucius.

"Only out of concern for your safety. A father's love. It was nothing," Joseph said.

"Nothing? What was it then? What did you say? To what did Pilate agree? He is dead, father," Miriam said. Her voice was cold and sharp.

"Brother, what have you done?" Deborah said.

Joseph looked from his daughter to his sister. He was quiet for a long moment.

"Pilate was only to watch, nothing more. If there was trouble, he was to inform me, and this Jesus would be banished from the city. Turned out and barred from returning. He was not to be harmed."

Everyone was silent, looking at Joseph who sank down onto a couch, elbows on his knees, head hanging between his hands. "He was not to be harmed," he said softly, almost to himself.

Miriam pulled away from Deborah and ran from the room. Deborah followed, looking back with pity on Joseph.

"Joseph, you had his assurances? His promise not to harm Jesus?" Lucius asked.

Joseph looked up slowly, blinking and focused on Lucius.

"Promise?" Joseph muttered.

"What did Pilate tell you?"

"He said that if there was trouble with the Galilean, he would inform me and he would have him sent away from Jerusalem, for good," Joseph said.

"You did this because of Miriam. Because she became one of his followers and you were afraid that she would follow him again? What did you think would happen if Jesus were banished and sent back to Galilee? That she would not return there too?"

"She would see that he is trouble, that he cannot even celebrate Passover with us peacefully, here in the holy city. That would be a beginning," Joseph said.

"The forbidden fruit is the sweetest. Surely you understand that?"

"But if the fruit grows spoiled, if it becomes long absent…"

"It will be forever absent now," Lucius said.

"She blames me for it."

"With cause. Who do you think you are dealing with? One of your Council?" Lucius said. "You thought to strike a bargain with Pontius Pilate, surely one of the most devious of men. You know why I am here. Pilate needs a watchdog if he is to be kept on the leash. He is a dangerous man.

"Now you have your wish. Jesus is gone and will trouble you no longer. You are in Pilate's debt now. He did what you asked, if not in the manner of your asking. If you reveal your secret dealing with him, one that resulted in the execution of an innocent man, that will go badly for you. Your power on the Council will be diminished," Lucius said.

"Perhaps."

"Worse, far worse for you, Miriam may never forgive you."

"No, in this you are mistaken. In time she will come to understand. She will see that I was duped, that I meant no harm."

"I do not think so, but whatever happens will go hard with you and her."

"I am a patient man," Joseph said. "I know you care for her. Will you not help us?"

"I will help. But I will help her. You must find a way to make your own amends."

The Plan

Lucius returned to Lazarus' house, where he found Kasha and the others. Mary, Jesus' mother, had taken to her bed. Near sundown they gathered to eat, except for his mother who remained in her room. After giving thanks in the Jewish manner, they sat at the table eating and talking softly when someone knocked at the door. Lazarus rose and opened it. Miriam stepped into the room. A large cloth bundle was slung over her shoulder.

"I will not remain in his house another night," she said.

No one spoke for a moment, then Martha went to her.

"Come, sit and take food," she said leading Miriam to the table.

"My thanks," Miriam said, "it has been long since I ate."

"Does your father know where you have gone, young daughter?" Kasha asked.

Miriam looked up from her bowl and said, "I care not what he knows."

Kasha looked across the table at Lucius.

They finished the meal in silence. Martha and her sister Mary cleared the table. Kasha and Lucius went into the courtyard with Miriam.

"Why have you come here?" Lucius asked.

"I will not go back. I am finished with him. It is his fault that Jesus is dead, and it is because of me that this happened."

Kasha took her hands in his. "Young daughter, one thing you must believe. This had nothing to do with you.

You have done nothing wrong. The blame lies with those who plotted to kill the young teacher, not with you."

"It was because of me that my father and Pilate…"

"No. It is because your father did not trust you, nor himself. He need not have struck a bargain with Pilate. That was not your doing. It was his. It was Pilate who arranged it all. Joseph is innocent of that. His guilt was in trusting the word of the Prefect."

"Kasha is right, Miriam," Lucius said. "You are blameless. Time will show you that this is true, but for now, you must listen to Kasha."

"Perhaps time will be kind to me, but I will not return. I cannot live in the same house with my father. He will always remind me of this day."

"Where will you stay?" Lucius asked.

"Anywhere. I will remain here, if they will have me."

"You will be welcomed by any of Jesus' followers."

"We will remain with you as long as it is necessary to do so," Kasha said.

"It will not be difficult for Joseph to discover where you are. If you truly mean to stay away from your father, it would be better to be away from the city," Lucius said.

"Who else is here?"

"Mary, his mother, Lazarus and his sisters. And us," Lucius said. "Magdalene is with Salome."

"Where are the others? Peter, Andrew, John, Judas…? Have they not come?"

"No one has seen them since Jesus was taken," Kasha said.

"They are afraid," Miriam said. "They think the Romans will kill them too."

"If Pilate wanted them, they would already be in the Fortress," Lucius said.

"Or nailed up on a beam," Kasha said.

"Do they know where Jesus lies?" Miriam asked.

"Only a few of us here know that he is in your father's tomb," Lucius said.

"He cannot stay there. My father will never permit it and I will not be there to persuade him. What can we do?"

"Perhaps one of the men will have a place…" Lucius began.

"No! They cannot have him. They will fight over the body. They are not worthy of him. Where are they? They are cowering in their holes, afraid. Where were they when he was suffering on the hill? No. I will never let them have Jesus," Miriam said.

"What then would you do?" Kasha said.

"I don't know. Something… I do not know," Miriam said.

"Perhaps..." Kasha said, "perhaps the Brothers would help."

"Brothers…?" Miriam said puzzled.

"That is possible. Yes, Kasha, that might be the answer," Lucius said.

"You speak in riddles. What do you mean?"

"Remember when we first met Jesus, at the river, with John? Where did we go afterwards and meet him again?"

"Qumran," Miriam said, "the Brothers at Qumran."

"It is far from Jerusalem. He was one of them once. Perhaps they would take him again," Kasha said.

Miriam looked at them both, her eyes open and direct. "You will help?"

"Let us start tonight," Kasha said. "We will bring his body here. I know enough of the Egyptian arts of preservation. I can prepare his body for the journey. I will need a few days and many herbs and ointments. Lazarus can help me to find what I need."

"We must act now before the others know where we have laid him and find him there," Miriam said.

"But his mother, Salome and the Magdalene, they know," Lucius said.

"We must tell them of our plan," Miriam said.

"No, it is best that we do not," Kasha said. "When anyone asks them where his body lies, they can answer truthfully. If we tell them what we plan, they will not be able to keep the secret for long. It is hard enough for one person to keep a lie. With three, it is impossible."

"But, when the men go there, Jesus will not be in the tomb. What will people say?" Miriam asked.

"That is of no concern to us. We must do this in secrecy and we must do it quickly or the chance will be gone," Kasha said.

"Come, let us talk with Lazarus. There is much to do," Lucius said.

They brought Lazarus into their plot, but did not reveal to him where they had laid the body, nor did they reveal its ultimate destination. Lazarus also understood that what he did not know, he could not reveal. He borrowed a large cart from a neighbor which they loaded with a long, stout pole, robes and a number of rush bundles that had been intended to repair the roof. Lanterns were lit and hung on the wagon. Miriam, Kasha and Lucius climbed aboard and they made their way to the city, circling the walls until they came to the tomb in the garden.

The moon was almost at the full, glowing brightly, casting dark shadows on the ground. The stone stood against the entrance. Kasha and Lucius took the long pole from the wagon and using it as a lever rolled the stone out of its socket and along the track far enough to open the way inside. Blocking it in place with a rock, they entered. Jesus' body lay where they had left it, cold and stiff with rigor. They carried it from the tomb and placed it in the cart, covering it with the robes and bundles. As Kasha slid the pole back into the cart, they heard voices in the distance.

"Come, we must go now. Quietly," Lucius said and sprang onto the seat. Kasha took the horse by the bridle and walked the wagon quietly out of the garden and onto the dirt track.

"The stone," Miriam said, "we forgot to roll back the stone."

They kept Jesus' body in a storehouse apart from the main dwellings while Kasha prepared it for the journey to the desert. He and Lucius persuaded Miriam to return to her father's house while Kasha worked.

"You will cause less concern, and certainly forestall any search if you return," Lucius said. "Otherwise, Joseph will have many people scouring the city and the towns nearby for you. We do not want them here."

"Very well. I will return for now. You must come for me when you are ready to travel. I must accompany his body to Qumran. Promise me," she said to Lucius.

"It might be best if your father thinks you have run away to be with Lucius," Kasha said. "Joseph knows of Lucius' feelings for you. What will he do if believes you have the protection of a Roman from a powerful family? That will surely temper his actions."

Neither Miriam or Lucius spoke.

"Or, so it would seem to me," Kasha said.

"You know my feelings, Miriam," Lucius said. "I do not know yours."

Miriam looked at him for a long moment. She touched his arm and said, "Let us do what we must now. We will talk of our feelings when we have done."

"Well said young daughter," Kasha said.

"I will ask Martha to accompany us. Let us return you to your father for now," Lucius said.

Refused

It took many days for Kasha to prepare Jesus' body for the journey. Finally, it was wrapped in heavy cloth that was then sealed, waterproofed and stitched closed. They laid it in the wagon and covered it. Over this, they stacked various boxes and jars.

Lucius had one last visit to pay before they departed.

"Lucius Qunitus!" the door guard announced as Lucius entered the baths and walked to the couches where Pilate and his familiars lounged.

"Ah, greetings Lucius. Will you join us?" Pilate said sweeping his arm wide to include everyone.

"I am pressed for time, but yes, Prefect," Lucius said.

"Prefect? Is this to be an official visit?" Pilate said chuckling and helping himself to more dates.

"No, a personal one, Pontius," Lucius said smiling, "but private."

"That is a different matter. A conversation among friends. Give us leave to talk," Pilate said gesturing to those around him. The others quickly left, wrapping their long robes about themselves and padding off to the other end of the baths.

"Tell me how I can assist you," Pilate said.

Lucius took a couch and leaned forward for a cup of wine. Taking a sip, he said quietly, "I need to rely on your discretion."

"Ah, something is afoot. Tell all," Pilate said.

"You may know that I have taken a fancy to a young woman here in Jerusalem. Miriam, daughter of Joseph, the Jew who heads their Council."

"I have heard rumors. Can't keep a secret in this place, too damn many ears about. Tell me, how does your, what did you call it, 'fancy', concern me?"

"Her father does not encourage it. To the contrary, he would as soon see me back in Rome. Alone. So, I find I must take matters into my own hands. Miriam and I will be leaving the city without his permission or blessing. However, once the deed is done, he will come around. What other choice will he have?"

"You wish me to intervene with this Joseph? Encourage his acceptance of the match?"

"That will not be necessary, although if he comes to you, calm him and tell him I will call on him when we return."

"I will do as you wish. You will give the old man time to settle down?"

"We will spend some peaceful days perhaps in the south, near the sea, then return after her father has come to grips with the fact that he can do nothing."

"With my best wishes. Anything I can do to make your journey more comfortable?"

"No, we have all we require."

"Quite so."

Lucius rose to leave and Pilate said, "Too bad about her holy man, that, who was it, Judas somebody from Galilee."

"Jesus."

"Can't keep these Jew names straight. Unfortunate for him, but good for you in the end, eh? You get the girl. He gets to meet his god. Fortune smiles on all."

"Farewell for now, Pontius. I will be certain to inform Tiberius of your dedication to duty and the peaceful Passover celebrations in Jerusalem. And, of course, of your loyalty to him. He will be pleased."

"Safe travels then."

Lucius smiled and walked away.

"Merits watching, that one," Pilate said to no one in particular.

When Lucius returned to Bethany, Lazarus stood waiting, the wagon beside him in the street outside the gate. Seated on it were Miriam and Deborah. Kasha greeted him with that raised eyebrow. He was smiling.

"We have another traveler," Kasha said.

"Deborah, you are welcome indeed, but will not your brother object?" Lucius said.

"He would object more if Miriam goes alone. I left a message that will give him pause. He will consider before he acts, so we have time to be away from the city, but still, we should not linger," Deborah said.

"All is ready," Kasha said.

"Then, let us depart," Lucius said.

Kasha and Lucius mounted their horses and the travelers slowly moved out of town and struck the road to Jericho. Kasha rode first, leading the draft horse, Miriam and Deborah on the wagon, and Lucius followed behind. As they went, they encountered fewer travelers as the day waned and darkness fell, most had by now found lodgings or set up camps alongside the road. They continued on into the night until they came to the north-south road leading from the Great Salt Sea to Jericho. There they turned toward the Salt Sea and soon found a camping spot nearby where they spent the remainder of the night.

After a quick meal the next morning they returned to the road which now dropped toward the Salt Sea. The land grew increasingly rocky and arid. To the west a long escarpment of tawny rock rose above the desert floor, cut with many wadis and defiles. It was a barren land where nothing grew and no one lived. Fine dust from their passage, and from those traveling north, soon coated the wagon and themselves.

To the east, the river Jordan ran, twisting and turning, its sluggish path marked by a line of trees and green vegetation, a narrow, life sustaining band flowing south to the Salt Sea. They did not leave the road, but kept on toward the settlement that was increasingly visible in the distance, a white and green presence on one of the rocky shoulders between the Sea and the escarpment.

"I can see it now," Miriam said. "Qumran."

The settlement was farther away than it first appeared. It was late, the afternoon growing into evening, when the travelers finally arrived. They stopped the wagon near the east wall.

"Who shall speak for us?" Miriam asked.

"Let us go as before. Deborah and Kasha remain with the wagon, and you and I approach the Brothers," Lucius said.

Kasha made a comfortable place for Deborah and stood beside her, his back leaning against the wall. Lucius and Miriam walked to the main gate and went inside. Word of their arrival had preceded them and they were met by one of the Brothers at the foot of the square tower.

"The Teacher has been told of your coming," the young man said giving a short bow of respect. "I am Simeon. I will take you to him."

He led the way, passing into the tower as before through the scriptorium to the room where the Teacher awaited.

"I am Caleb. I recall you are Miriam, daughter of Joseph, and you are Lucius Quintus of Rome," the Teacher said.

"You have a good memory. You were called the Teacher when last we were here," Miriam said.

"Only by the Brothers. To them, I am the Teacher of Righteousness. You may call me Caleb. What brings you to us?"

"We have journeyed from Jerusalem to seek a boon," Lucius said.

"A boon, is it? Something regarding young Jesus of Nazareth I would guess," Caleb said. He looked from his window down onto the scene below. The night was coming quickly. Many cook fires were lit outside tents. The wagon's lanterns were glowing. "I see you are traveling with the same companions as before, only now you bring a wagon."

"Jesus is dead," Miriam said.

Caleb did not move but remained by the window, looking out. "I feared as much."

"How could you know?" Miriam asked.

"I did not know, but when I saw it was you and that you travel with a wagon, my suspicions were aroused."

"He is dead. Crucified by the Romans in Jerusalem," Lucius said.

"Why? For what reason?"

"There was a fight in the Temple."

"That would not be Jesus' way. He could be angered, yes, but I have never known him to fight with anyone."

"He was provoked. As you say, he did not fight but he was accused, and he was executed for it," Lucius said.

Caleb moved from the window to his writing desk and sat, his arms flat on the surface.

"He should have remained here, with us."

"Perhaps, but no one sees their own fate. He made his choice, as we all must," Lucius replied.

"There are many who have come closer to God through Jesus' teachings. He has many followers, I among them," Miriam said. "If he had remained here, his light would not have shown."

"What is this light you speak of? Was it the same light that John claimed? Jesus left here as John's disciple, after that wild man lowered him into the river. John's light got him killed," Caleb said.

"He spoke John's message, that is true. At first. But after John was killed he taught that God's kingdom is here, before us, yet we do not see it. We should live it now, not wait for God to bring it to us," Miriam said.

"How are we to do that? Wander the country, speaking to anyone who cares to listen? Forsake our brothers and go about as penniless beggars? I do not think that is the way to righteousness," Caleb said waving his hand to ward off further conversation. "What is done, is done. Evil times. We live in evil times. It would have been better had he stayed."

Miriam and Lucius looked at one another, but remained silent. Caleb took a breath and said, "This boon you seek? What is it that you would have of me?"

"Bury him here. His followers are not worthy of him. His body would have been cast into the Valley of the Gehenna had we not brought him out of Jerusalem," Miriam said.

"Impossible! I cannot allow it," Caleb said sitting upright, his brows knit together.

"It is a small thing we ask," Lucius said, "and it can be done quietly. No one else need know."

"I would know, and so would the Brothers. All of them, in time. Secrets are impossible to keep here. He died a criminal, executed by the Romans. This is sacred ground and criminals cannot be buried here."

"He was not a criminal! He was blameless. Pilate and his Roman dogs did this. He should be here, with the Brothers," Miriam said.

"I cannot permit this," Caleb said. Turning from them, he looked again out the window. "He is in the wagon?"

"Yes," Lucius said. "All we need is your permission to bury him here, as he should be."

"No. I want no trouble with the Romans. Or with those idiots in the Temple. You must go. Take his body and leave and do not return."

"Where can we go?" Miriam said.

"Someplace where no one has heard of Jesus from Nazareth," Caleb said.

The Cave

They departed Qumran that night, taking the road north again. After a short way, they turned off and made camp, needing to talk, to decide what to do. The women built a fire and prepared food while Kasha and Lucius set up tents and cared for the horses. They had finished eating and were quietly talking when Kasha said quietly, "Someone comes."

Someone was moving in the darkness, approaching the fire. Lucius stood, drawing his gladius and spoke, "Show yourself. Move slowly!"

A tall man, not yet in his middle years, in the dress of the Essene Brothers walked slowly into the camp and stopped a short distance from the fire.

"I am Mordecai, from Qumran. I come peacefully," he said.

"Stay where you are," Lucius replied.

Mordecai stood still, his hands clasped before him, waiting. Lucius did not put away his gladius but stood also, waiting. Deborah and Miriam sat quietly by the fire. Kasha was nowhere to be seen. They remained like this for some minutes until Kasha appeared quietly from the darkness.

"He is alone," Kasha said sheathing his gladius, and Lucius did the same.

"Sit," Lucius said indicating a place nearer the fire. Mordecai moved closer and sat, cross legged. Lucius sat also, keeping himself between Mordecai and the women. Kasha continued to stand.

"You are obviously not a lost wanderer drawn to our camp," Lucius said. "Why have you come?"

"I have come to help," Mordecai said.

"What help could we need from you?" Lucius said.

"I know why you came. I know what was said between you and the Teacher. I know what you carry in the wagon," Mordecai said.

"Listening outside the door, perhaps? Why would you? Why would you go against the orders of your master?" Lucius said.

"The Teacher is not my master. We have rules, that is true, but we also have the Law. We also know what is right and what is not. In this, I believe the Teacher is mistaken. Although I cannot change his decision, I can help you with your burden."

"You must tell us, why would you do so? Why go against your Teacher's will? You have not given me reason to trust you," Kasha said.

"I knew Jesus when we were boys," Mordecai said. "We used to steal off to Sepphoris and play in the buildings, while the men were working. We learned a little Greek and sometimes the workers would give us sweets and a coin or two when we did errands for them. We often got into trouble at home, but still we went whenever we could."

"You knew him in Nazareth?" Miriam said.

"Yes, lady, we were both born there. My house was happier than his, but after my father was killed, he was one of the stone cutters who worked in Sepphoris, the happiness fled from my home. I believe it was our sadness that brought us together. His father was a hard man. There was little love between them.

"I left Nazareth and wandered, working where I could, existing on the kindness of strangers when I could not, and eventually found my way here, to Qumran. I found a home with the Brothers. After a few years there, I sent word back to him and he came. Not right away, but he came. We were brothers together. Not Brothers, but like brothers. He never took the vows, never completely accepted our ways. After he heard John speak, he was never the same. You know what the Teacher thinks of the Baptizer," Mordecai said.

Kasha and Lucius exchanged glances. Lucius looked over at Miriam and Deborah. Miriam nodded.

"We too were friends," Lucius said. "Tell us, how can you help?"

"I know a place nearby, a secret place that no one else knows. It is a cave, high up on the wall of Wadi Og. It is a place that can be gotten to, but not easily found. I visited the wadi many times before I found it. It is not visible from below."

"A cave. You think this would be a good place to put the body of Jesus? In a cave?" Miriam asked.

"I mean no disrespect. He was my friend too, but you cannot move a body around without arousing interest and suspicion. Look at you, two high-born women, obviously not from any village or town near here, a Roman nobleman and him, a large black foreigner, traveling together with a wagon. How long before someone becomes too curious, before you meet with a troop of soldiers that will not listen to your reasons but take you to their superiors? You must get off the roads and put your burden to rest," Mordecai said.

The others were silent until Kasha said, "He is right. It is too dangerous to stay on the roads and there is no place in the towns for us."

"Miriam, we must consider this. We do not know the country here. We must act soon. I believe Mordecai is here in good faith and we should trust him," Lucius said.

Miriam looked to Deborah, pleading in her eyes. "What should we do?"

"I see no alternative, my sweet. Let us follow Mordecai and find this cave. We can lay Jesus to rest there. If there should be need, we can always return," Deborah said.

Miriam looked at Lucius and nodded.

"When do we start?" Lucius said.

"At first light. The entrance to the wadi is on the road north from here. We will meet there and I will lead you to the cave," Mordecai said. "You must start alone in the morning. I return to Qumran tonight."

"Why? Is this necessary?" Lucius said.

"It will be noticed if I do not return tonight. Tomorrow, after the morning meal, I will have errands that will take me to Jericho. I will find you then," Mordecai said.

"Make sure you come alone," Lucius said.

"It will be only me. Now let me show you where we will meet. It will be better if you are not lingering on the road," Mordecai said.

He described the large wadi that cut across the road north of their camp. It had been formed long ago by seasonal runoff flowing down from the west, the water sometimes so strong and violent that the road was washed into the salt sea. It was easy to find. They were to wait for him a short way up the wadi after hiding the wagon from view of the road.

"Farewell. I will not fail you," Mordecai said and walked into the darkness.

After he had gone, Kasha said, "Let us rest. I will watch."

"Wake me later and I will watch until morning," Lucius said.

They found the wadi easily and turned up it. The dry bed was wide and covered with gravel and small stones. The wagon moved easily. After making two wide turns the wadi hid them from view, and they stopped in what shade they could find to wait for Mordecai. The women remained with the wagon while Lucius and Kasha moved back down the wadi to a vantage point where they could see the road well enough to have warning should trouble come from either direction. After a long, hot wait, Kasha spotted a lone figure leading a donkey on the road.

"Mordecai?" Lucius asked.

"Yes, it is him."

Mordecai and the donkey turned off the road, following the wagon tracks into the wadi. As he rounded the first bend Lucius called to him.

"You have brought a friend?" he said gesturing at the donkey that had a pack frame strapped to his back.

"Yes, a friend," Mordecai said scratching the donkey between the ears. "Where we will be going the wagon cannot follow."

The three returned to the wagon. The women climbed on board and they resumed their slow trek up the wadi, detouring more frequently around large rocks and boulders. After a long period of increasingly difficult travel, they reached a tall rock step that blocked further progress.

"This is a waterfall when the rain collects and rushes down from above," Mordecai said.

"The wagon can go no further," Kasha said. "Where now?"

"That way," Mordecai said pointing to the tall rock wall. "There is a path that men and this beast can follow." He led the donkey around to the rear of the wagon.

"I see no path, only rock and earth," Kasha said.

"The opening cannot be seen from here," Mordecai said. "We must tie the body firmly on the frame. Help me to get him out of the wagon."

They unloaded the boxes and cloths and slid Jesus' tightly wrapped body to the end of the wagon bed. Bringing the donkey close alongside, they gently placed the body on the pack frame and tied it securely.

After adding food and water skins to their packs they started forth. Near the wall, a large opening became visible behind a tall rock shoulder. As they entered, the space widened, opening into a large crevice that steepened into a wall of rock at the far end. On the east side, there was a narrow ramp, a feature of the rock, different in color, a dark cream colored rock swirled with veins of black. It sloped up at a steep but negotiable angle along the defile's side, topping out on a cramped plateau high above them.

"This is our path," Mordecai said. "Come. Walk slowly."

Although the ramp was steep, they climbed slowly to the top where it leveled out onto a plateau, littered with many boulders and rocks that had fallen from the heights above. There was no path. The only way out was down the ramp from which they had ascended.

"Where do we go now?" Miriam said. "How much further is it to the cave?"

"We are here," Mordecai said.

There was no sign of a cave or opening in the rock walls around them.

"The cave is behind the boulders?" Kasha asked.

"Yes, it cannot be seen from here."

Mordecai led them among the boulders until they came to the rock wall. In it was a dark opening, wide enough for two men.

"We are here," Mordecai said. "The cave is ancient. There are markings and drawings of animals on the walls. People lived here long, long ago. Probably before the rocks fell. No one comes here now. I am the only one who knows of it," Mordecai said.

"Since you found it, others may also know," Lucius said.

"I think not. The defile at the waterfall is the only path into this place. No one ventures far up the wadi since the waterfall step blocks all further passage. This place is secluded. It cannot be seen from below, or from above. See how the cliffs overhang us, and there is nothing but rock, sand and scorpions on the outcropping above. It goes for leagues, barren in all directions. No one goes there. Or here," Mordecai said.

"How did you find this place?" Kasha asked.

"I often hunt for certain plants that are useful to treat the sick and injured. I one day wandered far up the wadi looking for myrrh and the white thistle that sometimes grows where water flows and pools for a time. While I was here, near the waterfall step, I startled four ibex. They ran into the defile and disappeared. Curious, I went to look and found the ramp. I climbed it and found this. It was chance, nothing more," Mordecai said.

"Let us look inside," Lucius said.

They entered, pausing while their eyes grew accustomed to the dim light. The entrance opened into a high and spacious room. The floor was flat, covered in sand. Jutting from one wall was a natural bench of stone sloping at a slight angle to the floor. Next to it were ancient pieces of burned wood mixed in with the sand of the floor. One wall was streaked with soot from the fire. Faded symbols and crude animals had been drawn in the soot and scratched into the rock.

"These are very old," Deborah said peering closely at the figures.

"No one has been here for many ages," Mordecai said.

"Are we in agreement? Will this be the resting place of our friend Jesus?" Lucius asked.

Kasha was silent, waiting for the women to speak. Deborah and Miriam slowly looked around. "It is so dark and lonely," Miriam said.

"What other choices do we have?" Deborah said.

"None that are worthy of him. Yes, let it be here," Miriam said.

They retrieved the body and carried it into the cave and laid it on the stone bench. Kasha and Lucius stood while the the women and Mordecai said prayers over it and offered blessings.

"We are finished now," Miriam said. "We have said our farewells."

"Come, child, let us go," Deborah said and they left together with Mordecai. Lucius took a last look and stepped through the opening after them.

Kasha knelt by the rock bench, opened the pack that hung from his shoulder and pulled out a short, flat piece of wood and slid it underneath the wrapped body. It was a short plank with a splintered nail hole at the top edge. The dried blood splashed across the surface did not obscure the taunt scratched into the wood: INRI. King of the Jews.

At the wagon they said farewell to Mordecai. He led the donkey down the wadi and out of sight.

"What do we do now?" Miriam said. "Now that we are finished, now that he is at rest, I am at a loss."

"Let us pause for a while here. We should have nourishment. We must still make our way back to the road," Lucius said.

"Set up shade and food while I erase any signs that lead into the defile," Kasha said. "When the rains come, all traces of our passage will be erased."

They put up an awning while Kasha worked. After he returned, they ate and repacked the wagon.

"I have given some thought to where we should next go," Deborah said. "Let us return to the river, to the place where we first met the young teacher. It is not far and I desire to see it again. We may pass some time there before returning to Jerusalem."

"I do not wish to return to my father's house," Miriam said. "I will go to my uncle in Caesarea. He will have me."

"Yes, he would, but that would create yet more ill feelings within our families. Your father will press to have you return to him and if your uncle refuses, then…" Deborah said.

"I care not," Miriam said.

"You will. You do not see this now. You are young and it is easy to defy your family when your future is before you. Later, you will regret it, and your father may not be alive when you wish to reconcile with him."

"Deborah is right, young daughter," Kasha said. "Wisdom often comes to those who have time to reflect on life's lessons. Heed her words. She thinks only of the best for you."

Miriam looked at Lucius, who said, "They are speaking for your good, Miriam. Let us go where Deborah wishes, to the river. We will rest and talk and you can have time to think. Your father will be angry that you have gone without his permission, but you are with Deborah, and with us, and we have had his leave to travel together before. Your honor, and his, are still upheld."

"I care not for my honor. Jesus is dead. My father had a hand in it, witting or not. He has much to answer for."

Miriam stood and looked toward the defile, then down the wadi where the great Salt Sea glistened in the distance.

"Very well, let us go to the river," she said.

The four travelers moved slowly down the wadi, the wagon, lighter now, creaking and swaying over the stones, until they faded from view into the lengthening shadows of the day.

Part Three

Taos, New Mexico

Present Day

Chapter 1

Edith Donaldson's New Mexico house was located in the foothills southeast of Taos at seventy-six hundred feet. The land was dry with patches of early December snow among the sage, juniper and pinon. The day was cold, bright and clear and the private gravel road leading to the adobe ranch house from the highway was dry enough for the approaching car to kick up a following dust trail.

"They're here," Walker said turning back from the windows.

Edith sat in a chrome and leather wheelchair holding an earthenware mug of warm tea. Walker pushed the chair up to the windows.

"It has been so long since I have seen them," Edith said.

"Almost two years," Walker said.

"Yes, and they are bringing the twins," Edith said smiling at the approaching car. "Do you like babies?"

"Sure. Who doesn't?"

"It is odd. I think I know you so well, but I don't know what you like. I think when we are together, we talk more about me than you. Is that true?"

"Probably. I don't talk about me very much. If there is anything you want to know, just ask. I'll tell you," Walker said.

"Perhaps I will."

Edith touched his arm and said, "Wheel me out on the porch. I want to greet them outside."

Howard, the retired police officer from Santa Fe who had appeared with Walker the previous year to, as Edith complained, "baby sit me", stopped the big Jeep close by the steps and began unloading bags. Nat unbuckled the two infant carriers, passed one to Carol and lifted the other. Inside them, the twins were swaddled deeply in soft blankets.

Walker took a heavy shawl from a chair and pulled it around Edith's shoulders, opened the door and pushed her out into the cold morning air.

"Carol, Nathaniel, it is so good to see you!" Edith said.

"It is good to see you too. It's been too long," Carol said bending to give Edith a kiss. "You look well."

"No, I don't. No lies here, not among us," Edith said. "Nathaniel, fatherhood suits you. But, quickly, lets get these babies inside where it is warm."

Everyone trooped inside the house. Coats were shed and babies unwrapped, to Edith's delight. Walker peered at the twins closely but declined Carol's offer to hold them. Carol and Nat laid them side by side on a low sofa.

"We named them Mary and Jonathan," Carol said. "Mary for my mother and Jonathan for Nat's grandfather."

"How nice," Edith said.

"Actually, their full names are Mary Edith and Jonathan Walker," Nat said.

"Oh, bless you, my dears," Edith said touching her hand to her heart.

Walker looked at Nat, then at the twins, then back to Nat.

"Walker Burnett, at a loss for words?" Edith said.

"Which one is he? Jonathan?" Walker said looking at the twins.

"Here," Carol picked up a bundle of blue blanket wrapped around a tiny pink face. She walked over to him, offering the bundle.

"Why don't you hold him?"

She placed Jonathan in the crook of his arm and stepped back. He looked closely at Jonathan's rubbery smile and touched his chin with one finger. Jonathan immediately wrapped his little fist around Walker's finger and blurbled saliva down his chin.

"I think he's smiling at me," Walker said.

While Howard helped Nat and Carol settle into their rooms, Juana Sanchez, Edith's live-in nurse, wheeled Edith off for a rest. Walker sat in the big living room overlooking the deep Rio Grande Gorge where the river cut its way through the rift valley west of Taos. Nat came in and took a chair opposite him.

"How is she? She doesn't look good," Nat said.

"She is bad. Holding it together with drugs and guts."

"You been here long?"

"Got in early this morning."

"Has she talked much?"

"No, not much. I think she's saving her strength. She seems chipper, but it's only an act."

"What's wrong with her? I asked, but she didn't answer."

"I never asked," Walker said. "None of my business. She wants me to know, she'll tell me."

"You're not curious?"

"No. Doesn't make much difference. I'll do whatever she needs, but I can't help her that way."

Nat looked across the Rio Grande Gorge to the basalt plains and the blue mountains in the far distance. "Some view. I can see why she moved out here from San Francisco."

"Climate's good. Air is healthy. Lots of privacy," Walker said.

"I can't believe the way they hounded her back there. Reporters, cameras, demonstrations outside her house. Crazy people. They acted like she was responsible for putting the body in that cave."

"There are crazy people everywhere, but it got personal. That's why she left."

"Someone threatened her?"

"Two men broke into her house one night," Walker said standing and moving to the bar for a drink. "Want one?"

"No, thanks. What happened?"

"They were arrested and went to jail," Walker said.

"Were you there?"

"Yes."

"What did you do?"

"I told them they had a choice. I could shoot them or they could wait for the police."

As the sun dropped below the horizon and the light lingered on the edge of the sky, they took dinner with Edith. The cook had prepared dishes of the area's New Mexican favorites. Chile rellenos fried light and crispy. Blue corn buffalo enchiladas with green chile and goat cheese. Posole with pork, jalapenos and onions. Guacamole, pico de gallo, and warm corn tortillas. Afterward, they gathered in the living room warmed by the piñon flaming in the adobe fireplace.

"I am grateful we are all together again. I almost put this off too long. We four began this journey and it is fitting that we are together as it ends," Edith said.

"Edith, don't talk like that," Carol said.

"It is the truth, my dear. If there is one thing our discovery and its aftermath has taught me, it is the value of truth. We all must die. I am going before you, that is all."

No one spoke. Edith looked at each of them in turn, then said, "I once thought I knew what would happen after I died. No longer. Either the young teacher's god deserted him at the end, or he never existed at all. Either way, it's all the same. As Jesus taught, what we have is here and now and we must live it as it should be lived, loving one another. I am sad to be leaving you. My friends…" she paused, looking at each of them in turn. "My family. But, we did live for a time, didn't we."

They sat silently. Carol was crying.

"Now, look what I have done. At the end, I am giving a sermon. Quite odd, don't you think?"

"You may be right," Nat said, "but still, it isn't certain that the body we found was Jesus. There is no way to know absolutely. And the scroll. It is as old as the body, we know that, but there is no historical evidence of a Lucius Quintus who lived in Rome, or in Judea for that matter. Anyone could have written it."

"I believe it," Carol said. "If it isn't true, it must have been a plot, and who would have done that? If you wanted to prove that Jesus was not the Messiah, why hide his body? Why fake a history about him, then hide that with the body too? What would be the point?"

"Walker, what do you think?" Edith said.

"I'm not a believer in coincidence. Until we get some hard evidence, I'll pass."

Edith held Walker's eyes for a few moments, then said, "Enough of the past. Let's talk about the future. Tell me everything about the twins."

Nat and Carol talked of the children and about Nat's work with the University. Edith spoke of her love of New Mexico and the southwest. Walker was mostly quiet, listening, asking only a few questions now and then. The fire had burned low when Edith grew tired, her speech halting and her eyes wandering from time to time to the darkness outside. They said their goodnights and Jana came and wheeled Edith away.

Chapter 2

It was a few minutes past midnight when Walker slipped quietly downstairs. He walked softly to the study door, opened it and went in. Edith was sitting in her wheelchair, warmed by a crackling blaze in a corner fireplace.

"Thank you for coming," she said motioning toward a crystal decanter of Scotch on a side table.

"You're welcome, of course," he said pouring a glass then moving to sit beside her. "How are you feeling?"

"Like death warmed over."

Walker smiled.

"Pretty tough talk," he said.

"Not really. I can't say I'm ready to die. I suppose no one is. I'm scared, but I suppose that comes with the territory."

"What did you decide about the Padre? Juana said he called again tonight."

"I told him no. I've told him more than once, but he's stubborn and convinced it's for my own good. No, I have decided to make this last journey on my own."

Walker took a sip of the scotch and looked at her over the rim of his glass. "You didn't ask me here to discuss Catholic ritual."

"No, I didn't."

"You still have it?"

"Yes. It is there, on the table."

A narrow velvet bag lay on the coffee table by the fireplace. Walker stood and picked it up. Opening it, he drew out a long, thin piece of wood. Old and stained. INRI was scratched on one side.

"What now? What do you plan to do with it?" Walker asked.

"I don't know. It has been on my mind of late, you know, considering my situation."

Walker said nothing. He returned to his seat and placed the sign and bag on his lap.

"Considering your, 'situation', as you call it, I think you better make a decision pretty soon."

"That is why I wanted to see you tonight. What do you think?"

Walker took another slow sip of the scotch, turning the sign over looking at it closely.

"You know the sign is real, don't you?"

"Yes. I had it tested. DNA. The blood on that sign came from the body. It's him," she said, "Jesus of Nazareth's body."

"How long have you known?"

"I had the tests done shortly after we returned from Israel."

"You could have prevented a lot of trouble if you had said so earlier."

"There will always be trouble. It is a Pandora's Box. Once you found the cave there was no going back. You knew that."

"You want to know what I think? How about this?" Walker said. "You turn the sign over to, say, the IAA. They will want to know how you got it. You can say, 'I asked my friend Mr. Burnett to steal it for me'. They'll say, 'Mr. Burnett you are under arrest for stealing Israeli antiquities and taking them out of the country. Oh, and you are under arrest too, Mrs. Donaldson.' Assuming you are still around by then."

"Or, I can say, here is your sign and it is none of your business how I got it."

"Yeah, I suppose there isn't much they will be able do about that," Walker said.

"No, there is not."

"I need to know something."

"You want to know why I asked you to take the sign. I am no longer certain. When you called me from the desert, after you had killed those two men, I could see everything falling apart. I wanted something tangible that would prove what we had found. The body alone would not have been enough. It could have been anyone. Lucius' story could have been written by anyone. Many people think it is a forgery even now. But the sign, it ties them all together. The DNA is the key to the truth."

"So, why haven't you come forward with it?"

"Because of you, dear man. And for Nat and Carol, and the children's sakes. Theft, cover-up, lies. You would be exposed. Nat would lose his position with the University, and the children..."

"I see your point."

"And, there is another reason," Edith said. She paused and her eyes shifted inward to her thoughts. Walker waited.

"Pour one of those for me," she said after a few moments.

Walker brought a glass to her. She took a slow sip and smiled faintly.

"I have always liked a good scotch, even when I was a girl. My father would let me have a taste from time to time."

"Another reason?" Walker prompted.

"I am tired, Walker. I just can not keep it a secret any longer. Jesus was a man. He lived and died, like all of us do. He was special. Many people loved him, but he was not what people later made him into. He was human. One of us," Edith said looking straight at Walker.

"You're going to take the fall," Walker said.

"Yes, as you so eloquently put it, I am taking the fall."

"Edith you don't have to…"

"Yes. Yes, I do. Say what they will about me, they won't be able to hurt the rest of you. I have a deposition on file with my attorneys. It is to be made public after my death. It says that I am alone responsible for arranging the theft of the sign. It names no one else. Everyone will be questioned of course, but you are the only one who knows the truth."

"Then that will be the end of Jesus Christ. No more being raised from the dead or ascending to heaven on a cloud. No great commission to go forth and convert the world," Walker said.

"No, just the young teacher from Nazareth who wanted people to see that the world can be just and fair if only we would make it so."

Walker slid the sign back into the velvet bag and handed it to her.

"No, I want you to keep it until I'm gone. Then take it to Orem, that nice young man who helped us in Israel. I have made all of the travel arrangements. I don't trust Mayefsky or Menahem. Orem will do the right thing."

She handed him a manila envelope.

"These are the DNA results. He will need them too."

Walker took the envelope. Edith started to speak but Walker said, "You don't have to say it. It doesn't matter. I am going to miss you, Edith."

"And I you."

Chapter 3

Edith died quietly in the early morning hours. Walker did not sleep that night. Instead, he took a long moonlit walk and sat on the rim of a little canyon among the cedars waiting for the sunrise. As the light began to spread across the horizon, defining the canyon walls and the distant blue mesas, a pack of coyotes let loose a mournful chorus. When they were done, Walker walked slowly back to the house.

Chapter 4

The charter jet landed at Ben Gurion Airport in Tel Aviv early in the morning. It was a beautiful day, clear and calm, the sky a deep blue. Walker, carrying a black briefcase, strode from the jet gangway to a waiting policeman who escorted him into the customs area. Walker passed down a busy corridor into a large office. Orem rose from a wide cedar desk and extended his hand.

"Welcome to Israel once again, Mr. Burnett," Orem said.

They shook hands and Walker said, "It's still just Walker."

"Yes, you are not much for the formalities as I remember," Orem said smiling. "Allow me to introduce my assistant, Sharon Mazir."

A young, dark haired woman dressed in matching dark blue skirt and short jacket stepped forward, extending her hand. "Welcome, Walker," she said.

"Ms. Mazir," Walker said taking her hand.

"It's just Sharon," she said smiling.

Walker laughed as he released her hand.

"Please, sit," Orem said motioning to a chair close to the desk.

Walker put the briefcase on the desk as they took their seats.

"I understand you are here at the request of Mrs. Donaldson. We were all so sorry to hear of her passing."

"She asked me to deliver something to you that rightfully belongs to Israel and the Jewish people," Walker said. He opened the briefcase and placed the velvet bag and manila envelope on the desk, and set the briefcase on the floor beside his chair.

Orem and Sharon looked at each another. Orem opened the bag and drew forth the sign. They studied the inscription then looked at Walker.

"Before you ask, look in the envelope," Walker said.

Sharon opened the envelope and they read the DNA report.

"This is the sign that was taken from the laboratory?" Orem said.

"Yes," Walker said.

"How did Mrs. Donaldson get it? Why would she return it? Who took it?" Sharon asked.

"I can't answer that. I can say that she gave it to me before she died and asked me to deliver it to you."

"There are going to be questions," Orem said.

"I imagine there will be," Walker said. "Probably have to talk with her attorneys."

"Great. More lawyers," Orem said.

Walker smiled.

Sharon and Orem inspected the sign again, turning it over in their hands, getting the feel of it. Orem placed the sign carefully on the velvet bag, glanced at the DNA report and said, "This is going to create a lot of trouble."

"Yes," Walker said sitting back in his chair. "Yes, it will."

Chapter 5

The Lucius Scroll is permanently on display in the Rockefeller Museum in Jerusalem, resting next to the body and the sign found with it in the cave. The body remains officially unidentified. Even so, the sign and body draw thousands of visitors daily. Some of those who shuffle past pause a moment to ponder or to scoff. Others murmur prayers, clutch rosaries or other talismans. A few occasionally fall to their knees. They are gently helped to stand by the docents stationed there and are quietly moved along.

It was late in the day. The last visitors, an old man and his granddaughter, paused before the partially unwrapped body.

"Is it really him, Papi?" she asked, pressing close to the railing.

"No one knows for certain," he replied.

"But, do you think it is?"

The old man paused, looking at the still form before them.

"I don't know. But it doesn't matter. The scroll says he was a good man who cared for others. His friends wanted us to know that. This is what matters."

The old man and the girl left hand in hand. The guards turned off the bright overhead lights and locked the doors. A small amber beam of light remained, shining down on the scroll and the still form beside it.

Epilogue

Jesus

Many of his teachings were passed on by his followers to those who did not know him. As the stories went from person to person, they underwent many changes, as verbal traditions do. In the years after his death, when the kingdom he spoke of did not come, people explained to one another how this could be. The Kingdom of God did not come because he, Jesus, lives still, they told one another. He was raised by God who then took him to His kingdom. But, no matter, they said. He will someday return, bringing that kingdom with him as he promised.

Lucius and Miriam

After their sojourn by the Jordan River, Lucius and Miriam returned to Jerusalem where they announced their betrothal to Joseph. Joseph was bitterly opposed to this and suffered greatly when they, along with Deborah, left Jerusalem to live on a small country estate in Galilee, north of the Great Lake, near the Seven Springs where Deborah and the women had fed the people.

Lucius and Miriam were married there according to the Jewish rites, and, in time, became respected members of the community. Miriam bore two daughters and a son. The eldest daughter, Mary, died of the fever when she was a child. Their son, Yeshua grew to manhood and joined the Jewish rebellion against Rome in 67 CE. He was killed when the Romans took Jerusalem and destroyed the Temple. Their daughter, Rachel, survived the war and went into exile, joining Kasha and Larissa at the house of Quintus in Rome.

Miriam died in the spring of the year 61 CE. Lucius buried her alongside Deborah and their daughter Mary in the family tomb. Over the following three years Lucius remained at home writing his scroll. When he finished, he made one last journey south to Qumran accompanied by Rachel. With Mordecai, they journeyed again to the cave where Lucius left his scroll. Lucius returned to his farm and died the following year. Yeshua buried him alongside Miriam and sealed the tomb.

Kasha

The summer of the year following Lucius and Miriam's wedding, after the birth of Mary, Kasha returned to Rome, his daughter Larissa and the house of Quintus. He became master of the house after Rufus' death in 41 CE. Granted Roman citizenship by Tiberius, Kasha was respected and loved by his friends and family, and feared by his enemies. After Tiberius was murdered, Kasha, Larissa and Rachel returned to Alexandria. Larissa married a wealthy merchant from Crete, taking Rachel with her when she left for that island. Soon thereafter, Kasha walked out of Alexandria carrying only his bow and arrows, the ancient gladius, a bedroll and pack. He was seen now and then passing through villages along the river Nile, going always south, until he walked into the vast country beyond and was seen no more.

Deborah

Deborah remained with Lucius and Miriam and was a constant source of stability and love, a balm after little Mary's death, and a wise counselor to the family. She traveled once to Jerusalem to visit her brother Joseph, staying but a short while before returning to the farm in

Galilee. She would say little of her visit. After Yeshua's birth she became increasingly ill. One morning in the fall Lucius found her curled in her favorite blanket at the Seven Springs. She had died there in the night.

Joseph

Joseph never recovered from Miriam and Deborah's departure. He became ever more reclusive, going only to the Temple and meetings of the Great Council where even his good friends began to shy away from his bitterness. Deborah returned once to his house bearing news of his grandchildren whom he refused to recognize. Unable to sway him, she returned saddened to Galilee.

Pilate

Pilate's hold on Joseph was strong and provided him with much information and influence with the Great Council until the incident at Mt. Gerizim. Suspecting that a large group of Samaritans moving toward Mt. Gerizim were not going there to pray but to launch a rebellion, Pilate sent Marcus to suppress them. A pitched battle ensued and many Samaritans were killed and their leaders captured. Pilate had these men immediately executed. This was too much for Joseph and the Council who complained bitterly to Vitellius, the Roman Governor of Syria. Vitellius ordered Pilate to explain his actions to Tiberius. Before Pilate arrived in Rome, Tiberius was dead. Caligula sent Pilate to Gaul where he would cause less trouble. Pilate died there, some said by his own hand, although others said he was too proud to take his own life.

Peter

Peter grew increasingly angry and bellicose after Jesus' death. He was secretly ashamed that he had gone into hiding with the men. He never forgave Kasha for saving his life the night Jesus was arrested. Instead, he blamed Kasha for Jesus' capture. His dislike and distrust of women grew as did his influence with the steadily growing number of Jesus' followers. His jealousy of Magdalene soon knew no bounds. He hounded and argued with her at every opportunity, prompting many of Jesus' followers to go to her defense. Peter's actions were instrumental in splitting the original little band of Jesus' followers into opposing camps.

Then Paul appeared, also claiming discipleship from Jesus. Paul worked to convince people of his own interpretation of Jesus' identity and purpose. Those who were dissatisfied with Peter sided with Paul. After Peter, James and their followers in Jerusalem split from Paul, Peter launched his own campaign to recruit other Jews to what had become the Jerusalem church of Jesus. Following a bitter dispute with Paul in Antioch, Peter traveled to Rome where his hot temper lead to his death at the hands of Roman soldiers.

Magdalene

Mary Magdalene was revered by many of Jesus' followers as the one he loved the most. They would come to her often to hear stories of him. Many came to believe that Jesus had told her secrets he had not shared with the others, secrets that would help them come closer to the Father and enter the kingdom when it came, as it surely would soon. When the kingdom did not come and Jesus did not reappear, her influence suffered. The criticism of Peter and his followers toward her intensified. She left Jerusalem on the fifth anniversary of Jesus' death and returned to Magdala where she passed from the knowledge of men.

Mordecai

Mordecai was the last Teacher of Righteousness. After the revolt in 67 CE, heeding the advice of Lucius and his own experiences with the Romans, he began the effort to preserve Qumran's sacred writings by hiding the scrolls in caves near the settlement. Refugees who were fleeing south added to the collection and the Brothers worked continuously making and buying jars, sealing scrolls inside them and moving them to the caves. As the Romans marched south, Mordecai wrote a brief scroll recounting those final days and describing the location of Jesus' body, and sent it to be hidden with the rest.

The Roman Tenth Legion arrived at Qumran, briefly questioned Mordecai and the few remaining Brothers, killed them all and moved on, leaving Qumran to become yet another abandoned settlement in an inhospitable land.

Acknowledgements

When a writer sits down to begin a work like this, you may be certain that the influences, inspiration and help of many others led to that point. During the research, writing and rewriting of this book, help and inspiration were freely given. For those whom I have not recognized here, I ask forgiveness.

The story grew from the idea that truth, as much of it as we can know, is often found in history. Good history done right. For that ever-present insight I owe much to Dr. Sabetai Unguru. For this particular historical journey I was guided by the works of Dominic Crossan, Bart Ehrmann, and Joseph Campbell, among others, which pointed me in the right directions.

The way in which I have told my story owes much to the works of Annie Dillard, who writes without compromise, Norman Maclean who wrote from the heart, and Robert B. Parker, Elmore Leonard and John D. McDonald who taught me the joys of a well-told mystery.

Reading the Gospel of Thomas is like grasping a live wire connection to the mystery and awful strangeness of those times. I am moved by the mysterious presence of Mary from Magdala, a much loved disciple now often defamed, obscured and marginalized, which surely reveals her significance during the earliest days of Christianity.

Jill Dearman, who read and edited the first major version of this story, helped make it better, and gave me encouragement to continue.

Clark Dimond who stuck with me and offered essential advice and wise counsel.

My mother, who taught me to read and love it before the teachers got their hooks into me.

My daughter Kayla and my son Travis who are encouraging, helpful and ready with valuable advice and insights for which I am truly grateful.

Barbara, my wife, partner and friend of many years was always there with her support, encouragement, tireless editing and valuable suggestions as I worked through the many drafts and revisions of this story.

Like the boys said, "Love is all you need."

Michael Douglas Scott
Southern Colorado
September, 2013

Made in the USA
Lexington, KY
02 July 2014